BROADWAY
IN REVIEW

John Mason Brown

BROADWAY
IN REVIEW

W · W · NORTON & COMPANY · INC·

PUBLISHERS · NEW YORK

Copyright, 1940, by
W. W. NORTON & COMPANY, INC.
70 Fifth Avenue, New York City

First Edition

PRINTED IN THE UNITED STATES OF AMERICA
FOR THE PUBLISHERS BY THE VAIL-BALLOU PRESS

With Proud Affection
For The Two
PRESTON BROWNS,
The "General"
And
The Particular

Contents

Contents

"Whoever talks of excellence as common and abundant, is on the way to lose all right standard of excellence. And when the right standard of excellence is lost, it is not likely that much which is excellent will be produced."

MATTHEW ARNOLD

Foreword

TO many people, including professional reviewers, dramatic criticism must seem like an attempt to tattoo soap bubbles. That it is such an attempt is at once the glory and the challenge both of the job itself and of the theatre which provokes it and is provoked by it.

The dilemma—the special dilemma—of writing about plays and players in performance is that the subject written about is more variable than the person writing about it. The theatre (in the sense of what this or that playhouse may have to offer a patron during a season) is what it is only on the night this spectator happens to be in it, and then only to one person on that night. What critics attempt to put the fixative of their prose upon has ceased to be by the time they reach their typewriters.

Although the productions about which they write may, if successful or worthy of further attention, be revisited, what is seen a second time in the theatre is never quite the same as at its first seeing, if for no other reason than that the tingling impact of the initial impression is lost; the pleasures of familiarity, however

deep, are as unlike those yielded by novelty as settle-
ment is to discovery. The audience has changed. The
performance, to a degree no matter how infinitesimal
and often more psychic than material, has adapted itself
for better or for worse to the needs of this different
audience.

If dramatic critics function as defense attorneys for
their own reactions, they enjoy a freedom unknown
to lawyers. When they plead their cases (and always
win them, at least to their own satisfaction), theatrical
reviewers do so *after* the evidence has been destroyed.
It is time—the passing moments, the moments which,
whether they race or lag, have led inexorably to the
final obliteration of a dropped curtain—that has sab-
otaged this evidence. And time, both as an ally and
an enemy, though in reality more as an ally, merits
special attention in any consideration of the theatre of
the playhouses when it finds its way into print.

"It is somewhat late to speak of Amiel but I was late
in reading him," is the way in which Matthew Arnold
began his critical essay on the subject of the author
of the *Journal*. Confronted with such a lead, newspaper
reviewers are bound to admire the fine arrogance of
Arnold's disregard of a deadline and envy him his freedom. Dramatic critics must be more prompt in their
discoveries. No matter how personal their reactions
may be, what they are writing about is news, or was
news when they wrote it. And news in dramatic criticism is what has just happened in a theatre—last night,

or Saturday night in case the report cannot be printed until Monday. At the latest, if an article appearing on the theatre pages is not an obituary appraisal benefiting even then from a grim timeliness, it is apt to be a reconsideration of productions still current or players still seeable. Quite aside from the reportorial needs of a newspaper, the self-interest of three groups is the unconscious concern of all reviewing—that of the persons reviewed, that of the reviewer himself, and the possible self-interest, or purchasing desire, of those who read the article.

If theatrical reviewers are duty-bound to write against time, the mere fact that what they are writing about is news only adds to the popular confusions on the subject of dramatic criticism. The point merits clarification. Once correctly understood it would exonerate many a reviled reviewer, even if it would not free him from the special responsibility which is his because of the undeniable tyranny of print. In spite of an age-old and dangerous misunderstanding to the contrary, what a criticism, no matter how good or bad, is always *most about* is never what happened any night *on* a particular stage. It is always primarily concerned with what happened *in* the audience to a critic on, and after, the night he was a part of that audience. It is his spiritual, intellectual, emotional reflex to the given stimuli (if any) of the thing reviewed. This is why even when, in the interest of news, all the dramatic critics in a town are herded into one theatre on a particular evening, what they see, whether their verdict is unanimous or not, is always bound to be as many plays and performances as there are critics in the house.

Anatole France, who had the wisdom to realize we speak of ourselves every time we have not the strength to be silent, had criticism, not reviewing, in mind when he insisted that, to be quite frank, the critic ought to say, "Gentlemen, I am to talk about myself on the subject of Shakespeare, or Racine . . . subjects that offer me a beautiful opportunity." The excuses given American dramatic critics for the self-ventilation inescapable in what they may think is their most accurate and objective reporting differ nightly in scale and kind. Although the provocations range from Katharine Cornell to Gypsy Rose Lee, the reviewers, in their midnight journalism, cannot avoid the spiritual strip-teasing Anatole France spoke of when touching upon the autobiographical aspects of the higher criticism.

If all criticism, including the white-hot expression of opinion known as reviewing, is autobiographical without even meaning to be so or being so accepted, I beg forgiveness for daring to drop the customary, and misleading, mask of impersonality to speak quite personally about the following pages. The reviews and reappraisals they include have all of them appeared in the drama section of the *New York Post*, for which all but one of the following articles, and the introductions to the various chapters, have been written. The sketch of Professor Baker first appeared in *Theatre Arts Monthly*.

They have not all of them been left as they first appeared. Fully conscious that what is here arranged in book form is not the Holy Writ, I have not hesitated to be guilty of sins of omission and commission for which I would never have dared to be responsible had I been editing the Koran. If, even in the altered pieces, I have let the original date lines stand, I have done so only for the sake of what such untheatrical angels as the one who disturbed Abou ben Adhem's slumber would have referred to as the record.

What these pages seek to do is to paint the picture of the contemporary theatre as it was when it was accessible to audiences; to paint it as it was when, usually at the midnight hours, with a deadline to be met and every fresh detail crying for attention, it had possessed a particular playgoer. In fairness I warn such readers as may not have appreciated the profound sagacity of Heywood Broun's "It Seems To Me" as a choice for a column head, that when, in the following pages, I have said "you," the sentence ought truthfully to read "me," and that when I have sunk to that impossibility known as "we," "I" is always a judicious substitute. If what follows is as personal, hence as fallible, as all criticism is bound to be, it can at any rate claim one virtue. If it is not hot off the griddle, it is at least hot off the "grid." This, if I may say so, is not only the point of these pages but the theatre's point too.

One other item; an all-important one. Mr. Shaw, in the gloriously stimulating days of his reviewing, once tossed off a paragraph all readers and writers of reviews should recall and all provokers of bad notices memorize. "The artist," wrote Mr. Shaw, with a heat which on another occasion he humorously described as imperiling "the habit of studied moderation of statement which years of public responsibility as a journalist have made second nature" in him, "The artist who accounts for my personal disparagement by alleging personal animosity on my part is quite right. When people do less than their best, and do that less at once badly and self-complacently, I hate them, I loathe them, detest them, long to tear them limb from limb and strew them in gobbets about the stage or platform. . . . The true critic is the man who becomes your personal enemy on the sole provocation of a bad performance, and will only be appeased by a good (one)."

Personal as a reviewer's notice of a good or bad performance may be (and this depends no less upon what he hears with his inner ear, thinks with his lonely mind, and feels with his solitary heart than upon what he is as the victim of his birth and life), the splendor of the critic's dreams for the theatre's possible perfection is not only the best thing about him but his major excuse for being.

The dramatic critic is as much a watchdog for beauty as he is a dismisser of cheapness, a scoffer at mediocrity, a hater of incompetence, a seismograph responsive to worthy excitement. His duty is to be rational in the presence of emotion, to think his feelings and to feel his thoughts. His job, which often sentences him to leading the life of a happy leper on an island no Father Damien will visit, is to rationalize reaction, interest his readers, suggest quality, recapture mood and atmosphere, comment on the theatre in terms of the theatre no less than of life, be true to what he is personally while being impersonal with those upon whose work he presumes to pass judgment—and to do all of these things under pressure of time. While being true to himself, he must be true to such a vision of perfection as may be his and of which every false move in the theatre reminds him by denying it.

If the dramatic critic seems harsh, he is harsh only from affection. He does not, he cannot, think of persons as persons, or jobs as a means to livelihood. His duty is to consider his readers while considering himself. Ultimately he shows the deepest possible consideration for both by his awareness of what THE THEATRE, not a theatre, might be on the basis of what each offering in a particular playhouse tells him that it ought to have been.

John Mason Brown

NEW YORK CITY

JUNE, 1940

BROADWAY
IN REVIEW

One

THE THEATRE IN WARTIME

A cry rang out in the town,
  A shout of blood through the houses,
And a frightened child caught his mother's skirt
  And hid himself in her cloak—
Then war came forth from his hiding place.

THESE are not contemporary lines. Their unadorned strength and immediacy is deceptive. They may sound as if Archibald MacLeish had composed them for a drama more recent than his *Air Raid*. They were not written yesterday, even if, tragically, they could just now be the yield of any day's writing. They were written more than two thousand years ago. Although they are as old as that, they are as young as today's news and tomorrow's threats. They come from the greatest antiwar play dramatic literature has ever produced. As goes without saying, they come from *The Trojan*

Women * of Euripides. They are lines written in the twelfth year of a twenty-five year war which was ultimately to rob Athens of its grandeur and its glory. They were spoken in a play which cost Euripides his citizenship and sent him into exile. It is hard just now to exile them from one's mind.

Into the darkest of all possible black worlds, War has once again come forth from his hiding place. In such a time, at such a moment, the theatre may seem a subject at once trivial and irrelevant. It all depends upon what is the ultimate hope of our living; it all depends upon what the theatre means to those who patronize it. Although entertainment is its most frequent goal, and it must offer pleasure in its highest moments of tragic pain, the theatre, truly considered—even when it annihilates time—is more than the shortest distance between two hours. It is more than the flowering of a vulgar street; more than the by-product of warring vanities; more than a badly run business which in its commerce most generally abuses an art. It is an expression of the hunger of the free human spirit for joy no less than ecstasy; for self-discovery through forgetfulness of self. It is a weapon for protest; a provider of pleasure. Because of it senses are heightened, perceptions quickened, and laughter or tears released by a beckoning extension of life in which endowments and discipline must go hand in hand. In it, in terms of color and movement, sound and sense, a group endeavor

* Edith Hamilton's translation.

and a group response, are faced the challenges of a
medium as difficult as it can be pleasurable. For the
theatre is more than this or that night's fact. In its long
history it has been, and continues at its best to be, a
symbol of what is finest in the aspirations and achievements of civilized man.

Years ago, Edmund Burke once spoke a famous
paragraph, harrowing in its application to the imperiled
theatre in this still more tragically imperiled universe.
"Choose a day," said he, "on which to represent the
most sublime and affecting tragedy we have; appoint
the most favorite actors; spare no cost upon the scenes
and decorations; unite the greatest efforts of poetry,
painting, and music—and, when you have collected
your audience, just at the moment when their minds
are erect with expectation, let it be reported that a state
criminal of high rank is on the point of being executed
in the adjoining square—in a moment the emptiness of
the theatre would demonstrate the comparative weakness of the imitative arts."

Today those arts face a grimmer competition. Their
weaknesses pale in comparison with the weaknesses
civilized man has betrayed in himself. If the world of
make-believe seems pitifully insignificant compared to
a world all too real in the horrors and misgivings, the
fears and the disasters with which everyone is hourly
haunted, that make-believe world has gained a new
reason for our affectionate faith. If the future is not to
be the present, it is our urgent need just now, where

we are still able to do so, to cup our hands protectingly and without shame before whatever candles may still flame on civilization's threatened altars.

At such a black moment in history, the arts—including the theatre—justify themselves in ways spiritual no less than aesthetic. They gain a new strength, a fresh excuse by so doing. The greatest comfort, indeed perhaps the surest and most eternal appeal, the arts have to offer to mankind is not beauty nor color nor sound nor excitement alone, nor any of those sustaining pleasures which nowadays are so frequently dismissed as being escapist. Their final contribution, especially at such hours as these, is the illusion of order they momentarily create in a world which our living sorrowfully informs us is most often haphazard and disordered. Even as religions have been created to sustain us by shaping the irrational hopes of the spirit into a design born of our reason, so the work of artists delights us by disregarding the irrelevant, by relating cause and effect, by establishing a sense of sequence, by superimposing an arbitrary pattern on the patternless, and by at least endeavoring to bring some kind of sanity out of chaos.

It is not for nothing that men with a gift for design should have needed, since the beginning of recorded time, to believe in a god who, regardless of the name under which he may have traveled, has always had a genius for design. Man's yearning to console himself with a rational plan for the inexplicable joys and tragedies of his living has always resulted in one of the most glorious, if touching, operations of his reason. Destiny, Fate, Providence are all of them only man-made certitudes betraying man's uncertainty.

To some of us, at any rate, such words as balance, symmetry, composition, and their like are words which stubbornly refuse to be corseted in any lean aesthetic vocabulary. They belong to a more universal language, an Esperanto of human hope, and speak for the unquenchable thirsts of the spirit.

Not long ago a distinguished scientist was pointing out that, just as religion was born of the need to combat ignorance, so nowadays faith is needed to combat knowledge. One dares to mention faith and religion, even when writing about a subject capable of being so splendidly profane as the Broadway theatre, because all religions and the drama operate under a special mandate. This mandate, once identified as the "beneficent illusion," * is only the arbitrary pattern superimposed by the theatre upon what is patternless in our living.

Mr. Shaw, who stands in no danger of being called precious or pious, once trumpeted his pride in the theatre by saying that in belonging to it he belonged to a church older than the Christian Church. He gave his faith to it, said he in his most satanic days, because it was the only temple from which gaiety had not been excluded as a means of correcting the foibles of mankind. He counted himself among its communicants, he

* Joseph Wood Krutch in *The Modern Temper.*

confessed, because to him the theatre was "the Church where the oftener you laugh, the better, because by laughter only can you destroy evil without malice, and affirm good fellowship without mawkishness."

Appalling as are the times, the theatre has not failed its parishioners by forgetting to celebrate its high mass for sweet laughter's sake. Hazlitt once insisted man is the only animal that laughs and weeps because he is the only animal struck with the difference between what things are and what they ought to be. At such moments as these, the theatre cannot be blamed if, in the sublimest sense of tragic writing, it has not often paused to remind men of what they ought to be—indeed what they could be—if only they were better than their clay.

Not unnaturally of late the theatre has also hesitated before doubling on the news and showing men and women what they are. If it has turned more escapist of recent months than it has been during many fruitful years of peacetime protest, it is not hard to find its justifications for so doing. Removed, at least geographically, as we are from the scene of the war, our theatre has not been untouched by the conflict. It may have lacked the courage to ask audiences to look without relief upon the head of the Medusa, but it has responded to the world's disaster by joyfully fulfilling its wartime function as a palace of forgetfulness. Whether it has operated as a place of reminder or of escape, it has continued to offer the consolation of the arbitrary pattern.

Infinite as are the distempers of the present, one is forced to take hope so long as somewhere the arts persist in freedom; and, while trembling at the more sinister diseases which today threaten the future, to sympathize as never before with the man who once said he trembled to think Shakespeare and Cervantes could ever have been exposed to measles at one and the same time.

Two

AS SPARKS FLY UPWARD

THE TRAGIC BLUEPRINT

IN NO way are the differences between what is patternless in our living and the pattern which the drama can superimpose upon life made clearer than in those differences which exist between death, as most of us are bound to face it, and death as it is encountered by the heroes and heroines of so-called high, or formal tragedy.

The finest statement of what is enduring in high tragedy's timeless blueprint is not to be found in the *Poetics* but in the Book of Job. Although Aristotle was on the threshold of truth when he spoke of tragedy's being an imitation of an action, serious, complete, and of a certain magnitude, and insisted, however erroneously, upon its effecting through pity and fear the proper purgation of these emotions, the sage of Stagira halted at truth's portal as Eliphaz, the Temanite, did not when he was exhorting that prince of suffering known as Job.

"Man is born unto trouble," said the Temanite, "as the sparks fly upward. I would seek unto God, and unto God would I commit my cause: Which doeth great things and unsearchable; marvelous things without number. . . . Behold, happy *is* the man whom God correcteth: therefore despise not thou the chastening of the Almighty: For he maketh sore, and bindeth up: he woundeth, and his hands make whole."

In all tragedies concerned with the unsearchable, hence high because of the altitude of their search no less than because of the elevation of their agony, the sparks fly upward as men and women, born unto trouble, are made whole by their suffering. By these sparks, which are great words struck from the anvil of great sorrow, are we kept warm in the presence of the pain endured by those wounded men and women who are tragedy's favorite sons and daughters, and illumined in what would otherwise be the darkness of their dying.

That we are able to attend their deaths without tears; that the yield of their anguish is in us a pleasant ecstasy greater than is our sympathy with their distress; that we experience no desire to save them from their fates and would, indeed, feel cheated were they to be robbed of the self-realization which, on the brink of oblivion, is so often theirs—should warn us of how far the Stagirite was from truth when he spoke of tragedy as an imitation of life. One thing is certain. Regardless of the extent to which they may pretend to imitate life as their heroes and heroines are hastened to their deaths, high tragedies discard all pretense of such imitation when death, not life, becomes their high concern. If they extend life while dealing with the living, they transcend it when death is their subject. Then it is most markedly that their feigned reality, however slight, surrenders to the "beneficent illusion" and the arbitrary pattern is consolingly superimposed upon the patternless. The lies they tell at such supreme moments are among the most resplendent and sustaining truths they have to offer.

Whatever our deathbed fates may be, this much we know. Our dying will not be similar to the dying of the heroes and the heroines of high tragedy. When they die, these men and women are apt to be possessors of a talent for verbalization such as we can never aspire to even in our hardiest moments of health. By a convention, born of beauty and of our need, they are fated to leave this earth spiritually cross-ventilated. Furthermore, they die without benefit of hospitalization. Always they go as victims of a design, with a toll to be paid either for a defect unmistakably established or a misdeed meriting punishment.

Our bodies, not our characters, are to blame if we have weak lungs or weak hearts. Thrombosis can switch off our consciousness at any moment without giving us

time to light up spiritually or signifying divine dis-
approval. The arteries of saints no less than sinners can
harden with old age. In everyday life longevity is the
result neither of moral grandeur nor of Sunday-school
applause. The good are asked to suffer with the bad,
usually more often and to a greater extent. Cause and
effect do not need to be on speaking terms to have
any one of us snuffed out. Infantile paralysis is not an
affliction which the innocent at five or eleven or at
any age can be said to have earned. Death rides through
life, not as a moral logician, inexorable in his demands,
but as a hit-and-run driver. We who live in cities are
aware that, while crossing the street—any street, at any
hour, and even with the lights in our favor—to do the
best good deed of which we are capable, we run the
risk of being struck down by a truck, the driver of
which will never have had anything against us except
his truck at an unfortunate moment of impact. We say
these haphazard misfortunes are beyond our understanding.

So they are, even as they are beyond the possibilities
of high tragedy. Melodramas, when hard pushed, may
enjoy dalliance with such disasters; never high tragedies. Although their concern is often the inexplicable,
they take pains to state their gropings in understanda-
ble terms. They take few chances with chance. Where
we, as actual men and women, may be confused by the
injustice of our lot, the heroes and the heroines of high
tragedy live lives and die deaths clearly motivated.

They are not ruled by coincidence in our fashion. They are deliberate parts of a visible design, even when, in our manner, their search is to comprehend their place in a larger design, infinite as it is inscrutable.

For them the tree of life is always cut with a single purpose—to make a cross. If they shape their crosses for themselves, it is because they belong to a race apart, these men and women who, by their suffering, give high tragedy its grandeur. In spite of what the church basements may have told us, there would have been no such thing as high tragedy had the world been peopled exclusively by Boy Scouts and Girl Scouts. More often than not the record of high tragedy is the record of splendid sinners who, always *after* sinning— if to no other extent than shirking their manifest duties, or surrendering to their defects—redeem themselves spiritually just before the moment of their taking off. This is but a part of the pattern of high tragedy, and of its moral obligation, too.

We, in our living, are aware every time we pass a hospital, magnificent and indispensable as it may be, that we are in the presence of a brick-and-stone re- minder of the frailties of the human body. The body, and all its sickroom failings, figures to an humiliating extent in our more leisurely deaths. In high tragedy what matters is always the flame and never the lamp; never the body and always the spirit.

This lifts high tragedy beyond tears even as it lifts it beyond pain. Run over the long list of the heroes and heroines of high tragedy and you will find that though these men and women have died from multifarious causes—have stabbed themselves or been stabbed, been poisoned, fallen like Romans on their swords, or died from snakebite, more classically known as aspbite—not one of them, at the moment of intense pain and imminent death, has ever surrendered to the mortal luxury of an "ouch." This is why even in an age of realism, no attempt wisely is ever made to deal realistically with their wounds. Their spirits spill the only blood that matters; and it is life-giving even when life is being taken.

Sinners or not, the heroes and heroines of high tragedy belong (as Edith Hamilton has pointed out) to the only genuine aristocracy known to this world— the aristocracy of truly passionate souls. In spite of economists or the most hopeful of Utopians, there is one respect in which men and women are doomed forever to be unequally endowed. This lies in their capacity to suffer. If this capacity is among the most ineradicable of mortal inequalities, it is among the most notable gifts of high tragedy's heroes and heroines. Their genius is to suffer greatly, and in their sufferings to ring music from the very dissonances of life.

By convention they not only feel acutely and speak greatly for their authors and all the rest of us while speaking for themselves, but always have what we shall never have when our lungs are exhausted on hospital cots, and that is the last word. A poet's endowment enables them to sing their way into heaven. They trumpet themselves into paradise, releasing such verbal splendors that we forget their agonies and are sustained by the music with which they orchestrate death.

Pathos is everywhere one of the most common of emotional commodities. In no country is it held in higher esteem than here where we have Sealpack handkerchiefs to keep up with it and Hollywood to see to it that what might be our sympathetic dust bowls are in no danger of not being moist. Although it is as widespread as are the mishaps briefly reported in every daily newspaper, the pathetic is never the tragic. It is only the tragedy of the small-souled, the average, the commonplace. Its dividend is at the least sighs, at the most tears, and never ecstasy because it is no more than unhappy and can claim no fortune in misfortune.

The theatre knows a host of pathetic plays. It knows its tragedies, too—welcome enough, often dissolving, sometimes provocative, occasionally exquisite in their poignancy—which seek to deal with nothing more than the worries of men and women as they hurt, or are hurt by, one another or their neighbors. But high tragedies are more than earth-bound. They are translunary as opposed to terrestrial, if for no other reason than that their heroes and heroines are bent upon facing imponderables. They extend their interest beyond their neighbors to the forces controlling their destinies. There are more things in the heaven and earth of these turbulent worldings than are dreamt of in the philosophies of the tamer Horatios of this planet, however good or kind. If as characters these heroes and heroines take on spiritually the dimensions of their interests, their interest is not unrequited. The gods, the stars, and nature itself may direct their misadventures, but they care for these people as these people care for them. Cries Hecuba:

> *O thou who does uphold the world*
> *Whose throne is high above the world*
> *Thou, past our seeking to find, what art thou?*
> *God, or Necessity of what must be,*
> *Or reason of our reason,*
> *Whate'er thou art, I pray to thee,*
> *Seeing the silent road by which*
> *All mortal things are led by thee to justice.**

And her cry, in one form or another, addressed to Jove, to God, to Destiny, to Heaven, to Dat Ole Davvil Sea, Mother Dynamo, or the godhead in one's self, is apt, sooner or later, to be the cry of all the men and women whose authors have sought to follow the tragic blueprint. Part of the greatness of these characters is that with their eyes they at least dare to look for the unseeable, and with their ears they hear harmonies to which most of us are deaf.

When they die, self-realized by their suffering, they do not relinquish life but are at last released from it. They fall as mortals so complete that they have lost both their desire and excuse for living. Death for

* Edith Hamilton's translation.

them is not a cessation of life. It is a fulfillment of self. Their living on, when the book is closed, would only mean for them and us the letdown of a sequel. Hence they and we can be happy in their dying. Macbeth is the only one of Shakespeare's major tragic characters who dies unworthily, self-despising and despised. The others feel to varying degrees, in language appropriate to their natures, the exaltation of Mark Antony's:

> *I will be*
> *A bridegroom in my death, and run into't*
> *As to a lover's bed.*

Or they die as monarchs of their own spirits in Cleopatra's fashion, when she utters the superb speech beginning:

> *Give me my robe, put on my crown; I have*
> *Immortal longings in me. . . .*
> *husband, I come.*
> *Now to that name my courage prove my title!*
> *I am fire and air; my other elements*
> *I give to baser life.*

No wonder, in the presence of such a spirit, one feels that Death himself has struggled for its surrender. Or that Charmian, when the asp has done its tragic duty, can say as she surveys the body of the dead queen:

> *So fare thee well,*
> *Now boast thee, death, in thy possession lies*
> *A lass unparallel'd.*

If those words form the finest caption for the "beneficent illusion" of high tragedy known to our language,
there are plenty of others scarcely less noble or sustaining. When Kent salutes the body of the dead Lear
with:

Vex not his ghost: O, let him pass! he hates him much
That would upon the rack of this tough world
Stretch him out longer

he is speaking one of these, and following the pattern of
death, made painless by its verbal and spiritual splendors, in high tragedy. Although many have tried and
only a handful have succeeded, all dramatists, before
and after Shakespeare, seeking to write high tragedy
have worked, however variously, from the same blueprint. Recently, for example, in *Murder in the Cathe-
dral*, a play which managed to become a play in spite
of T. S. Eliot, Mr. Eliot had his Thomas à Becket
sing, and sing beautifully, tragedy's timeless song.
When his Becket knew his murderers to be at the gates
of Canterbury, Mr. Eliot had him send away his protecting priests with these magical words:

I have had a tremor of bliss, a wink of heaven, a whisper,
And I would no longer be denied; all things
Proceed to a joyful consummation.

In our living we know only too well that, New Deal
or no New Deal, few things ever proceed to a joyful
consummation. The moral pleasure, and one of the
aesthetic delights, of high tragedy is to persuade us that

all things might so proceed, if only we were or could be better than our clay.

In the following pages three tragedies written according to the tragic pattern are discussed. Two of them are by William Shakespeare; one is by Maxwell Anderson. If *Romeo and Juliet*, however acted, is no more than a youthful groping after the tragic, *Hamlet* is of course one of the wonders of our literature. Hamlet may be an indecisive prince, but he is a great soul in distress. His interests are not limited to the court at Elsinore. Flights of angels sing him to his rest.

No contemporary understands the exaltation of the tragic pattern better than Maxwell Anderson. No one has written about it with more fervor or eloquence. Mr. Anderson is well aware that if we save our necks by losing our souls we might better be six feet under. As a dramatist whose understanding of the tragic is profound, however disappointing his tragedies may be, he knows the mere act of being alive does not mean any one of us is living. He is as conscious as we all are that the number of unburied living who clutter up the earth's surface is legion. He is no less aware that the spiritual and intellectual zombies to be met with daily are countless. As a dramatist, at least aiming at the tragic, he is not interested in these zombies except as they redeem themselves. As such a dramatist, he knows it is only by losing our necks that we can save our souls.

Mr. Anderson shows his wisdom in *Key Largo* by realizing that in high tragedy, or tragedy which aims at being high, the geographical whereabouts of God matters as little as does the name He may be given. In his prologue, the best part of an unsatisfactory play, Mr. Anderson has one of his young Americans, fighting at the front for Loyalist Spain, speak a speech in the best tragic manner. He is the young American who refuses to desert when Mr. Anderson's hero tries to persuade him to do so by telling him he and his comrades have been betrayed. What the young American says is:

*I have to believe
there's something in the world that isn't evil—
I have to believe there's something in the world
that would rather die than accept injustice—something
positive for good—that can't be killed—
or I'll die inside. And now that the sky's found empty
a man has to be his own god for himself—
has to prove to himself that a man can die
for what he believes—if ever the time comes to him
when he's asked to choose, and it just so happens
it's up to me tonight.—And I stay here.
I don't say it's up to you—I couldn't tell
about another man—or any of you—
but I know it's up to me.*

When in the last act of *Key Largo* Mr. Anderson's hero is dying, after saving his soul by losing his neck in a silly gangster plot on the island off Florida which gives the play its title, Mr. Anderson once again follows the tragic pattern. "Is this dying?" his hero asks, when the gangster's bullet is in his stomach,

> *Then it's more enviable than the Everglades,*
> *to fight where you can win, in a narrow room,*
> *and to win, dying.*

Mr. Anderson follows the same pattern again when, after his hero's death, the detective, playing a faint echo to Shakespeare's Kent, says:

> *You can't be sorry*
> *for a man that planned it, and it all worked out,*
> *and he got what he wanted—*

Much as one may regret that the fly of this emotion has not been embalmed in the amber of great language, one is also forced to realize that when Mr. Anderson follows the tragic pattern he is too well aware of its theory for his own creative good. He writes of ecstasy by rote rather than inspiration. And the pattern shrinks whenever it is memorized, not felt and rediscovered by the spiritual needs of each dramatist who feels the great need of employing it.

Hamlet UNABRIDGED

TIME in the theatre cannot be told by what the hands of clocks, or watches, or even sundials say. A minute there is elastic. It is as short as our interest in it, or as long as the boredom it may have brought us. Although every playgoer knows this, only those who have attended Maurice Evans' production of *Hamlet* in its entirety are apt to know how brief, yet how exciting and unforgettable, almost every minute can seem of five long hours passed in the footlights' presence. Those five hours race by at the St. James. They are as brief as they are full of memorable pleasures. One leaves them not fatigued but filled with an uncommon exhilaration. It is an exhilaration born of, and kept alive by, the ever-present knowledge that what one is seeing is a great play so greatly done that all its innumerable greatnesses are made incessantly communicative.

When last night's audience had hoarsened itself by such cheers as Americans are apt to release only at football games or when more Relief appropriations have been announced, and the actors had taken enough curtain calls to stiffen their necks with bowing, Mr. Evans finally gave way to the inevitable. He made a curtain speech. It was a model of graciousness. It contained, moreover, one sentence which sums up in a line the unique virtue not only of his production but also of his performance of the Dane. "I have long wanted to produce a *Hamlet*," said he, "which would be a play rather than a case of dyspepsia."

This is precisely what he and his excellent company have done with the brilliant aid of Margaret Webster's

direction before David Ffolkes' helpful settings. By
bringing the whole of *Hamlet* to the stage for the first
time in our history, Mr. Evans as a manager has performed a signal service both to William Shakespeare
and to contemporary audiences. By acting the Prince
as admirably as he does, Mr. Evans has added overnight
many cubits to the reputation his Romeo, his Dauphin,
his Napoleon, and, particularly, his Richard II have
already won for him.

Mr. Evans' determination to present the uncut *Hamlet* refuses to be described as a stunt in showmanship. It
comes as no attempt to steal for Shakespeare the long-
distance bays hitherto held by such marathon runners
as Mr. Shaw and Mr. O'Neill. For once, the text comes
across with all its wonders intact. Hamlet remains Hamlet, though even he has grown. The drama's most famous piece of living sculpture is given an appropriate
pedestal and background. Hermione-like, his "natural
posture" becomes a source of wonder. The tragedy
ceases to be vehicular in the traditional sense. It
emerges as a thrilling entity, a work of art in which
the supreme artist who fathered it has his unimpeded
say. No hacks have dared to prune his script pretending they knew his business better than he did. No star
has used his actor's vanity as a blotter to absorb the
secondary characters.

Shakespeare speaks at the St. James as he wanted to
speak in the form he had made his own. It is fascinating
to see how his tragedy grows as an undwarfed Hamlet

is brought into contact with a Claudius, a Gertrude, a Polonius, an Ophelia, a Laertes, a Rosencrantz, a Guildenstern, and even a Marcellus fully grown. These so-called subsidiary characters now explain themselves to theatregoers as in the past they have done only to readers. You can almost hear the blue pencil being lifted from them, as if it were a barrier at a racecourse. So released, they run an interesting race which more than justifies their inclusion in it.

Too much cannot be said in praise of Miss Webster's direction. It is at all times original without being "stunt-y," and inventive with an invention which can only spring from a profound comprehension of the text. In scene after scene it ignites the action with a fire which I, for one, have never seen equaled in Elsinore, and I have seen every major *Hamlet* staged in this country since the twilight days of Forbes-Robertson. Not one of these productions has surpassed, or in any way approached, Miss Webster's for pictorial loveliness in its groupings, for revelatory byplay, or for sheer melodramatic excitement.

Mr. Evans has surrounded himself with an astonishingly fine company. Even the smaller parts, with one or two very minor exceptions, are handled with the skill with which Donald Cameron plays Marcellus. Most of the important secondary characters are played with unrivaled excellence. Augustin Duncan is an effective Ghost. Whitford Kane is once again a lovable First Gravedigger. George Graham, though he muffles some of his words, is by all odds the most humorous, human, and individualized Polonius whose garrulity I remember to have enjoyed. Henry Edwards is a superlative King; a fellow troubled by the crime he has committed, and yet able to establish his villainy the more forcefully by keeping it deep within himself.

Although at rare moments Mady Christians may relapse into an accent almost as thick as Modjeska's is reputed to have been, her Gertrude is a triumph of acting. It is beautiful to look upon, played to define her as an innocent and compassionate bystander, and deeply moving except in its somewhat stiff recitation of "There is a willow grows aslant." As for Katherine Locke, she is, both before and during her mad scenes, the most poignant, clearly spoken, and intelligently conceived Ophelia I have so far encountered. She is the first Ophelia who has not waited for her "Mad Margaret" moments to establish her real character; and the first to explain how deep was her love for Hamlet. As a matter of fact, the Laertes and the Horatio of Mr. Evans' revival are the only pivotal parts which are disappointingly played. Although he betters perceptibly toward the end, Sydney Smith leaves much to be desired as Laertes. And the Horatio of Donald Randolph manages to make a blank out of one of Shakespeare's most charming creations.

It takes a few minutes to become adjusted to Mr. Evans as Hamlet, even as it did to surrender to his Romeo. At first sight he seems to lack physical presence.

During the initial court scene he is haunted inescapably by memories of John Barrymore's lean regality and Mr. Gielgud's fiery unhappiness. Soon thereafter he establishes himself triumphantly in the part. His Prince escapes detailed comparison with recent Hamlets by being a Hamlet very much Mr. Evans' own. It does not follow tradition; it creates a new and, if I may say so, very welcome one.

The Hamlet he acts, in colors unorthodox in their gaiety, is not outwardly the melancholy Dane we have come to expect. His sadness is in his heart rather than on his face. Although at the outset he may seem to be uncerebral, the proofs of his thinking are constant and stimulating. Unlike most recent Hamlets, Mr. Evans is not a neurotic princeling with a pale visage who strikes despairing poses under spotlights. He is the first entirely masculine Hamlet of our time. He has wit, gaiety, vitality, and charm. Watching him, one understands what the King means when he describes Hamlet's spirit as being "free and generous"; why dueling should be something at which he excels; and why Fortinbras insists after his death that "the rites of war speak loudly for him."

Mr. Evans' Dane is, in other words, not the introvert Mr. Gielgud disclosed so brilliantly. He has a consistency Mr. Gielgud's Hamlet never dreamed of achieving, and a brilliance of his own which is no less rewarding. Mr. Evans, moreover, is an actor who does not lose control of himself. His performance shows

careful planning and is always in hand. He saves himself for his more torrential outbursts and realizes them
superbly. His voice is a beautiful instrument, capable
of doing justice to the magnificent beauty of the lines
he speaks.

Exceptional as he is throughout, in such moments as
the scene with Ophelia which he turns into a heartbreaking love scene, or as in the tempestuous excitement of the "play-within-a-play," or as in the glorious
tension of his closet scene with Gertrude, Mr. Evans
proves himself to be the finest actor of our day in a
production which is by all odds the most satisfying and
most moving *Hamlet* has received within not-so-recent
memory.

This man Evans is a superlative performer, a genius
the stage is fortunate in claiming as its own. What Flagstad is to grand opera he is to the theatre. Should proof
be needed nowadays of the theatre's greatness and of
the fact that great acting has not vanished from the
earth, this proof can be found in abundance at the St.
James these late afternoons and nights in the person of
Mr. Evans and his revival of *Hamlet* in its entirety.

October 13, 1938

MR. EVANS' DANE

MR. EVANS' Hamlet, so unconventional in its vigor,
so extrovert in its virtues, so contrary to tradition in

its very masculinity, has burst upon this town as a new and welcome interpretation of a Prince usually played as if he were a fugitive from a psychopathic hospital, a cross between Dr. Caligari and Rodin's Thinker, and the first male interior decorator.

To maintain that Mr. Evans' is the only interpretation of the part would be to tell a lie, for one of the proofs of the play's greatness is that it refuses to admit a final Hamlet. Also it would be to turn one's back churlishly on those actors who, in our time and in their own ways, have illumined the cut texts in which they have chosen to appear. Forbes-Robertson's Hamlet was a notable creation, the vocal beauties of which still ring in the ears of those who saw it. But when seen, as I happened to see it, at the time of the farewell tour, Forbes-Robertson's Dane was so unmistakably autumnal that, as one listened to him talking about having just come down from college at Wittenberg, even a playgoer as young as I was then was forced to wonder if Hamlet were not a sad case of arrested development. Mr. Mantell's performance had about it more of the feeling of a poetic undertaker than of a noble mind in deep distress. Mr. Sothern, though expert both as Malvolio and Petruchio, always acted a stolid Prince, a sort of early broker, in mourning for his losses, who had just voted for Landon.

To claim the aforesaid finality for Mr. Evans' Hamlet would also be to overlook the excellent and touching tragic figure Mr. Hampden created in his early matinees, before his Dane had become so scholarly that he substituted a Phi Beta Kappa key for a rapier. It would be to forget the dynamic splendors of Mr. Barrymore's realization of the Prince as a hot-tempered neurotic capable of magnificent theatrical effects. It would be to ignore Basil Sydney's memorable modern dress performance which was expertly read, especially in the Speech to the Players, and did much to rediscover for contemporary audiences the wonders of the play as a play. It would be to discount, as one cannot, the brilliant flashes of cerebration by means of which Mr. Gielgud's fiery weakling cast a new and brilliant light upon many familiar passages.

Yet a major glory of Mr. Evans' Prince is the hitherto unrevealed and unsuspected Hamlet he establishes. Between all the previous Hamlets, good and bad, that I have seen, a certain bond of orthodoxy has existed. Dissimilar as they may have been because of the gifts and temperaments of their projectors, most of these Hamlets have either been, or sought to be, brothers in much the same kind of melancholy. They have been solitary fellows, white-faced squatters on Savonarola chairs, black mourners, spotlight searchers, tragic poets in a rough age, or heartbroken soliloquizers. All of them have been men of inaction, condemned by fate to do deeds for which they had no liking and were ill equipped.

They have taken literally Hamlet's description of himself as being "so poor a man a Hamlet is." For them the time has been out of joint, as out of joint it must

be no matter how the play is interpreted. Their special
tragedy has always been the "curséd spite" that ever
they were born to set it right. On this line they seem
to have built their whole characterizations as surely as
Peter's church was built upon a rock. Moreover, they
have often so superbly justified their morbid Danes on
the basis of the cut text that, until Mr. Evans came
along justifying his extrovert Hamlet on the authority
of the unabridged script, no other Hamlet had seemed
quite possible.

Now at least we know the tragedy can yield a Prince
totally different from the Prince we had begun to take
for granted. We have also come to realize with much
joy not only that the part, but also that the play as a
whole, gains enormously in freshness and vitality when
it is given the benefit of a re-evaluation as exciting as
the one which Mr. Evans, Miss Webster, and their
actors have given it at the St. James.

Mr. Evans' Hamlet is very much a man. He bounds
into Elsinore with the vigor of a Legionnaire. In part,
at least, he is the soldier Fortinbras deems worthy, after
death, of military honors. His is the "noble heart"
Horatio salutes. He is one of the few Hamlets of our
time who has waited for his soliloquies before beginning to soliloquize. He is the only Hamlet I have seen
who has explained why he should have made friends
in college who would have bothered to look him up
afterwards. If he despises Osric, it is because he makes
clear, as many contemporary Hamlets have failed to

do, the differences in type and temperament which set him apart from "this water-fly." It is easy to understand his dashing Prince's eagerness to test his skill with Laertes upon hearing of Laertes' prowess with the rapier.

From the first, however, he is unhappy in his heart. Unlike his predecessors, he does not wear his sufferings on his sleeves. Thoughtful as he is, he is not a sandwich man for melancholia. He has wit. He has charm. He is normal, though distressed. With all the beauty of Mr. Evans' voice and the controlled surety of his excellent readings, he does justice both to the poetry and the passion of the text. Mr. Evans' Hamlet is a Prince born of the whole play. He is not a creation made possible by whittling it down until only a stellar part is left.

It is the full-grown Hamlet of the full-grown tragedy Mr. Evans seeks to explain. Just as surely as the secondary characters are permitted to grow on the authority of such a text, so does Hamlet himself take on new dimensions. Mr. Evans is, for example, the only Hamlet of our time who, in addition to his gifts as a thinker and a poet, is a Prince in the executive sense. One feels that, if everything had gone well around the palace, as he might have hoped it would, Mr. Evans' Hamlet could have succeeded his father and become an admirable ruler in his own right. Obviously his spirit has been touched, as an Elizabethan princeling's would have been, by Machiavelli's. Whereas most of the Hamlets of our time, at the moment of their dying, would have been right in reaching for the collected works of Freud, Mr. Evans is the only Hamlet I have seen who died thinking about the state and the Danish equivalents of such political issues as the Third Term and the New Deal. In other words, he is the only Prince whose misadventures I have followed in Elsinore who is statesman enough to make one understand why Hamlet, before crying, "The rest is silence," should be curious about the election news from England, and trouble to give Fortinbras his dying voice.

Then, too, unlike most Hamlets, he does not wait until after Ophelia is safely dead to make known his love for her. No moment in the play gains more by its disregard of stage tradition than does Mr. Evans' scene with Ophelia. By postponing Hamlet's glimpse of the hidden king and Polonius until "Where's your father?" Mr. Evans and Miss Webster change the whole meaning and value of "Get thee to a nunnery." In their hands it ceases to be the usual bitter, almost hysterical cry of rage. It becomes a tender and protective declaration of love. For Mr. Evans speaks the speech in a voice heavy and sweet with affection. His arms are around Ophelia; his head is buried in her bosom. His one pathetic hope seems to be to protect her from the world full of sinners he has been forced into knowing.

You may wonder why so vigorous a Hamlet as Mr. Evans creates can be so slow in revenging his father's murder. Certainly, his Dane is colored with a "native hue of resolution" which is never *"sicklied o'er"* with

a "pale cast of thought." Yet he finds as much justification for his active Hamlet as the pallid, indecisive
Hamlets have been able to find.

Although Mr. Evans' Dane is no coward, he has a
conscience. It is this conscience which turns awry his
enterprises of "great pitch and moment" until they
may seem to "lose the name of action." Like every
Hamlet, Mr. Evans' healthy young intellectual curses
the spite that has doomed him at his birth to the doing
of bloody deeds. When he utters this complaint, however, it does not come from the heart of a weakling
incapable of action and filled with neuroses. Both his
dilemma and his "dull revenge" are fully explained in
his "How all occasions do inform against me" soliloquy.
It is on this speech, rather than on the more familiar
cry against spiteful doom, that he builds his Hamlet, and
by means of which he seems to justify it. One believes
implicitly in Mr. Evans' Dane when he points out he
has the "cause," the "will," the "strength," and the
"means" to do what he has been fated to do. The only
thing delaying him, as Mr. Evans makes clear, is "some
craven scruple of thinking too precisely on the event."

November 8, 1938

THE LESSER ROLES IN *Hamlet*

FINE though his performance is, Mr. Evans' Dane is
not the only untraditional and illuminating feature of

the uncut *Hamlet*. Margaret Webster shares with Mr. Evans the honor of being the hero of the occasion. Her direction is an almost constant source of wonder and delight. Freshening as it is, however, its revelations would remain unrealized were it not for the supporting cast with which Mr. Evans has been both wise and generous enough to surround his Prince. The extensions and innovations in the following secondary characters are typical of the new theatrical qualities gained by the play at the St. James. They may serve to explain why some of us have not hesitated to maintain that no one can claim to have seen *Hamlet* who has not sat before the play as Mr. Evans and Miss Webster have presented it in the unabridged version.

THE KING. Anyone who recalls the Claudiuses in the *Hamlets* of the last twenty years must remember they have been acted as deep-dyed villains. They have tended to wear brass crowns around the palace at all times of the day or night to establish their kingship. Most of them have gone so far as to cover their chins with blood-red beards in order to advertise their divine right to be hated as potential murderers. They have always looked as if they had just stolen the Brooklyn police records. They have been Desperate Desmonds in ancient dress. They have wandered around the castle as if they were looking for some room in which they could fingerprint themselves. Spotting them as the public enemies they have so aggressively been would never have caused Mr. J. Edgar Hoover's men any difficulty. The wonder has been that they have ever fooled the Court. Or that Gertrude (innocent or an accomplice) should ever have consented to marry them after having lived with such a nice old fellow as King Hamlet must have been.

Henry Edwards' Claudius is fortunately not sprung from the Krimsky Brothers' line of hissables. Instead of resembling one of the regal Jack-the-Rippers of tradition, he is wise enough to mask the wickedness of his Claudius. His King is spiritually a slyer fellow than the Musica family could boast. He is a suave man who, as all temporarily successful villains must be, is capable of committing a crime and hiding his guilt without arousing the suspicions of everyone except a house detective. He is a courtier and a king. He shows how heavy his crime hangs upon him (in other words, how right the Ghost is) only when he attempts to pray or watches the play. He is a palace intriguer attractive enough to feel safe in gratifying his ambitions. The Comte de Provence and the Comte d'Artois, those Iscariot brothers of Louis XVI, could have exchanged fraternity grips with him.

Furthermore, Mr. Edwards' Claudius is the first I have ever seen who either feels, or is justified in feeling, the physical attraction for his brother's wife about which young Hamlet minces no words. His love for Gertrude is so poignantly established that one is forced to wonder why, at the very moment the Queen is drinking from the poisoned goblet, Miss Webster should have missed one of her few humanizing values by allowing Claudius to cry to the whole Court the aside reading, "It is the poison'd cup; it is too late," without rushing sadly to her side.

THE QUEEN. Most Queens in the cut versions have sauntered through the text as if they were mute sisters of Lady Macbeth who, among the duties of their high office, had been obliged to become honorary president of the Garden Club. Or they have pouted around the palace resembling nothing so much as pigs searching for truffles.

Mady Christians is a brilliant exception. One look at her is almost enough to explain why Claudius wished to get his older brother out of the way. Obviously the Queen Miss Christians creates did not mean to be unfaithful to her first husband when she married her second. Plainly she is the kind of woman who did not bother to distinguish between them, because of her group interest in men. Miss Christians' Gertrude is a forerunner of the female lean-to Chekhov had in mind when he wrote *The Darling*. In the frosty Court of Denmark she burns on the overtime schedule of the midnight sun. She is unaware of the dirty work in the garden which has changed the seating of her breakfast table.

She is attractive, interested, and queenly—at least on state occasions. She is at once a doting mother, a considerate queen, and a more than doting wife. She is a compassionate and seductive Gertrude who is the more ardent because of her age. If she is capable of tragedy in the closet scene, she indulges in coquetry throughout. She is so busy ordering dresses and keeping her "men folk" happy that it is little short of miraculous she does not find time to sing one of *India's Love Lyrics* while reading the *Boston Cook Book* on the throne.

OPHELIA. Most Ophelias, of course, either succeed in their earlier episodes of sanity or in their later mad scenes. None to my recollection has ever succeeded in both to the extent that Katherine Locke succeeds. She is the first Ophelia I have ever watched who did not act as if the entire Court had anticipated her lunacy all these many years. She is the first Ophelia who, when her madness has descended upon her, has not rushed to her room upstairs to get down from her closet that sort of public nightgown which can only be described as her little mad dress, and which apparently she has had hanging there for many seasons along with her other clothes for every occasion.

Most Ophelias, of course, when they return to the stage so dressed, have always taken pains to let down their hair. When a woman lets down her hair in the theatre, needless to say, it always means one of two things, and the second of these is insanity. Although Miss Locke may bow to convention by deranging her coiffure, she creates something of a precedent by not forcing one to look forward to her lunacy when she is sane, or to her death when she is mad. In her introductory scenes she appears as a young woman both intelligent and charming. She is intelligent enough to have been to Vassar, and charming enough to win forgiveness for having gone there.

She is the first Ophelia I know of who so fully projects her passionate love for Hamlet that she explains his no less passionate love for her. The country dances she executes with her back turned to the King and the Queen, while singing her mad songs, are welcome escapes from the traditional Raquel Meller "Will-you-buy-my-violets" business and even Miss Gish's effective stocking tuggings.

What is true of the King, the Queen, and Ophelia as they are revitalized at the St. James is no less true of the process of vitalization which quickens the whole of Mr. Evans' *Hamlet*. Small wonder, therefore, when so superb a play is realized in such superb and tingling terms, that Mr. Atkinson should write in his most classical style, "Only the dopes will stay away from this one!"   *November 9, 1938*

MR. OLIVIER'S AND MISS LEIGH'S
UNFAIR VERONA

IN A manner William Shakespeare did not anticipate, Romeo and Juliet were lovers star-cross'd and misad-

ventur'd in Laurence Olivier's and Vivien Leigh's
hands last evening. Although the mask of night was
not on Juliet's face, it was on almost everything else at
the Fifty-first Street. It had settled like a heavy fog on
nearly all the beauties of a play which, however irritat-
ing it may prove in the silliness of its avoidable catas-
trophes or infantile as it may be as a groping after true
tragedy, boasts its lyric wonders and its acting challenges that for centuries, and with reason, have persuaded audiences to be forgetful of its faults.

Potentially Mr. Olivier might scale the difficult garden wall all Romeos, especially all modern Romeos,
have to climb. Potentially, too, Miss Leigh might prove
a Juliet worthy of admiration in and out of her balcony. Miss Leigh is a pretty woman, even if her features fail to project in a backstage Verona the beauty
an enlarging camera gave them at Tara. She has a body,
slim as it is graceful, which in a silent movie could meet
the age requirements in this case of a cruelly specific
text. Mr. Olivier is a handsome fellow, whenever he
stands still long enough for one to catch a fleeting
glimpse of his full face. He is, moreover, an actor who
in England has not only enjoyed considerable experience in playing Shakespeare but who has won plentiful
devotees.

The two of them, as I suggest, might make an ac-
ceptable Romeo and Juliet if only an excellent director
were present to see them and the play from out front,
and, above all, to listen with loving ears to what Shake-

speare has written. Mr. Olivier, however, has elected to
stage the tragedy in addition to presenting it and playing Romeo. From the distressing evidence turned in
all too plentifully last night, I am forced to gather Mr.
Olivier is not the ideal director for Mr. Olivier, Miss
Leigh, or William Shakespeare.

Under his supervision, *Romeo and Juliet,* so hot in
its impulses, so youthful in its spirit, so tumultuous in
its fatuous action, becomes a dead march from the
rise of the first curtain. Not its last scene alone, but all
of it is laid in a tomb. Satisfactory as are many of Mot-
ley's Fra Angelico settings when they spin around on a
revolving stage, the fire of the narrative is extinguished
at every pictorial moment by the dampening fussiness,
the tedium, the downright irrelevance of all the Hollywood business Mr. Olivier has painstakingly intro-
duced. In every sense of the word he has gone in for
dumb show, forgetting that what gives wings to the
love story he is staging is not its camera possibilities
but its verse.

So unaware of the melodic values of Shakespeare's
poetry does Mr. Olivier seem to be that, in addition to
gulping down most of his lines as if they were so many
bad oysters, he overcrowds the backstage with unseen
musicians and choristers at many significant moments
to create the music he and Miss Leigh fail to find in the
music of the lines they are speaking. The result is less
like carrying coals to Newcastle than toting violins
to Stradivarius.

Mr. Olivier is all over the place as Romeo. His amorous Montague is part Fairbanks-Robin Hood, part Jitterbug, part Bela Lugosi, and all of them well shaken by more scenery-clinging, crouching, handwaving, and posturing than has been seen hereabouts in many comparatively tranquil theatrical years. If in the farewell scene and some of his later episodes, Mr. Olivier begins to show what his Romeo might be with some kind of direction, he does unfortunately seem to spend the rest of the evening dodging his own shadow and Shakespeare's verse.

Pretty as she is, lovely as is her pliant body, Miss Leigh appears to be no less tone-deaf than Mr. Olivier in the presence of Mary Arden's boy. She is all motion and picture and no real sound. Although her voice is pleasant enough, especially in its less flat moments of emphasis, she never responds to the cadences of the verse she utters. Even her moonlit lines in the balcony scene emerge from her throat as prose—arid, muted, pedestrian.

If a director could work wonders with Mr. Olivier, one suspects he could work more wonders with Miss Leigh. Her Juliet may be young and still lack the warming spirit of youth. It may bump about on one of the O'Hara's postwar nags when it is meant to soar on Pegasus. It may lack humor, tenderness, pointing, variety, and the distinguishing qualities of true lyricism by means of which, for example, Miss Cornell embodied all tremulous young love. Still it is more satisfactory than Mr. Olivier's Romeo. Somehow one is ready to believe that, with a director to teach her the ABC's of blank verse and to go over each line with her, Miss Leigh would make a satisfactory Juliet.

Of the rest of the cast, the less said the better, especially in the case of Halliwell Hobbes' preposterously jocund Capulet. Dame May Whitty, of whom much was expected, misses every comic value and all the rich qualities of the Nurse. Edmond O'Brien is the worst of all imaginable Mercutios. Only the Peter of Raymond Johnson, the Benvolio of Wesley Addy, and Alexander Knox as Laurence, that flat-footed friar, that Neville Chamberlain of Western Union boys, are passable. The pity is that Mr. Addy, the company's only Shakespearean actor whose skill is known to the New York stage, should have been given so little to do.

One wonders how the Prologue, in the face of such a slow-moving production, ever dares to speak of "the two hours' traffic of our stage." For the proceedings, more dismal than exciting, last much longer than that and seem twice as endless as *Gone With the Wind*.

May 10, 1940

MUSIC AS THE FOOD OF LOVE

ONE virtue of debatable merit can be claimed by Miss Leigh's and Mr. Olivier's *Romeo and Juliet*. By its very ineptitudes it succeeds, as no other professional revival of the tragedy in our time has succeeded, in exposing all those shortcomings, in tragic profundity no less than in logical plotting, which are blemishes, usually obscured, in the staging of Shakespeare's play.

That the script has its beauties no one can deny. They are beauties of such an ingratiating kind that they have not only won immortality for the play but continue to win forgiveness for its faults. These beauties include what can be (but is not at the Fifty-first Street) the hot turmoil of the active introductory scenes by means of which the story itself is swiftly unfolded and the feudist passions of the Renaissance are dramatically established.

They number, too, the flaming malignity of Tybalt; the bawdy humanity and prankish spirit of the Nurse; the sententious lullabies of Friar Laurence; the sheer glory of such an aria as the Queen Mab speech; the roistering heartbreak of Mercutio's dying; and, as goes without saying, the moonlit quality of all young love which hovers above the script like a heavy perfume and finds its most magical expression in the balcony scene and the farewell in Juliet's chamber.

What is irresistible in the play is its song. It can be —it often is—a melody of such sweet persuasion that the ears are fiddled into a delight absolute enough to lull the reason to a well-earned rest. Without this music *Romeo and Juliet* suffers cruelly. It becomes as

blossomless as a cherry tree in midwinter. It is all trunk
and no foliage. And the trunk of the play's plotting
does not bear inspection. When one can no longer
surrender to the drama's sound, one has too much time
in which to object to the sense.

It becomes impossible not to protest at what is incredible in the play's tale of all-too-sudden love at
first sight. It is no less difficult not to be made aware
of the emotional immaturity of the two young lovers,
or to realize how much more they are in love with
love than with one another. One is forced to admit
that, except for the misfortune of their birth in warring houses, these same hot innocents are never so
much star-cross'd as they are author-doomed.

To Bardolaters it used to seem a sacrilege that,
after the Restoration, when *Romeo and Juliet* was
revived, " 'Twas Play'd Alternately, Tragical one Day
and Tragicomical another; for several Days together,"
so that playgoers could choose between Shakespeare's
horizontal ending in the tomb and a happier vertical
conclusion, written in by the management. But if the
truth must out, there is no good reason why Romeo
and Juliet should ever have died. If either they or
Friar Laurence had had their wits about them, they
would have thought of either fleeing to another town
or putting themselves under the protection of such a
peace-loving prince as Escalus instead of trusting to
the phial. An undelivered message to Romeo and the

fallen arches upon which Friar Laurence hies himself
to the Capulet mausoleum are the only excuses for the
final sadness.

I say "sadness" instead of "tragedy" because the
action of the play is always (in Shakespeare's phrase)
more "misadventur'd" than tragic. No sillier example
of hurried plotting can anywhere be found than
Romeo's sudden remembrance of the whereabouts of
an Apothecary in Mantua and the coincidence of his
finding himself, as he recalls this Apothecary, in front
of the selfsame beggar's shop.

Then Romeo is too much of a lovesick crybaby to
be possessed of tragic grandeur. His soul is never as
large as his self-pity. As for Juliet, in spite of the
beauty of her lovely phrases and the shimmering
quality of her youth, she seldom thinks a thought a
girl of fourteen might not think without straining her
brain.

Listen to her in the famous potion scene, and her
spiritual insignificance as a tragic heroine becomes
clear. Though faced with the possibility of death, not
once does she have anything to say about life or dying
such as Hamlet or Cleopatra manages to get said.
Properly enough, considering her age, she is kept in
an emotional kindergarten. In terms of verses, preeminently actable however shoddy they may be, all
Juliet does is to surrender to such worries as might agi-
tate the mind of a mortician's youngest daughter. What
she asks herself, in the presence of eternity, is will she

be cold in the tomb, will her ancestors be fragrant, will she perhaps play with her forefathers' joints, or encounter Tybalt's ghost.

If the potion speech is a poor one as poetry, the parting soliloquies of the lovers in the tomb are on the whole no less inadequate. Shakespeare was right when in the second Prologue, usually omitted, he described his play as "tempering extremity with extreme sweet." The "extreme sweet" is his verse and all that is most haunting in its lyricism. Denied this lyricism, nothing remains to temper the extremities to which *Romeo and Juliet* goes in its shoddy plotting.

May 25, 1940

MR. ANDERSON'S *Key Largo*

NO DRAMATIST writing for the contemporary theatre can claim a nobler vision of the timeless function of high tragedy than Maxwell Anderson. That slim Nabisco of a volume, known as *The Essence of Tragedy*, in which he has collected his prefaces and addresses, is eloquent proof of this.

In theory he understands, as few men do, the spiritual elevation of the tragic. His pessimism, his disillusionment, his insistence that the rats shall inherit the earth and that men build only to build ruins have not blinded him to the exaltation of high tragedy's ideal.

He has himself confessed that, as he sees it, the reassuring hope offered to mankind by the authors of tragedy is that men can rise superior to physical defeat and death. The message of high tragedy, he has pointed out, is simply that men are better than they think they are. This, says he, is a message needing to be repeated in every time and place lest the race lose faith in itself entirely.

He has recognized, too, the importance of language. During many years of worthy effort, if uncertain achievement, he has sought to restore the poet to his proper place in the theatre; to take playgoers off a "starvation diet of prose"; and to give the wings of great words to great emotions.

Between Mr. Anderson, the theorist, and Mr. Anderson, the doer, a disconcerting difference has often existed. The two have not always been on speaking terms. Although they bowed to one another at times during *Key Largo* last night, they by no means established what can be described as a happy intimacy.

Obviously Mr. Anderson's new play is the work of a dramatist whose aims are high. Obviously it is the product of a proud spirit, of a man who can think his own thoughts on issues which must everywhere be faced today. Obviously, too, as it tells its story of an American who died spiritually by avoiding death with the Loyalist forces in Spain only to come to life again when he is prepared to die a sacrificial death in some gambler's scrape in Florida, it shows that Mr. Ander-

son's understanding of the tragic ideal is as exalted as it
ever was. No less obviously his new drama erupts at
moments into speeches worthy of his best poetic efforts.

Even so, when its Spanish prologue is over, and its
first passionate conflict of credos is past, *Key Largo*
soon fails to live up both to Mr. Anderson's aspirations
as a preface writer and to its own potentialities. It comes
across as an honorable intention rather than a good play.
If it has its intermittent moments of interest, it never
rises to excitement. It is all ripples and no waves, and
frequently its ripples are far apart.

In *Key Largo* Mr. Anderson is saying a very simple
thing. He is insisting that to live men must be ready
to die for their ideals. He is indicating that men who
may no longer believe in God must, to endure themselves and life, take on some of the attributes of the
godhead themselves. And he is establishing, obliquely,
that, to his thinking, his Florida gambler and General
Franco are both of them destructive forces of the same
kind; gangsters differing only in degree; challenges to
be dealt with in the same way.

Simple and decidedly worth-while as are Mr. Anderson's points, he does not make them simply or dramatize them with the interest they deserve. After the fine
tension of his prologue his tragedy shows Mr. Anderson to be a poetic dramatist who in his writing has never
been sufficiently influenced by Margaret Sanger. His
poetry begins to betray a woeful lack of verbal control.
In his dialogue is missing the firm discipline which in a

poetic drama the dramatist must exercise over the poet.

Shakespeare could, after all, treat dictionaries as if they were so many iceboxes to be robbed at midnight. The feast his words supply is bounteous and inexhaustible. He was, however, more than a mere master of the thesaurus. He could toss words into the air with a juggler's skill, keeping each one of them shimmering there. But one of the sources of his theatrical strength was that Shakespeare, when he had fully bloomed as dramatist, knew that he had to look with suspicion upon his verbal prowess. Such was his instinct, such his wisdom, that he realized he must at times hush the organ of his poet's speech to make silences and pauses as fateful as only pauses and silences can be in the theatre. Mr. Anderson, unfortunately, keeps on writing, writing, writing purple passages with the regularity with which he once wrote editorials for the *World*.

His ears are more attuned to arias than action. His cadenced prose can, when well spoken, sound like poetry. Mr. Anderson's, however, is the mistake of failing to halt the steady onrush of his language with the hot give-and-take of emotionalized speech, with the serpent's hiss of short interruptions, the single phrases picked up and repeated until their insinuations vibrate, the naked words dependent upon actors' intonations for their clothing, which grant a timeless glory to such a scene as Iago's poisoning of Othello's mind.

Furthermore, in spite of Mr. Anderson's admirable theoretical understanding of the tragic, he endeavors in his concluding acts of *Key Largo* to cap the tragic with the ironic. This proves to be a combination unhappy and impossible. To combine the tragic and the ironic is to commit in the drama the same mistake of which a chemist would be guilty who mixed bromo and seltzer expecting them to live happily ever afterwards.

One virtue beyond dispute *Key Largo* can claim— its bringing of Paul Muni back to the New York stage. Mr. Muni is a gifted and exceptional actor. He sets about playing Mr. Anderson's regenerated hero with a modesty matched only by his brilliance. His is a memorable characterization of a part which can hardly be called tempting.

Uta Hagen as the girl in Florida, Harold Johnsrud as her blind father, Jose Ferrer as her brother who died in Spain, Ralph Theadore as a bullying sheriff, and Frederic Tozere as the villainous gambler all contribute to the Playwrights' Company's first production of the winter. Still the evening comes as more of an honorable failure than as a success. It leaves one admiring Mr. Anderson and his high intentions but disappointed in his results.

November 28, 1939

Three

THE PURSUIT OF HAPPINESS

WIT AND THE WISECRACK

A CHASM separates the comedy of good manners from the wisecracking comedy of bad manners which in recent years has represented so superlative a flowering of American wit and humor. The Comic Spirit as Shakespeare gave it a ruddy, roistering health; as Molière endowed it with a courtier's graces and made it, beneath its peruke, outshine the Sun King at Versailles; as Congreve rouged it and bedecked it with the diamonds of his prose; as Sheridan teased it into new life on a diet of shamrocks and roast beef; as Wilde decorated it with string after string of his epigrammatic cultured pearls; or even as in its honor Mr. Behrman lights bright rows of graceful candelabra that have been electrified, is different from the Comic Spirit George Abbott knows or that Mr. Kaufman and Mr. Hart have served so well, and that Americans have come to recognize as their native own.

The laughing expectation in most high comedies, even in comedy both high and low such as can be found in the Falstaff scenes in *Henry IV*, has always been the give-and-take of equal minds. In such plays as *Much Ado*, *The Misanthrope*, *Love for Love*, *The School for Scandal*, *The Importance of Being Earnest*, or *No Time for Comedy* one not only listens to a witty character's statement with pleasure but looks forward with equal pleasure to another character's rejoinder.

Verbally, high comedy has by tradition always been a series of sallies, of skirmishes, of forays. It has not been a matter of bullying into silence but of exciting into response. Its wit has served an antiphonal purpose. Its characters have not been so much rude as provocative. When they have been rude, they have been so almost out of courtesy, in the hope that by their provocation they would lead to a worthy exhibition of a worthy opponent's powers.

Our wisecracking comedies have not only deviated from the older comic tradition in this respect but established a new, often wonderfully funny, one of their own. When, for example, such a character as Sheridan Whiteside in *The Man Who Came to Dinner* has had his lethal say, no answer is as a rule possible. He uses speech not as a rapier but as a Flit-gun. The whole joyous and effective purpose of his wisecracks is that of a Maxim silencer.

Our wisecrackers wage verbal Blitzkriegs against their opponents. They show a genius not for observation so much as for impoliteness. The source of the abundant pleasure they provide comes not from parrying but from bullying; from annihilating, not encouraging; from writing "finis" upon the forehead of the interlocutor.

About American wisecracks there is a boisterous lack of mercy. In terms of words they manage to find audacious equivalents for the bodily hurly-burly of the comic strips. A major source of their wit is their very lack of inhibitions. Quick as is their thinking, devastating as their comment can be, vivid as are their extensions of slang, they break with the older traditions of comedy by coming as the ultimate in frankness, not in artifice.

They burst upon us as diverting examples of spontaneous combustion rather than as proofs of illumination well thought out. They serve their joyous purpose as lingual reflexes rather than as the results of reflection. They are not so much wise as smart, and in them what wisdom they possess deliberately goes slumming, rejoicing in the vernacular. They not only orchestrate the mucker pose but swing it. Their brevity is more than the soul of their wit; it is its body, too. If they have no echo, it is because each one of them is spoken as if it were meant to be the comeback to end all comebacks. Naturally such a purpose proves disconcerting even to an echo.

Our wisecracking comedies find vigilantes in the home rather than courtiers in the drawing room. They bespeak more physical than mental exuberance. About the most convulsing of their words (and this is their point and glory) there is the "blop," "wow," "bop," "ugh" sound of funny-paper distress. Although our wisecrackers may bludgeon inferiors rather than converse with equals, they do so with such zestful invention that they turn what conversationally amounts to a mass murder into a joyous American holiday.

MR. EVANS' PLUMP JACK

BANISH plump Jack, and banish all the world, indeed. For dramatic literature has produced no comic figure of the same huge dimensions as those to be claimed by this great tub of guts, this gorbellied knave, this fat-kidneyed rascal, this ale-soaked rogue, this capon-filled coward, this whoreson candle mine, this obscene, greasy, tallow catch, this bolting-hutch of beastliness, this swollen parcel of dropsies all of us love, and in exchange for whom we would outdo Prince Hal himself and not take a battalion of better men.

No wonder Falstaff has been placed in the happy lands of laughter upon a throne no less exalted than is the one Hamlet occupies in the black regions of despair. Falstaff's girth measures more than the circumference of his body. At its most bloated it is but an inadequate symbol for what is comic in his spirit.

It is not ale and capon which have swollen Sir John until he resembles a convention of tumors. He is a rascal who has grown fat on reason. The plump knight has a wit as nimble as his body is becalmed. His person is full-blown with good nature and knavish resourcefulness. Although his sword may be sheathed, he can out-parry the best of men—sitting down. Two steps taken, except in flight, may exhaust him, yet mentally he is never winded.

We love him for his faults as we are supposed to admire heroes for their virtues. We love him—cheat, idler, sponge, and coward though he is—for more than his abundant humors. We love him because bundled up in his mountainous flesh is the sweetest expression this world has known of unsweet reason. If he is ignoble, if he is joyously independent of all those ideals we have been taught to venerate by calendars, recruiting officers, night courts, Sunday-school teachers, and aspirational philosophers, it is because he dares to raise his ale-soaked voice to give each man's private fears their most hilarious and unanswerable expression.

There is nothing totalitarian about him except his person. He never speaks for the group or considers anyone save himself. The only welfare which concerns him is the welfare of Sir John. He is the arch-individualist who lives by laws drawn up for no other purpose than to insure his own comfort and safety. He is more than a man. He is a huge and wise Trust; Sir John Falstaff, Incorporated. His enemy is not only the state but all small and large competitors. His own pleasure, which he makes ours, is the only friend to claim his unswerving loyalty. In superb fashion Sir John articulates those misgivings which communal considerations have had to hush in all of us. He is one of the greatest realists of all time. His cowardice is due not to the weakness of his heart but to the strength of his mind.

Any man who can insist the better part of valor is discretion, and counterfeit death with as little pride as he does during a battle that finds his prince's throne at stake, or lie in his all-inventive manner about undone deeds of bravery, is not apt to die a hero's death. Yet it is because he dotes upon life with such shameless courage—and such wit—that we dote upon him. His eyes are dangerously clear even if his hipbones are hidden in flesh. Grand company though he is, he is a rogue of the most antisocial sort. His very timidity is deceptive. He is no well-stuffed Caspar Milquetoast. About the unorthodoxy of his fears there is the conscientious objector's bravery. All he lacks is a motive nobler than self-preservation for the sheer joy of living, even if living most unworthily. He finds this sufficient reason and can justify it brilliantly.

Mr. Evans is sage enough to make his Falstaff much more than a mere tallow catch of the taverns. Although the size of his rotunda is such as to fill graduates of the University of Virginia with envy, his spirit is rich with all the unflinching comic wisdom of Sir John. He is more than a plump clown. He is a huge, gross hedonist; a fellow to whose lips fine, glowing, bawdy words taste as sweet as does the best of ale or the juiciest of roast beef.

If physically Mr. Evans' Falstaff is less untidy than some of his predecessors have been, he is mentally more alert. It is, of course, an extraordinary thing for an actor to be able to turn from Hamlet to Falstaff in a lifetime, much less in one short season. Yet Mr. Evans is able to make this Jack Spratt-and-his-wife change triumphantly.

His voice is a different voice from the one he used in *Hamlet* even as his Hamlet voice was different in its pitch and intensity from the silvery one with which he revealed the lyric beauties and tragic overtones of Richard II. His Falstaff does not employ those singing head tones Mr. Evans can use to superb effect. His speech is deep-seated. It leaves his lips like the roar of a lion who has just dined well on Androcles. Base it may be, still it is genial, because his very tonsils appear to have been dunked in ale. Mr. Evans is now a comic roisterer where once he was poet and tragedian. His words, however, are indulged in once again for all their round and glorious beauties. Now they air a different mind, and speak not only for a totally different body but a totally different spirit.

His production gains incalculably because of the all-quickening imagination Margaret Webster has brought to it as director. There is no sense mincing words. Miss Webster is a genius—as much a genius in her own way as Mr. Evans is in his. The two of them are fortunate in David Ffolkes' settings and costumes; in Henry Edwards' playing of the crowned Bolingbroke; in Mady Christians' vivid characterization of Lady Percy; in Edmond O'Brien's engaging Prince Hal; and in Wesley Addy's admirably vigorous Hotspur. All of us are very lucky to have plump Jack brought back to us by such an actor and in such a revival.

March 22, 1939

CONGREVE AND BOBBY CLARK

IN A charming speech between the acts at the Hudson last night Otis Skinner pointed out how different from life as he knows it in his home in Woodstock, Vermont, is life as it was lived by the fops and ladies in *Love for Love*. Mr. Skinner was as right as he was ingratiating. The Congrevean universe is a special world. Mr. Coolidge's shade stands in no danger of wandering into it. It is the Utopia of gallantry, the cuckold's paradise, the happy hunting grounds of the unprudish which Charles Lamb knew it to be.

Those who trespass past the sign at its gates reading "Danger" have to be sophisticates to survive their visit with impunity and without blushes. Conversation they must prize—not small talk for the sake of gossip, but tattle for all the glories with which a superlative stylist could lighten his innuendoes, vary his comments upon infidelity, and in general so dispel the shadows of the alcove that its secrets, thus illumined, became literature.

The hue and cry in Congreve's world is for the *double-entendre;* the scene that takes serious domestic virtues lightly; the line that never admits the existence of virtue and gets along quite brilliantly without it. Othello would have been maddened by jealousy and committed murder long before the fifth act in such a setting. The people for whom this setting is designed are characters whose manners are too exemplary to indulge in jealousy. They are as innocent of jealousy as they are of scruples. These are their only innocences.

Polite as they are, they live by their wits. In their presence we must be prepared to live by their wits, too, no matter how impolite they may be. Hazlitt knew that wit is the eloquence of indifference. He knew, too, that, though Congreve's characters could all of them speak well, they were machines when they came to act. Correct as Hazlitt was, he failed to remember that, if one is really listening to the talk of Congreve's people, there is little time left in which to bother about what, as he put it with delicacy, is mechanical in their actions. They all of them—the Scandals, the Tattles, the Bens, and the Mrs. Foresights, the Miss Prues, the Angelicas, and the Mrs. Frails—shine like naughty deeds in a not so good world. What is left of their reputations when the curtain first goes up hangs upon a phrase, and only the delight in the phrase survives when they are done with one another.

If they are a bawdy crew, the ladies no less than the gallants, they are nonetheless a delightful one by virtue of their witty amorality. The men are hot-blooded dandies, who, to an uncertain extent, are air-conditioned by the glories of their small talk. The ladies spend their time holding up the flaming candelabra of their conversation to an artificial exposure of their natural frailties. They are intriguers, every one of them, to call them by the gentlest of ungentle names.

If the very effulgence of their prattle, pleasurable as it is, can grow wearisome because of the relentless straining and blinking it invites, its quality has nonetheless been admirably suggested by Robert Edmond Jones in the glittering setting, all mirrors and flashing candles, which first he used in his revival of the same play back in 1925. In more ways than one the mirrors in Mr. Jones' backgrounds are the perfect symbol of the comedy they reflect and of the special world reflected by that comedy. They have an appropriate gaiety and style. Even when Congreve is lagging, they continue to give visual significance to his intentions.

The Players Club has been fortunate in more than Mr. Jones' settings. Its members have been lucky in his direction, too, and are to be congratulated upon their cast. That the women are on the whole better than the men is no doubt only a subtle expression of the Club's gallantry.

Cornelia Otis Skinner is an admirable Angelica. Miss Skinner plays with a genuine mastery of the difficult artificial style. She neither overstresses nor underdoes. Her voice is attuned to the niceties of a conversational elegance and sparkle long since a literary treasure. She acts, moreover, with grace and charm, and perfect co-operation with her fellow players.

Violet Heming as Mrs. Frail makes vital and tantalizing every implication in a shamelessly fascinating creature. As the country-bred, innocent Miss Prue, to whom fall some of the comedy's best scenes, Dorothy Gish gives an excellent performance, insouciant and wittily established in its mock innocence. Peggy Wood strains herself trying to subdue her goodness to the wickedness of Mrs. Foresight, and strains the audience by being asked to sing more songs than the traffic will bear.

It is Bobby Clark, however, who walks away with Congreve and Congreve is quite an author to walk away with. Although as Ben, the rough-spoken sailor, Mr. Clark does not wear his painted spectacles, he could not be better even if he did. His footwork remains unchanged. He scrapes and trots his way through the comedy with a terrier's glee. His blue eyes shine like lakes at noon on colored postcards. He functions as a happy dust blower in a classical library. His comic spirit is something Congreve cannot subdue or alter.

He swoops down on innuendoes with the full posse of his superior music hall tricks. Much as one admires Congreve and the Players Club revival of his comedy, Bobby Clark's roistering antics are more than welcome in a world of sustained artifice; they are downright convulsing.

June 4, 1940

MISS CORNELL IN MR. BEHRMAN'S COMEDY

ALTHOUGH the theatre often throws money away, its comedians seldom throw away laughs. They do more than hoard them. They can create them where no laughs exist. Are there those who, as the expression runs, can get money out of thin air? Well, there are also those who can get laughter out of the thinnest of thin lines. They are the natural-born comedians, the men and women truly possessed of the Comic Spirit. They are the gay souls of the earth whose very faces have witty lines, whose eyes are epigrams, and whose mouths seem formed to protect a jest or to discover one. That they are rare goes without saying. They could almost be counted on the fingers of one hand, if in their presence both hands were not so busily engaged applauding them.

Although theirs is a God-given genius, to be effective

it, more than most, must also be man-made. If they are
high comedians, they cannot warble any native wood-
notes wild. They dare not trust to impulse alone. Their
instinct leads them to developing, each one of them
according to his or her personality, a technique—spar-
kling, precise, unfailing in its watchfulness.

Their very spontaneity is the product of elaborate
study. For comedy—real comedy—is the child of planning, the product of foresight. Its hidden artifices are
among its guarantees and delights. To overdo would
be as fatal to the joyous work of genuine comedians as
it would be to underdo. Their concern is always the
effect; the anticipated effect by means of which they
surprise us.

They give laughter no rest. They stalk it where no
one would guess a cause for it existed. When they come
upon it, they point as instinctively as a bird dog points
in the presence of a quail. They have a hundred tricks
to let us know they have scented what is our game and
theirs. They ferret out their prey for us by means of
dry inflection, shrewd vocal underscorings, lifted eyebrows, perfect timing, sly facial expressions, and a score
of other proofs of how unrelenting is their search for
comedy and their ability to transmit it. Dullness is their
only enemy, sincerity their infrequent friend. They
swoop down on laughter as tireless, yet utterly charming, aggressors.

So special are the attributes, the approaches, and

manners of those who through long servitude, plus
their own endowments, have become masters of the
comic that Miss Cornell's participation in such a script
as Mr. Behrman's *No Time for Comedy* cannot fail to
interest playgoers who derive pleasure from the niceties
of acting. Unlike Lucile Watson, or Grace George, or
Lynn Fontanne, or Ina Claire (or Mrs. Fiske before
them), Miss Cornell has not risen to pre-eminence because of her skill in serving comedy. Although she admits in her autobiography she has acted in smiling
dramas with Jessie Bonstelle, and everyone affectionately remembers the compassion of her Candida, Miss
Cornell has won her crown—and a real and resplendent
crown it is—as an emotional actress, which is an entirely
different matter.

She has achieved her high position in our theatre by
virtue of the tragic power, the sense of fascination and
foreboding, of importance and beauty with which she
has illumined the tawdry plays she has graced no less
than the significant ones. Where comediennes shine
with the brightness of the noonday sun, she has been a
daughter of the night; pallid, glowing, and compelling.
Il Penseroso and *L'Allegro* could not be less alike, for
example, than Miss Cornell and Miss Claire.

Passion, not wit; emotion rather than laughing reason
have been Miss Cornell's concern. No jest has sum-
moned her to appear. She has entered at Sorrow's command. She has suffered, not bantered; felt instead of

sparkled. Yet fateful as her acting has been, it has never found her turning Melpomene in a cold or forbidding manner. Her sadness has not been tainted with self-pity. What has set her apart has not been a gift for easy tears, but an emotional intensity—controlled, though omnipresent—which she possesses more than any of our actresses. Always, too, there has been about her a radiance, a warm compassion, a sense of good nature mingled with foreboding, which have granted her per-formances a special glow.

With such rare endowments in her favor it is doubly interesting to watch Miss Cornell desert the serious and tragic domains she has made her own and invade the realms of laughter in *No Time for Comedy*. That the evening presents her with a challenge is undeniable. But that, as the actress-wife who regains her playwright-husband in Mr. Behrman's moderately entertaining tri-fle, Miss Cornell undergoes a transformation and sud-denly bobs up as a comedienne cannot be maintained.

She gives a charming performance; wise, affectionate, ingratiating. As always she is fascinating to look at and listen to. She plays intelligently. She is properly gay in spirit, and at all times pictorial. By her very sincerity, which is transparent and winning, she succeeds in en-dowing the script with a quality, familiar in her case but always welcome, no comedienne could have brought to it.

But to say that overnight Miss Cornell has turned

comedienne is to misunderstand the true nature of playing high comedy no less than Miss Cornell's own gift. What she does is to bring a new-found joy to her playing, or rather to heighten that joyous good nature which has lurked charmingly beneath the surface of her Candida, the eager Juliet of her earlier scenes, and her young Joan. Yet, though she lightens her heart, she does not lighten her tongue.

She throws away laughs as profligately as Madame Ranevsky threw away money. With the strategies of comedy she will have nothing to do. She does not give a line that triple exposure—that sense of harking back to what has just been said and anticipating what is to come even while she is speaking—in the alert manner of the true comedienne.

She wins the major laughs Mr. Behrman has placed at her disposal without creating any of her own. She is relaxed, not vigilant. Although she smiles, her spirit is gay, and she irresistible, she is not witty. She has found her satisfactory substitutes for comedy, chief among which is her all-conquering sincerity. She puts this sincerity to admirable uses. By means of it she makes us gladly accept oleomargarine as if it were butter. But this very sincerity, lovely and shining as it is in its own way, is a sure proof that Miss Cornell is a welcome traveler rather than a resident in comedy's bright but merciless kingdom of artifice.

April 24, 1939

MR. WOOLLCOTT COMES FOR DINNER

THAT Alexander Woollcott is the author, lecturer, critic, and radio performer Moss Hart and George S. Kaufman drew upon for their central character in *The Man Who Came to Dinner* is about as much a state secret as that Franklin Delano Roosevelt is the person people have in mind just now when they speak of the President of the United States. Yet there is another truth we hold to be self-evident—the Messrs. Hart and Kaufman have been uncommonly fortunate in their choice of a hero.

If, at the Music Box, Sheridan Whiteside sounds and behaves suspiciously like Dr. Woollcott, this in itself is a guarantee of excellent talk and entertaining antics. As everyone must know by now who can turn a dial or read the language, the good doctor is one of the most colorful personalities of our day. In any of his roles— as arsenic or old lace, as fugleman or executioner, as murder addict or humorous raconteur, as drama critic or book trumpeter, as charity lover or prestige destroyer, as sentimentalist or "old meany"—he is a figure not in one million but in one hundred and thirty-three million.

Mr. Woollcott has had more than the inclination to be an individualist. He has had the gifts, too. All

of us have long rejoiced in this knowledge. If Mr.
Woollcott has made it practically impossible for anyone in these United States not to have heard of him,
the reason is, of course, that he has long since become
a jubilant part of the public domain—practically an
annex to Yellowstone Park. Although his intellectual,
or rather his cardiac, possessions are as far-flung as the
British Empire, Mr. Woollcott has never allowed the
sun to set on Woollcottiana. What he possesses, he
possesses joyously and no less joyously shares. Everyone knows he owns Christmas. To be sure, he has, on
occasion, shared Christmas with Dickens, just as, on
occasion, he has shared Dickens with the *New York
Post.* Everyone knows, too, he has so staked his claim on
murder as a fine art that one is tempted to feel De
Quincey must have left it to him as a special bequest
in his will.

Anyone who has ever heard Mr. Woollcott on the
air or enjoyed the rare privilege of hearing him speak
in person, must be familiar with the Town Crier's voice
—that voice which can persuade you there are truffles
on his tonsils. Anyone who has heard him is likewise
happily aware of how he betrays not only his fondness
for language but his excellence at it, by the very way
in which he bites out his words. Both Mr. Woollcott
and Raymond Gram Swing (that admirable war com-
mentator who can sound so much like Mr. Woollcott
on the air) have a happy precision in their speech. They
can nibble at English with the same relish with which a

rabbit nibbles at fresh lettuce. The two of them can chew off with such neat dispatch so short a word as "It" that, as they utter it, it can sound more important than "Fate" itself. All writing persons jealous of Mr. Woollcott (and this, with reason, includes nearly every member of the profession) may insist Mr. Woollcott's style is based upon a trick, as if all art did not depend upon a trick happily disguised. The interesting thing is that though everyone can tell you what the Woollcottian trick is, no one except Mr. Woollcott is able to make it work.

Among his many gifts Mr. Woollcott can claim that he writes like only one person in the world—Alexander Woollcott. There is no other who to an adjective can give such a final shot of hyperthyroid as Mr. Woollcott can administer. To cold print, read by strangers, he can lend the warmth of an anecdote told among friends. There is not a bridge builder in the country who has his gift for suspense. By the sheer excitement of his story-telling, he can send his readers, with their tongues hanging out like bloodhounds on Eliza's trail, in hot pursuit of the identity of those unidentified maidens who are apt to figure prominently in his introductory paragraphs.

Mr. Hart and Mr. Kaufman have been more than fortunate—they have been downright inspired—in their choice of Mr. Woollcott (by his or any other name) as a hero. In addition to being one of the wittiest men of his time Mr. Woollcott is one of our most expansive and arresting personalities. He is not only a figure of rare gifts and contagious loves and hates but a happy accumulation of paradoxical qualities. As everyone knows, his heart is one of the country's largest public gardens. There is not a kinder writing man alive. Still, as any victim of his wit would also acknowledge, Mr. Woollcott's talent to turn conversation into insecticide ceases to be talent and becomes a very high order of genius.

If few can match him as a sentimentalist, none can equal him in the sudden accuracy with which he can dispatch an enemy. What makes him doubly service-able as the central figure of such a comedy as *The Man Who Came to Dinner* are the very contradictions in his nature which add to his delights as a personality. He is a mixture of Santa Claus and Flit-gun, of adder nest and bonbon box, of learning and spontaneity, unique among the present-day tribe of pen-pushers. Not since Mr. Sherwood leaned on Lincoln for a certain Pulitzer Prize winning drama of his, has an actual person done so much to support a play as Mr. Woollcott, just by being Mr. Woollcott, does to serve *The Man Who Came to Dinner* as its unseen caryatid.

Although we have known that, in addition to being an author, Mr. Woollcott has also functioned as an actor when he has lent his owlish person to the playing of such Woollcottian raisonneurs and couch-dwellers as Mr. Behrman has written for him, it was not until last night that the Messrs. Hart and Kaufman forced us to realize Mr. Woollcott is also a play. And what a play *The Man Who Came to Dinner* proves to be!

It is as gay, giddy, and delectable a comedy as our stage has seen in years. The surest proof of its hilarity no less than of its skill lies in the fact that it is a *drame à clef* to which no key is really needed. The door is wide open upon laughter the whole time, regardless of whether or not you can read Noel Coward into Beverly Carlton and Harpo Marx into "Banjo," or are intimately acquainted with the legends of Woollcottiana.

Having a passkey is always flattering, and one can be turned to advantage even in this unbolted door. Without such a passkey, it is still possible to enter into the joys of *The Man Who Came to Dinner*. It is a self-contained piece of writing for all its sidelights on a special group. Its characters are developed with such witty persuasion that, unless he is very careful when next he goes on tour, Mr. Woollcott stands far more in danger of being accused of modeling himself on the play than he does of hearing the play has been modeled on him.

What Mr. Hart and Mr. Kaufman have done is to imagine and develop all the complications which might arise if, while having dinner with a small-town Ohio family during one of his lecture trips, Mr. Woollcott were to slip on the ice, fall, do an even crueller pelvic damage to himself than if he had sat through *Gone With the Wind,* and thereby be compelled to spend several weeks in a startled household. With mustard gas oozing from his mouth in the form of speech, with his finger in every pie, with broadcasts to deliver, the family exiled upstairs, love affairs cropping up all around him, strange Christmas presents arriving by the score, and transatlantic calls possible on the telephone beside him, what would such a legendary character do? Plenty. Of this you may be certain, especially after seeing Mr. Hart's and Mr. Kaufman's sidesplitting imaginings which add up to form a kind of *Hellzapoppin* of the literati and prove a joy throughout.

Their comedy is a joy not only because in it the "Master" speaks as unmistakably as if his words were coming from a Victrola record. It is a joy because one knows a master is speaking even if one should not happen to know who the actual "Master" is. The wit, the malice, the invention, the sentimentality, the gift for phrasing, the lush purr of his words give more than a unique quality to the dialogue. They spill over into the action, directing its course and granting it a similar fleetness.

It should not be assumed that *The Man Who Came to Dinner* is a one-character play. It is anything but this. It includes some of the maddest as well as some of the best-drawn of Mr. Hart's and Mr. Kaufman's eccentrics, and some of the most adroit of their developed scenes. Then, too, it gains because of its smooth-running direction, because of Donald Oenslager's exceptionally helpful setting, and the genuine contribution of its actors.

It is Monty Woolley * who supplies this *drame à clef* with its Yale lock. Mr. Woolley is not Mr. Woollcott. Although he is blessed physically with the comfortable insulation helpful for comedy, he lacks the final dimensional amplitude of Mr. Woollcott. Nonetheless, he has his own delectable brand of astringent comedy to offer as the semivertical Woollcott who whiles away his invalidism by being an autocrat at someone else's breakfast table. It is Mr. Woolley as an actor who pushes the play beyond the realms of eavesdropping and guarantees its functioning as a self-reliant example of comic dramaturgy.

Mr. Woolley is a distinguished fellow in his own

* Clifton Webb, who plays Sheridan Whiteside in the Chicago company of *The Man Who Came to Dinner*, is at first thought, no less than at first sight, an impossible shadow for Alexander Woollcott to cast. Dimensionally at least Mr. Webb is all-too-slight to fall heir to either the Woollcottian belt or to Monty Woolley's. He beards his Whiteside as does Mr. Woolley. Still, in his presence, it is impossible not to feel that for the first time in Shakespearean history Sir Andrew Aguecheek is trying to impersonate Sir Toby Belch. Mr. Webb is amusing, but amusing in a way quite different from Mr. Woolley. One is forced to think back to Mr. Woolley's lustier quality and his Edwardian urbanity when confronted with the cattier, more petulant, somewhat Cassius-like, but still entertaining Sheridan Whiteside of Mr. Webb. Good as he is at comedy, Mr. Webb still seems something of a spare rib, lacking the hearty rotundity possessed both by Mr. Woolley and that elfin Falstaff—Mr. Woollcott—who, after all, is the final authority on Sheridan Whiteside. Always, too, Mr. Webb appears to be a dancer protected from his profession by having to stay in or near a wheel chair.

right. As our Alexander the Great he may look like an Edwardian. For the benefit of such tiny tots as may have read this far may I quickly add that when I say Edwardian, the Edward I have in mind is, of course, Edward VII. Although none of us can be certain how historians of the future will distinguish between these two gay reigns of the House of Windsor, we can hope for their convenience no less than for ours, that these chroniclers will identify the later period as Simpsonian. If Mr. Woolley's smart gray beard is so Edwardian that you expect Lily Langtry to bob up from under Mr. Oenslager's chintz, the effect is fortunate. For Mr. Woolley's individuality (in other words his un-Woollcottian quality as Sheridan Whiteside) manages to stress the divorce always needed to separate creation from stenography.

Mr. Woolley throws himself manfully into an heroic task. With uncanny skill he plays a part, almost as long as Hamlet and consisting entirely of talk, which must be the most difficult invalided character to be acted hereabouts since Miss Cornell accepted the challenge of taking to her sofa to dominate and sustain the whole of *The Barretts of Wimpole Street.*

Considering such a combination of talents, it is no doubt inevitable that men should find it easier to come to dinner almost anywhere these nights than to get into the Music Box.

October 17 and 28, 1939

DAYS WITHOUT END
Life With Father

IF, AS seems indisputable, the late Clarence Day was fortunate in his parents, all the rest of us stand in the elder Days' debt for their son. It was he who, in *Life With Father*, *God and My Father*, and *Life With Mother*, kindly removed brownstone by brownstone the front of the Madison Avenue home he had known in the New York of the eighties, and allowed the nation's readers to claim Father and Vinnie as household gods, if not indeed as household pets. It is Howard Lindsay and Russel Crouse who have had the courage to dramatize Mr. Day's inimitable domestic sketches. And all things considered, including the bothersome preconceptions playgoers are bound to bring with them and the slowness of the introductory scenes, a heart-warming and delectable job Mr. Lindsay and Mr. Crouse have done.

As all people in this country must know, who can read and have been able to get beyond McGuffey's, Mr. Day's family portrait was a book of unusual charm. Its happy mixture of tenderness and malice, and of the universal with the individual, was uncommonly felicitous. If the results in the theatre are not quite the same as they were in print, *Life With Father* is nonetheless hilarious. We have Mr. Day's own lines to thank for this. And truly sustaining lines they prove to be, when spoken no less than when read.

As was to be expected, there is a difference. Mr. Day's family on the stage has ceased to be quite so much his own personal property. It has lost, to a certain extent, the special breeding which distinguished it. It no longer seems quite so securely anchored in a period. It has become everybody's family, and the change, at least from the audience point of view, is helpful. If, instead of saying, as we did when we read *Life With Father*, "How like the Days our families are," we now, as theatregoers, are apt to say, "How like our families were the Days," it is because the ripple of application has been widened. The book has had to be Katzenjammered up a bit for audience consumption. Even so, the entrance requirements to enjoyment are very simple. All one needs to have had in order to relish the play is either a father or a mother.

What *Life With Father* is, is a dramatization of all happy home life AND the male ego. If these two are mentioned in conjunction, it is because that is precisely where they belong. The male ego, needless to say, is a subject in which all women are doomed to get at least a bachelor's degree, and most of them are fated to acquire a Ph.D. All males not descended from Caspar Milquetoast are sandwich men for the male ego. A typical moment of their operations is the one which occurs between five and five-thirty during the afternoon of any working day. Then it is that a key can be heard in the front door. Then it is that the front door opens, and the male ego stands hatless in his own front hall, with some such salutation as "Well, here I am"—as if something had to be done about it right away.

If the returning male is returning to a happy home, he will, of course, have been met by a female Machiavelli who will have already begun to massage his vanity. The husband knows in every case he does not really rule the home. The wife never needs any information on this score. However, in the interests of domestic cricket (especially in this country where men have long since lost their equality) it does seem fair for the returning male to be allowed to operate under the beneficent illusion that he dominates his home as a mixture of von Hindenburg, the elder Rockefeller, and Santa Claus. The happy homes are those in which male egos are encouraged to nourish this illusion.

Such a home was, of course, the Days'. What one gets as one watches Father complaining about meals, losing servants, grumbling about expenses, objecting to visitors, reading the newspapers, exploding into endless tempers, suffering during his wife's illness, urging his oldest son to be firm with women, scoffing at his minister, and resolutely avoiding baptism, is a picture into which every family man fits, whether he likes to believe so or not. It is a full-length portrait of the aforesaid male ego, with all of the laughable petty tyrannies exposed

which that ego exercises within the fortress of those
four walls over which he is artfully encouraged to believe he rules.

Clarence Day knew male sovereignty was more a
matter of noise than of fact. So did Vinnie. This is
where the fun—the abundant fun—comes in for all
members of any family wise enough to journey to the
Empire these nights. For *Life With Father* proves to
be a play of tremendous gaiety, and of sudden interludes of tender observation. Although as a play it may
be unimportant, as a biography of everyone's family it
is shrewdly drawn and ingratiating. It deals with those
crises which occur on the first of the month when bills
not only have to be paid but explained; in fact with all
those crises, at once minor and major, which keep domestic bliss from ever becoming monotonous.

"Father" may no longer be the meticulous, forbidding, though lovable tyrant he was in Mr. Day's narra-
tives. Vinnie may have lost some of her subtlety. But
the male ego, so childlike in its delusions, lives in such
endearing terms in *Life With Father* that all families
can feel at home in the presence of Mr. Lindsay's and
Mr. Crouse's play. If the book has, as hinted, lost certain
of its values as transferred to the stage; if especially its
period anchorage has been disturbed, such alterations
were doubtless inevitable. The comedy has merely kept
pace with the changes in a changing world. For example, since the elder Clarence Day lived and died,

the new woman has come into being. And, as no one can dispute, the new woman has, to a large extent, done the old man in.

Although Mr. Lindsay faces an almost impossible task as "Father," he plays him so acceptably in an actor's way (which would, no doubt, have sent "Father's" blood pressure soaring) that one is more than willing to accept him as a substitute for Mr. Day's courtlier parent. Mr. Lindsay * is industrious, frequently skillful, and almost always satisfactory enough as the red-wigged chieftain of a red-wigged tribe. At no time is he funnier than when, in moments of final exasperation, he cries out loud to his Creator.

Miss Stickney is a pleasant, chirrupy, and effective Vinnie, even if she is unfortunately given to stealing "actress-y" glances across the footlights from time to

* As acted by Percy Waram and Lillian Gish at the Blackstone in Chicago, *Life With Father* forces a New Yorker, who has relished the play at the Empire, into the disloyal and ungrateful position of confessing that the production in the Loop is superior so far as its principals are concerned to the one Broadway has enjoyed hugely. Percy Waram, after all, is a more experienced actor than Mr. Lindsay. He may not have been able to function in Mr. Lindsay's capable manner as coauthor of the play, but he acts what Mr. Lindsay has written for him with no stock company exaggeration.

As Vinnie, Miss Gish gives the first comic performance of her career and shows an admirable gift for comedy. She endows Vinnie with charm and a shrewd, acquiescent authority and pantomimes with rare effectiveness. When the road is enjoying a company of such excellence as the Chicago company of *Life With Father* it is almost as silly to talk about the road's being dead as it is to talk about "the road." Aesthetically at least, the drama's "sticks" are wherever a bad play or a good one is being badly produced.

time. John Drew Devereaux is exceedingly good as young Clarence Day. And Dorothy Bernard is charming as Margaret, the cook.

Although a sign may be written across the stage at the Empire saying "Actors at Work" rather than "The Days at Home," there is no resisting the enchantment of Mr. Day's sketches as Mr. Lindsay and Mr. Crouse have adroitly assembled them in dialogic form. For in this country, as in all countries, and to an extent even Mr. O'Neill did not seem to realize, there are Days without end.

November 9 and 18, 1939

The Male Animal AND MR. THURBER

NO ONE familiar with *The New Yorker* needs to be reminded of the slightly spectral quality of James Thurber's drawings. All readers of that delightful magazine are doubtless better acquainted with Mr. Thurber's jubilantly cockeyed sketches than they are with the *Notebooks of Leonardo da Vinci.* Everyone is well aware of how, in these modern cave drawings dealing with contemporary cliff dwellers, men, women, and dogs are almost always to be found, even if no one can ever be certain as to which is which. The only sure thing is that all of the aforesaid creatures are apt to have

pendent lower lips which hang down like the lower
lips of hungry whales. Everyone knows, too, from the
same magazine, the humorous penetration distinguishing Mr. Thurber's moonstruck writings.

Combine some of the un-Homeric qualities of the
war between the sexes, which Mr. Thurber has uproar-
iously chronicled, with the homespun unpretentious-
ness Elliott Nugent brought years ago to *The Poor
Nut*, or which distinguished Frank Craven's *The First
Year*, and you may have some notion, however hazy,
of the qualities of *The Male Animal*, that comedy in
which Mr. Nugent and Mr. Thurber have turned collaborators.

It would, of course, be unfair to expect even Equity
members to look like the creatures who drip from Mr.
Thurber's pen. That they have done so in the past is a
matter of unkind record, as is the fact that they have always managed to do so in the wrong plays. What is remarkable and delightful about *The Male Animal* is that
its characters, while happily resembling the most human of simple human beings, often do manage to sound
very much the way Mr. Thurber's drawings look.

Although *The Male Animal* would never have been
the darling of Sardou's *Good Housekeeping* eyes, it
does manage to be both more endearing and more diverting than are many tidier comedies. If its qualities
are paradoxical, it is not only because they are mixed
and often contradictory; it is because Mr. Thurber's
and Mr. Nugent's script is several plays at once. This is

a part of its likable madness and its no less likable sanity.

To the sociologically inclined it is a plea for liberalism. To those interested in education it is a satire of those thickskulled Babbitts who, as university trustees, think if they have built a stadium they have established a college. Again to those interested in learning, it comes as a welcome attack upon the trustees, alas all too numerous in this country, who feel that because they have succeeded in the shoe business or the corset business they are *therefore* equipped to be the arbiters of the education of the next generation. Its two-fold plea, radical only in Parent-Teachers Association circles, is that the nation's instructors be allowed to do at least some of the teaching, and that students anxious to read good English be permitted to read good English by whomsoever it may have been written, whether Lincoln or Vanzetti.

To those tirelessly concerned with the problems of love, marriage, and the triangle as it exists away from Princeton, it offers a bifocal—younger and older generation—fable of small-town campus courtship which is often very funny. And for those whose sole search is for laughter it provides, along with some typical Thurber field excursions into unnatural history, the most convulsing drunken scene to be witnessed hereabouts since Noel Coward and Alfred Lunt took to their cups in *Design for Living*.

Mixed as its qualities are, and decidedly calico as is the feel of Mr. Thurber's and Mr. Nugent's play, *The*

Male Animal bears the unmistakable imprint of Mr. Thurber's comic spirit. It has about it that quality of joyous derangement and sensible goofiness which has made Mr. Thurber one of the first humorists of our time.

Leon Ames, Robert Scott, and Elliott Nugent approach their Thurberan assignments with the right kind of gravity. In their normal way they have about them some of the same earnestness which can be found on the faces of even the most madly distorted of Mr. Thurber's brainless children.

Mr. Ames catches to the full every breezy, extrovert characteristic of the ex-football hero and gives a hugely comic performance. As a professor now instead of the student he used to play, Mr. Nugent again demonstrates how excellent he is in farce comedies of this sort. Although the evening's blend may be that of *The New Yorker* crossed with a stock company, the results are in general gratifying and sometimes uproarious.

January 27, 1940

Four

"THE ONLY HONEST HYPOCRITES"

WHAT'S HECUBA TO US

THE actor's temperament has probably not changed much since Socrates inquired of Ion if he were not the best rhapsodist in Greece and Ion answered with an immediate, almost automatic, "By far, O Socrates." No doubt players have to believe doubly in themselves to make us believe they are on stage the people they would have us think they are. Once for us, once for themselves.

"What's Hecuba to him, or he to Hecuba?" is more than a question which has been tantalizing theorists since the first audience assembled. It is the source of that wonder, as old as the theatre, as young as last night's performance, which playgoers feel in the pres-

-:C 105 :}-

ence of good actors and which critics are trying feebly to express when they say, with a surprise the *cliché* cannot hide, "So-and-So played *with conviction.*" Plato's Ion was not an actor as we understand the word or as the Greeks knew it. He was a reciter of epics. But, though only a rhapsodist, to give him his professional name, he belonged to that great line of "Pretenders" which, unlike history's other claimants to the title, have to be on their thrones, not off them, to prove they are "Pretenders."

Ion merits close attention. He was not an artist through whom life spoke directly. He won the contempt of Plato, as actors have been fated to win the halfhearted approval of some critics and a secondary place in the ranks of true creators, by being an interpreter of an interpreter; in other words, a sort of first cousin once removed in aesthetics.

Furthermore Ion anticipated the dilemma of those players for whom only one kind of part is right when he confessed he went to sleep when any other poet except Homer was discussed. He stated, too, the eternal requisite of professional employment for actors when he pointed out that, though sometimes when he saw his audiences weep at him, he laughed, taking their money, still "if they should laugh, I must weep, going without it."

"When I recite of sorrow," said he, saying what many a player, self-persuaded in his or her feigned grief might say today, "my eyes fill with tears; and, when of fearful or terrible deeds, my hair stands on end, and my heart beats fast."

You can almost hear the pause that follows in the *Dialogue*, and see the quizzical look on Socrates' face when such a confession of willful delusion sends questions trooping through his rational mind. "Tell me, Ion," he asks, "can we call him in his senses, who weeps while dressed in splendid garments, and crowned with a golden coronal, not losing any of these things, and is filled with fear when surrounded by ten thousand friendly persons, not one of whom desires to despoil or injure him?"

What Socrates was getting at, of course, was that, to recite Homer well, Ion did not have to be learned on the subjects of which Homer wrote, but that he did need to be inspired to capture in himself, hence in his listeners, the reality those subjects had possessed for Homer. The rhapsodists and early actors, as Socrates saw them, and as we see their descendants to this day, are the middle links in the magnetic chain of a public performance of a written work, in which the author is the first link, the auditor or spectator the last.

Although divine inspiration is certainly not needed to do a greater justice to most contemporary scripts than they deserve, actors continue to need to have something added to their everyday selves if they are to hold our interest and win our gratitude in the theatre. Even to be on-stage what they are off, they have to have technique. A player with inspiration, however small, but without technique, is bound to be at best like a galleon without sails or at worst a rowboat without oars.

When we assemble to see particular actors or actresses, we come to see them when, behind the footlights, we know they will have been given a name other than their own which has drawn us to the theatre. Although we see them *in person,* our desire remains, in this day of type casting and scrupulous realism, not to see them at least entirely as themselves but usually as characters whose names we will have forgotten, while treasuring theirs, when the final curtain is lowered.

What they are themselves—in size, coloring, temperament, voice, and face—is to a large and uncontrollable extent what their careers are fated to be. What they are able to do with themselves as other people is the result of their technical skill, and determines the rank and nature of their playing. They are portrait painters who have had to swallow their own paints and canvases and have no other choice than to be their own models even when a dramatist has placed another model before them.

That they are better than most of the plays in which they appear, may indicate that the gift for their special kind of make-believe is more common than the talent for conviction-through-pretense which is the dramatist's function. This, however, in no way decreases our gratitude to them when they succeed in making their grease-paint Hecubas something to us. No wonder

Hazlitt called actors the only honest hypocrites, or that ours can be an honest happiness when they manage, as he put it, to be *beside themselves*, and thus achieve the ambition which continues to be their nightly business.

MISS HAYES AND MISS CORNELL
COMPARED

FOR some time Katharine Cornell and Helen Hayes have been players so outstanding in merit and importance that theatregoers, out of the most genuine but ungrateful kind of gratitude, have been tempted to express their admiration for the one in terms of superlatives tossed off, by implication at least, at the expense of the other.

Those of us who are reviewers have been subject to the same well-meant fickleness. When, for example, Miss Hayes opens hereabouts in a new play, there are those who seem to know no other way of expressing the pleasure they have found in her acting than by saluting her as "unquestionably the First Lady of our theatre." Then a season passes to find Miss Cornell once again in town, and in the fullness and haste of our midnight approval, we reviewers, who suffer from amnesia as most mortals do, rush to our typewriters to proclaim "Miss Cornell is unquestionably the First Lady of our theatre."

Although I admit to my shame that I, too, have on occasion surrendered to this form of Injun-giving, I must
confess I have never been deceived as to what is at once
silly (because meaningless) and ungracious (because
unnecessary) about it. The passion for a theatrical First
Lady is one I do not understand, unless it to be that a
"best," once established beyond dispute, can be taken
as a welcome means of saving critical thought.

There is plenty of room on our stage both for Miss
Hayes and Miss Cornell. And no reason at all why
either one of them should be forced to wear Eleanor
Blue to the other's discomfort or disadvantage. When
all is said and done, the real business of criticism is not
crown-giving. Such a role may suit the Archbishop of
Canterbury at Coronation time, but since when have
dramatic critics been willing to think of themselves as
archbishops or has Canterbury functioned as a dramatic
critic?

Criticism is not so much concerned with the final
bestowal of a diadem as with a rational explanation or
re-creation of the qualities justifying or distinguishing
its possible recipient. Even when it presumes to reach
for the anointing oil, criticism should be wise enough to
know that just as there is more than one deserving head
so there are all kinds of crowns of every shape, size,
and material in the crowded ranks of talent. Certainly
it ought to be sensible enough to realize that between
talents as fascinating in their differences as are Miss Cornell's and Miss Hayes' there can never be any choice of

an ultimate "best." As well try to establish that a painting as such is more beautiful than a statue as such, or that a symphony, merely because it is a symphony, is more satisfying than a building because it is a building.

What is most interesting about Miss Cornell and Miss Hayes when they are jointly considered is not which is First Lady (whatever that may mean dramatically) but the wide disparity distinguishing their endowments and their work. Truly they have few things in common, except that both of them happen to be preeminently excellent actresses in their totally dissimilar ways.

Each of them has of recent months taken a vacation from the more serious work of her career in scripts unworthy of her finest efforts. Certainly Miss Cornell enjoyed something of a holiday in *No Time for Comedy*. Unquestionably Miss Hayes is embarking on a sabbatical just now by having consented to appear in *Ladies and Gentlemen*.

Still, what is more to the point than their scant likenesses are the illuminating differences by means of which these two performers are set apart. What I, for one, admire unstintingly in Miss Cornell is everything exceptional about her, everything uniquely hers, which sets her apart from all other women on or off the stage. I prize her Mrs. Siddons tension; her tragic majesty; her dark allure; her midnight pallor; and the sense she gives of being so fateful in her own person that when she comes through a door you are gladly persuaded she could never have entered to answer anything so mundane as a telephone but must have emerged because she has a date with destiny.

In the presence of Miss Hayes it is just the opposite qualities I admire. She, too, is exceptional and in no way more so than in her radiant averageness. I like the woman in her as opposed to the goddess; the simple humanity which has no connection with the unearthly attributes of the muses; the technical virtuosity she unquestionably possesses; the feeling she so reassuringly creates that she is just like any number of earnest, attractive, intelligent, and hard-working young American women—with this glowing exception—she happens to be the one who made good, and who for countless reasons deserves to have done so.

When it comes to which of the two is First Lady of our theatre, this strikes me as being a compliment both empty and gratuitous. Washington, not Broadway, should be at least the starting point of First Ladies.

December 23, 1939

JOHN BARRYMORE'S RETURN

OBVIOUSLY Mr. Barrymore is having himself a very good time in *My Dear Children*. He is all over the place, moving about with that exaggerated energy which has to be used to keep oneself warm at a picnic held in the late autumn. He makes more faces than a rubber doll. He rolls his eyes about until they begin to bounce like dropped marbles.

He leers and sneers; he ogles and capers. He rubs noses with the ladies of the ensemble until it seems as if his one desire were to destroy "The Great Profile." He is not even content to act with his tongue *in* his cheek. He is in so affectionate a mood that he embraces some of the men in his company in a way that would embarrass a French general. He heckles the audience whenever he happens to hear it yawning. He asks play-goers from the stage (with more reason than they or he appear to realize), "What the hell are you laughing at?"

He hoists his eyebrows with hydraulic vigor. He laughs with painful conscientiousness to sustain the illusion that his notorious ad libbing is spontaneous, although at this late date the majority of his jokes, which are pretty feeble at best, are better known than they deserve to be and better remembered by Mr. Barrymore than his authors' lines. Most of all, however, the Mr. Barrymore-who-is devotes what remains of his once great talents not to acting the character asked for even in a peculiarly dull script but to playing musical chairs at the funeral of the John Barrymore-who-once-was. He practically slides down the banisters of his own reputation.

To those of us who cherish the memory of that other Mr. Barrymore, who saw him and can never forget having seen him, in *Justice, The Jest, Redemption, Peter Ibbetson, Richard III,* or *Hamlet,* the recollection of what he was is far too valued a memory to have the present-day Mr. Barrymore force us to "look here, upon this picture, and on this." That erstwhile Mr. Barrymore was the most exciting male acting talent the American theatre has produced in our time, the most splendidly endowed, the most magnificently magnetic, and by all odds the most pictorial.

There are moments even now, while Mr. Barrymore is permitting his features to enjoy a well-earned rest, when the John Barrymore of the earlier, palpitant years, of the Bruguiere photographs and the Sargent sketch stands palpably before us. The ghost of Hamlet continues to stalk the ramparts. But he is no longer armed cap-a-pie. The present-day Mr. Barrymore appears to resent his past reputation and to resent it bitterly. Watch him as he hurls unuttered, though clearly formed, curses at the portrait of his Hamlet which hangs upon the stage of the Belasco, and you are made painfully aware of how little the present Mr. Barrymore—who is the greatest huggermugger of our day—thinks of the Barrymore-who-was.

In *My Dear Children* Mr. Barrymore shows that, when he puts his mind to it, he can even now read the Hamlet soliloquy well. Heard as it is at present in the middle of such a play and such a performance, "To be or not to be" takes on an unbearably tragic note such as it has never before been able to claim in the midst of

Shakespeare's tragedy. Mr. Barrymore is still handsome. His personality remains compelling. He continues to move with extraordinary grace. His voice,
however, has lost its beauty, his diction its distinction.
Even when he is employing farce (at which he once
excelled) to mock the tragic Barrymore of his great
years, Mr. Barrymore appears to have misplaced his
skill. His pace as a *farceur* is slow beyond endurance;
his overplaying uncontrollable and unprecise to the
point of being a major depressant; and his pauses are so
long that, between the lines he delivers, one almost
reaches for a cigarette, convinced an intermission is at
hand.

How his fellow actors survive his roughhousing is
beyond comprehension. They do so, however, with a
bravery worthy of Congressional recognition. How
audiences can be cruel enough to find pleasure in seeing
Mr. Barrymore make a midway exhibition of himself
is another question difficult to answer. Their eagerness
to laugh at him, to encourage him into making a spectacle of himself and a joke of his name, is no less cruel
than Mr. Barrymore's apparent desire to bury alive the
fine legend of his own creation.

Most of us, as warm admirers of the Barrymore we
remember, have gone to the Belasco asking, like Os-
wald, for the sun, and have been given to our sorrow
only a fallen star. Between jokes in *My Dear Children*,
Mr. Barrymore might profitably read the essay William
Hazlitt wrote when once upon a time Mrs. Siddons at-

tempted to return to the stage. Reading that essay he might well congratulate himself upon the good fortune he at least enjoys in having William Hazlitt safely dead. It was Hazlitt who, when Sarah Siddons ventured to reinvade the realm of her former triumphs, asked, "Would she remind us of what she was by shewing us what *she was not?*"

March 9, 1940

MISS BANKHEAD AND *The Little Foxes*

IF *The Little Foxes* gave us no other cause for gratitude, the mere fact that it at last provides Tallulah Bankhead with a part in this country which reveals her full splendors as an actress would be enough to put us all in Miss Hellman's debt. Miss Bankhead is a player who has abundantly deserved her present good fortune. The faults of her Cleopatra have long since slipped into ancient history and been forgotten. Even at their worst they had nothing to do with Miss Bankhead's extraordinary powers as a realist.

For some years, in such insufficient scripts as *Dark Victory, Forsaking All Others, Something Gay,* and *Reflected Glory*, she has been giving tantalizing glimpses of these powers. All of us have admired her sullen beauty, and applauded the versatility she has shown in realism as she has turned emotional cartwheels from tragedy to comedy and back again.

As we have listened to her husky laugh, or heard her release her throbbing voice, we have sensed the vibrancy which is hers. We have noted the restless energy which has granted uncommon strength in her playing. We have observed her grace and responded to the explosive force of her personality. We may have regretted the lack of discipline which has marred some of her effects. Always, however, we have realized, as we have watched her pacing through unfortunate plays like a caged pantheress, that before us was an actress so gorgeously endowed that it would be one of the true theatrical misfortunes of our time were she to be unable to find a script permitting her to do justice to herself.

Fortunately for all of us, *The Little Foxes* brings Miss Bankhead her long-awaited opportunity. As the despicable Southern wife who is the central figure of Miss Hellman's drama, she gives the performance we have been waiting impatiently for her to give. She creates the kind of villainess even the Grand Guignol has never matched. Her technical resourcefulness is put to superb use. Her smoldering strength galvanizes the attention. Her quality of immediate ignition, of incessant combustibility enslaves the interest. In her torrid presence one understands why it is that theatres have to have asbestos curtains. One watches her fascinated, as if confronted by a cobra. To see her is to see Sargent's

Madame X come to life, possessed of a clammy heart into which flows the black blood of Clytemnestra, Medusa, Lady Macbeth, and Mrs. Danvers.

If one has the time, even while sitting breathlessly before *The Little Foxes*, to keep on thinking of how magnificent a Hedda Gabler Miss Bankhead would make, the fault is not Miss Bankhead's. Hers is a brilliant performance throughout. It is Miss Hellman who by her very overcompetence forces the mind to wander.

It is Miss Hellman because, engrossing as is her play, it suffers from being far too well contrived for its own enduring health. Much of its writing is too expert in the worst manner of Ibsen, which is only another way of saying in the best manner of Pinero. It is not only a play that is well-made (as if that in itself were not something to date it); it is a play that is too-well-made. This in no way detracts from its fascination in production. But as a drama which pretends to sociological significance and abiding literary importance, it does put *The Little Foxes* in precisely the same category in the theatre which *Rebecca* occupies on the list of best-sellers in fiction.

Just as *Rebecca* forces you to feel as if you were about to shake hands with the Brontës on any page, so *The Little Foxes* seduces you into believing that at almost any minute all of Ibsen's and Strindberg's most unattractive heroes and heroines, having crossed the Atlantic without suffering a sea change, will suddenly bob up on the stage as Sons and Daughters of the Confederacy, in convention met near Atlanta. Do not misunderstand me. The literary skill of both Miss Du Maurier's novel and Miss Hellman's melodrama is such that, while their spell is upon you, you are willing to believe you are getting literature, although in both cases your better judgment insists upon informing you at every turn that all you are receiving is super-Crime Club stuff.

As a *fleurs du mal* dramatization of the profit motive below the Mason-Dixon line, I do not for a moment doubt that, if it were badly acted, Miss Hellman's absorbingly unpleasant guignol would evoke snickers because of the very boldness with which she has dipped her pen in sulphur. Miss Hellman has a genius for plotting. Such close-knit plotting as she is adept at is more than slightly old-fashioned in the theatre; it is a lost art.

One grows suspicious of it, even as one tires of the way in which Miss Hellman unrolls a red carpet before every scene in her play, hell-bent upon turning each one of them into what, in the language of "Sardoodledom," used to be called a "big scene." Her costumes of the turn of the century help her in protecting the excesses of her storytelling. So does the commendable validity of much of her observation and the way in which she *seems* to look into the hearts of evil characters and goad these people into action.

Most of all, it is Miss Hellman's actors who endow

her play with its final effectiveness. It is Charles Dingle as a sinister brother. It is Carl Benton Reid as a loathsome husband. It is Patricia Collinge who gives one of the season's most poignant performances as a silly Southern wife driven by despair into becoming a secret drinker. Above all, it is Tallulah Bankhead. These players are all of them so expert that, even while they keep Miss Hellman's play the superlatively "good theatre" it is, they are able for the most part, with her Machiavellian aid, to make it seem much more than that. The result is an evening of extraordinary interest and almost anguishing tension.

March 11, 1939

SUSAN WITHOUT GOD

GERTRUDE LAWRENCE IN *Skylark*

WATCHING Miss Lawrence is always entertaining. She is as much of a side show as she is an actress. She is more than a comedienne; she is a one-woman Luna Park—ferris wheels, roller coasters, merry-go-rounds, shoot-the-shoots, bright lights, and all. Joy spills from her eyes. Her smile is beguiling. She moves with uncanny grace, is charming to look at, dresses smartly, and has a voice of velvet which she can wrinkle as amusingly for laughter's sake as she does her upturned nose.

Then there is about her acting an energy which makes a windmill in a hurricane seem lethargic. Like Mrs. Roosevelt, Miss Lawrence is unquestionably blessed with a happy thyroid. Her wrists, though slender, must be as strong as Bismarck's will. Otherwise her hands, which have a way of galloping off in all directions like Mr. Leacock's horseman, would be compelled to obey the law of gravity they so constantly challenge. If her gestures take to skywriting for emphasis, they are nonetheless felicitous. Her strides may reveal a pelvic ease worthy of Martha Graham, and, like Miss Graham, she may seem to conspire to keep one knee from knowing exactly what the other knee is doing. Her archness may suffer from strain; her winsomeness become Gargantuan.

Yet even when she is led into overplaying, when she suddenly reverts to her musical comedy past and is misguided by the generous abandon of her acting to treating a comedy scene as if it were a black-out in *Charlot's Revue*, Miss Lawrence does not lose her fascination. Hers is neither an ordinary personality nor a skill usually encountered. Her performance may get out of hand. She may seem to dizzy herself by the tailspins into which she goes, but such uncomfortable moments when they do occur (as they did last night at the Morosco) prove no more than air pockets encountered during an otherwise delightful flight.

Miss Lawrence is unquestionably the mistress of a hundred and one enchanting comic devices. Then, too, hers is the distinction of having done what very few women have ever been able to do and more ought to try—that is, of course, being able to sound English and look French. In her own trim person she has succeeded where even the most ingenious engineers have failed—in other words, in doing away with the English Channel.

If in *Skylark* Miss Lawrence can almost be said to be playing the title role, watching her nonetheless holds its ample rewards. Mr. Raphaelson's comedy is custom-built for Miss Lawrence. It fits her as if Valentina had designed it with her demands for physical freedom in mind. Truly it is as vehicular as the Holland Tunnel. In every sense, except the moral, *Skylark* is something of a deaconess' one-horse shay in which Miss Lawrence takes her audience for a joy ride. Miss Lawrence may continue to be Susan, which is one way of saying she may continue to be flighty in her celebrated and justly appreciated manner, but at the Morosco she bobs up as Susan without God—with Mr. Raphaelson doing his best to take God's place.

Mr. Raphaelson's play is the kind of drama which need not fear winning the Pulitzer Prize. It is a comedy, light, hard-working, and almost arrogant in its triviality. It is a machine-made product which, though it is serviceable, can claim neither the sensitivity nor the charm which distinguished the same author's *Accent on Youth*. It does its laughing duty for those not expecting too much. It boasts its felicitous lines and some adroitly handled situations. Especially as played by Miss Lawrence and most of Mr. Golden's well-chosen cast, it holds the audience's attention. But just as one trembles to think of *Skylark* without Miss Lawrence and Glenn Anders, so one prefers to think of them rather than of the comedy they adorn.

Although Mr. Raphaelson's story must be older than the Alps, it will unquestionably long be a favorite resort of both dramatists and audiences. It is concerned with nothing more or less original than the happiness which finally comes to a married couple which thinks it is ripe for divorce. As is entirely justifiable, Mr. Raphaelson attempts to make this venerable fable his own by having the husband in question a man who loves his business so ardently that his deserted wife threatens to name it as corespondent; by peopling his fable with representatives of other families also in advertising; and by introducing a disillusioned lawyer whose bitter comments prove hilarious as they are excellently drawled out by Mr. Anders.

The pity is that all of Mr. Raphaelson's writing in *Skylark* is not on the level with his play's happier interludes. Much of his comedy sounds like a very inferior imitation of Philip Barry. Then, too, even in his more entertaining scenes, Mr. Raphaelson has unfortunately assigned to the lawyer that Mr. Anders plays so well some would-be poetic lines which must cause Mr. Anders as much embarrassment to speak as they did some of us to hear last night. Also Mr. Raphaelson's final act still seems unsatisfactorily resolved, even when from the rise of the first curtain its cheerful outcome is as plain as the nose on Jimmy Durante's face.

Although *Skylark* may have its plentiful shortcomings as a play, it passes the time agreeably, largely because of Miss Lawrence. She has lost none of her cyclonic energy, but she gives a better, more ingratiating, and, on the whole, more disciplined performance than she gave in *Susan and God*. As the phrasemakers have it, it is her evening. And she makes more than the most of it, which, needless to say, allows us to do the same. It is she who keeps *Skylark* off the ground.

October 12, 1939

THORNTON WILDER TURNS ACTOR

WHEN at Cohasset's summer theatre Sinclair Lewis, as the editor in his own *It Can't Happen Here*, put a sheet of paper in a typewriter and proceeded to tap the keys, audiences felt rewarded. They had had their money's worth. If they had not seen a professional actor, they had at any rate seen a distinguished novelist IN PERSON. More than that, they had seen him *at work*. Theirs was the illusion of being present at the birth of a book. Had they been permitted to peek through a glass panel in Mr. Lewis' study as he was writing *Babbitt* they could hardly have been happier.

At the Morosco these nights playgoers with a literary turn of mind can experience not only an equal, but a far greater pleasure. Because there Thornton Wilder is to be seen playing the philosophical Stage Manager in his own *Our Town* during Frank Craven's brief absence. Mr. Wilder, if I may say so without offending partisans among the novel readers, acquits himself much more creditably as an actor than Mr. Lewis succeeded in doing.

Trying to step into Mr. Craven's shoes was a brave thing for Mr. Wilder to do. If he does not quite fill them, remember no one could. Mr. Craven has his own dry brand of humor. His face might be overlooked in an Atlantic City beauty contest, but it is as American as Yankee Doodle or Uncle Sam. It is quizzical, shrewd, tender, and humorous. Although it seems familiar with poker, it could be just as well acquainted with Gideons. Its smile has about it the affability of Midwestern locker rooms; its benignity is the goodness of the country doctor or the small-town banker, in those days when it was still safe both to say and to assume bankers were good.

His voice is no less indigenous than his Rotarian face. In its quiet way and with its eloquent flatness, it speaks for the average small businessman in this country who is a capitalist in wit and experience. Then, too, as goes without saying, Mr. Craven is a fine professional. His understatement, apparently so casual and colloquial, is the result of a skill which long years behind the footlights have brought him. It is at once as cunning as it appears to be artless.

To follow Mr. Craven, Mr. Wilder had to have his courage with him. He was not foolhardy. He has merits of his own to offer. You may miss certain gentle touches of the Craven humor in Mr. Wilder's playing of the Stage Manager. You may detect a certain nervousness at first, particularly in those introductory moments during which Mr. Wilder must set the stage by arranging the few required properties. You may wish Mr. Wilder spoke a little louder throughout, and feel the insecurity of a few of his pauses. Certainly you are bound to miss Mr. Craven's pipe, which as he puffed at it seemed visibly to link Grovers Corners with the ancient Greece in which smoke escaped up the chimneys.

Mr. Wilder grows in poise. He has a musical voice and great charm. His cultivation is so manifest, in his diction and inflection, that the few "ain'ts" he has given the Stage Manager to say may sound as out of place on his scholar's tongue as a reference to Plato would be in Tony Galento's mouth. Still Mr. Wilder's charm is a thing of the spirit which syntax cannot obscure. It springs from his sincerity, is born of his simplicity, is heightened by the fact that, as he stands before an audience speaking his own lines, he becomes a symbol of all the virtues of his own rare play.

Its gentleness, its beauty of mind, its wisdom, its humor, and its heartbreaking insight into what is common to all our living take on a special interest when

Mr. Wilder himself plays the Stage Manager as simply as if he were conducting a class at Lawrenceville in a subject he loved. You can almost tell he is the author by the way in which he caresses (with reason) some of his finer speeches. His heart is in his work. What is more, the heart of his play is visibly at work in him.

September 17, 1938

MISS HEPBURN IN *The Philadelphia Story*

THAT there have always been two Philip Barrys has long since been well known to those who have followed Mr. Barry's double life as a dramatist. One of these has been the cosmic Mr. Barry who has fought an anguishing, often arresting, inner struggle as he has gone searching for his God in such scripts as *John, Hotel Universe, The Joyous Season,* and this winter's *Here Come the Clowns.* The other Mr. Barry, the first to be heard from and the one his largest public has always doted upon, is the dramatist who has shown a genuine flair for badinage and written such perceptive tearful comedies as *You and I, White Wings, Paris Bound, In a Garden, Tomorrow and Tomorrow,* and *The Animal Kingdom.*

It is this second Mr. Barry, the smiling one with a lump in his throat, who has tossed off *The Philadelphia*

Story, that play, so pleasant at times but so unimportant throughout, which can boast as its truest and most commanding virtue the fact that it brings Katharine Hepburn triumphantly back to our stage. Although Mr. Barry's new script is not in his best comic vein, through it shine those qualities, literate and ingratiating, which have distinguished his better comedies. It is the work of a man, sensitive and witty, who, even when he has embarked upon what proves to be something of a dramatist's holiday, turns up bearing his special gifts.

As he relates how a rich young Philadelphia divorcee, a chill perfectionist, a married virgin who has no understanding in her heart, is awakened to love and life by a drunken incident with a writer the night before she is to marry another man, Mr. Barry has difficulty starting his fable and nods at times, in the best Greek fashion, while keeping it going. Yet when once he has established his wealthy family, and abruptly indicated that they are supposed to be on their best behavior because their country home is being invaded by a writer and a lady photographer representing a magazine thinly disguised as *Destiny*, Mr. Barry's play begins to show agreeable signs of his authorship.

If his comedy is not a good one, if it forces one to think back to the superiority of *Paris Bound* which it often brings to mind, it has its commendable points. At least it passes the time, often very pleasantly. It bristles with amusing lines. It has scenes which indicate Mr. Barry's surety as a comic dramatist. It makes clear what

a gay and intuitive mind is his and how polished can be
his gift for dialogue. Even at its feeblest and most aim-
less, it is warmed by a winning sense of tolerance. Once
again Mr. Barry may be turning Congreve into a cardinal, and advancing his old argument that a single
transgression is no justification for divorce between
two people who really love one another. But to this he
adds a welcome and timely plea to the effect that people,
not classes, are what matter; that poverty does not spell
virtue any more than riches necessarily spell meanness.

At its best Mr. Barry's play is no more than a rich
cloak which Mr. Barry, in a moment of Raleighesque
gallantry, has spread wide for Miss Hepburn to walk
upon. Miss Hepburn is not an actress easy to describe.
It is difficult to distinguish between what she is and
what she does. It is more than difficult; it is irrelevant.
To an almost unmatched extent what she is, is also what
she does.

What she is, as playgoers came to know in *The War-
rior's Husband*, and as movie-goers realized in such
films as *Morning Glory*, *Little Women*, and *Alice
Adams*, is one of the most beautiful young women on
our stage and screen and also one of the most fascinating. That on the screen she has wavered between performances of high excellence and those which have
been said to be downright embarrassing by people who
have had the heart to see them, only indicates, as does
her more recent stage record of failure in *The Lake* and

triumph in *The Philadelphia Story*, that Miss Hepburn is a performer who, more than most, needs to find the right script, to be protected by expert direction, and to have her very special gifts displayed to equally special advantage. As an actress she bears a greater resemblance than the majority of her rivals to the little girl with the curl in the middle of her forehead. Certainly when she is good, she can be very, very good indeed.

That she is blessed with uncommon endowments no one can deny who has seen her at her best or at her worst. She has intelligence, breeding, fire, a voice which in its emotional scenes can be satin, a body Zorina might look upon with envy, and a personality of such compulsion that, without meaning to do so, she can make the center of the stage wherever she happens to be. There is grace—a lovely and arresting grace—about her very awkwardness; about the tomboyish attitudes she strikes from time to time; and, most especially, about that free-limbed quality of hers which can turn her very crosses into the poetry of motion.

Most of all, there is Miss Hepburn's beauty. Dramatic critics, of course, have a way of pretending that an actress' beauty is of no importance either to them or to her art. What has led them to do this is at once a desire to seem judicial when appraising technique, and the fact—the melancholy fact—that so many of our actresses have had to get along (and done very nicely, thank you) unaided by beauty.

Miss Hepburn is not one of these. Beauty is decidedly

in league with her. Nor is her loveliness of that languid,
bovine sort so dear to the elder Edward with his
well-known fondness for Lilys who, though eye-filling
in their serenity, were apt to be more Jersey than Lily.
Miss Hepburn's face is as interesting as it is pretty, as
flexible as it is well-modeled. It has strength no less than
temperament behind it. Above all, its decisive modeling
enables Miss Hepburn to project her expressions on-
stage with the clarity of a close-up. With its high cheek
bones, its almost equine spread, its generous mouth, and
its sculptured features, it is the mask of a Bryn Mawr
Garbo whose visual fascinations are endless. Moreover,
Miss Hepburn can act. And act she does with agreeable
results, not only by being what she is but by doing
very nicely what she is called upon to do in Mr. Barry's
script when, in the last act, he gets around to asking her.

March 29 and April 1, 1939

Five

AMERICA'S YIELD

BACKGROUNDS

SHADOWBOXING has always been a favorite form of critical exercise. Once Goethe, when indulging in the sport, played Eckermann to himself (which is only a way of saying he played fox terrier to his own Victrola) by putting himself a question he was eager to answer. "What are the conditions that produce a great classical national author?" he demanded. Gobbo's reply to Launcelot's query was prompt and remains instructive.

The emergence of such an author, said Goethe, depends upon several things. He must be born in a great commonwealth. That commonwealth must, after a series of great and historic events, have become a happy, unified nation. The author must find in his countrymen loftiness of disposition, depth of feeling, vigor, and consistency of action. The national spirit must thoroughly pervade him. Through his innate genius he must feel capable of sympathizing with the past as well as with the present. In order to encounter no difficulties in obtaining a high degree of culture for himself, he must find his nation in a high state of civilization. The spade work in literature must already have been done. Much material must already have been collected and be ready for use, and his predecessors must already have made a large number of more or less perfect attempts. Finally, conditions must be such that, instead of having to pay too dearly for his mistakes, he will be able, in the prime of his life, to see the possibilities of a great theme and to develop it according to some uniform plan into a well-arranged and well-constructed literary work.

No wonder, after so formidable a parade of "musts," Goethe had to admit to himself that the emergence of such an author is the result of what, with immoderate moderation, he described as "a happy conjuncture of outer and inner circumstances." No wonder such authors are rare, and even rarer in the theatre than outside of it. In the theatre there are additional "musts," equally exacting, which antedate the appearance of a dramatist entitled to wear the triple adjectival crown of "great," "classic," and "national." As a matter of fact many are the playwrights, successful and respected, who, though they are expert contrivers and articulate enough in that telegraphic form of emotional communication known as dialogue, cannot pretend to be authors in the literary sense of caring for words, using them well, or having achieved the personal possession of them known as style.

Goethe, in the role of Goethe's ventriloquist, may, on the subject of "the man and the moment," have been able to explain many of the conditions making "the moment" possible, but neither he nor anyone else has been able to explain the mystery of "the man's" emergence. Although the works of a man of genius are additions to the world's natural resources, open to everyone's inspection, the whys and wherefores of genius are unnatural wonders which remain secrets that doomsday itself will probably not give away.

If we in our theatre have produced as yet no great classic national author; if to the hopeful even Mr. O'Neill, so bold of spirit, so worthy in his gropings, so exciting in his better theatricalism, and so innovational in technique, is, because of his lean language, bound to appear more like a mute Marlowe heralding some Shakespeare to follow, than the full flowering in drama of which America is capable, the justifications are nonetheless numerous for our taking a pride in our modern theatre equal to the many pleasures we derive from it.

Although ours is a vigorous theatre—the most vigorous in the world today—one cannot in honesty ascribe that vigor to its youth. Youth happens to be a fetish in this country. For centuries during which we have bat-

tled against age as if it were the last frontier we had to
conquer, youth—not the young so much as the in-
domitable persistency of the legend of our national
youth—has been to us what ancestor worship is to the
Chinese. We have Peter Panned our way through the
years. As time's draft-dodgers, but still banded together
on almost every front, we have waged the longest, most
stubborn of our national wars against maturity. In the
flush of victories, won with appalling ease, we have forgotten that youth itself is no virtue save as a guarantee
of health, of energies unspent, of curiosities unsatisfied,
of courage unbroken, wonder unexhausted, and potentialities not fully realized.

We have forgotten, too, that the excellence of what
is done, not the age of the doer, is art's chief concern
and the point at which the lovers of that art and Shirley
Temple's fans part company. Oscar Wilde realized the
youth of America is our oldest tradition. So it was when
he visited these shores almost sixty years ago. So, though
considerably older, that youth remains to this day. But
the theatre, at least as we know it and respect it, is one
of the youngest developments in a country, slow to
grow up, which still delights in being a Mrs. Moonlight
among nations.

In its aims and assumptions, its standards and objec-
tives, this theatre of the playwright we now enjoy is
—as opposed to the theatre of the actor in which our
forefathers rejoiced—younger than the motion pictures,
the incredible youth of which is so often advanced as an

excuse for their misdemeanors. If Hollywood can be said to have grown up technically in 1915 with *The Birth of a Nation*, then 1918 (when the Provincetown Playhouse moved to Macdougal Street) and 1919 (when the Washington Square Players reopened as the Theatre Guild) can with safety be named as the years during which, at least spiritually, the "new" American theatre was born. If this theatre had broken with native tradition in no other way, it would have done so by asking us not to praise it for its youth but to admire it as an adult that just happened to be young. This is one of its encouraging distinctions.

In the nineteenth century we had, as a nation with a considerable past, sufficiently met the demands of Goethe's inexorable "musts" to produce Hawthorne, Melville, Poe, Emerson, Whitman, and Mark Twain. But the America which had expressed itself greatly in the novel, in poetry, and the essay was unrecognizably different from the America which at the same time was enjoying itself with a modicum of self-expression and no literary distinction in the theatre. The solitary minds of readers were trained to expectancies they willingly abandoned when they came together as audiences.

Make-believe was to them make-believe. Nothing more. It was not life so ordered in dramatic form as to make them believe in the reality of this observation. It was falsification so overstated in its farcical or melodramatic exaggerations as to compel them to forget reality. The stage's truth was neither life's nor literature's. What the gaslights flickered on was a world the sun had never shone upon.

Writers, who understood and respected the integrity of letters, turned panderers to the lowered group taste with Bronson Howard's cheerfulness when they wrote for the stage. There they functioned not as authors, true to themselves, their subjects, or their vision, but as merchants of amusement, providers of happy endings, thrill-concocters, brewers of "big" scenes.

They had their theories with which to bolster up their self-respect and explain the concessions they made, at the turn of almost every phrase, to popular taste. They spoke of the laws of dramatic construction and truth, and said, even while admitting the precise nature of these laws to be unknown, that when it came to breaking any one of them, "you might as well show your originality by defying the law of gravitation." *

What these mysterious rules of the drama boiled down to was a fearful regard for what the public wanted; in other words, for what its group morals and its group wishful thinking were willing to accept. Obedience was the law of laws—obedience to the mass prejudices, the mass preconceptions, the mass orthodoxies, and the mass mythology of audiences which did not want to be disturbed, which did want to be entertained, which refused to take the theatre seriously as a reflection of their living, and treated it as if it were no

---

* Bronson Howard, *The Autobiography of a Play*, a lecture first delivered at Harvard in 1886.

more than an extremely well-played game of emotional
charades. If these audiences boasted of their national
youth outside of our playhouses, they never surrendered to that youth with more fervor than when in
them.

The rising of the curtain meant for them the lower-
ing of adult standards. The eagle they worshiped dramatically was hatched from a bluebird's egg. On-stage
they wanted the simplicities respected, not the verities.
They loved "Mother" as dutifully as they suspected
foreigners, believed slickers city-born, and goodness
an undeniable rural product. They wanted villains
hissable, heroines ill-used but undefiled, heroes heroic,
virtue rewarded, vice punished, and the Sunday-school
precepts made exciting. Although they did not mind
having the mortgage foreclosed in the second act to the
accompaniment of tons of paper snow, they insisted in
the last act upon the farm's being regained by its poor
but honest owners. Papier-mâché disasters they wel-
comed, but they sought the solace, even while enduring
them, of realizing in advance that the frontiersman, the
Union troops, the fireman, the policeman, or the marines (depending upon the vintage) would always arrive in the nick of time, not before, not after. The most
unhappily married member of the audience believed
that behind the footlights wedding bells were inevitably
a guarantee of enduring bliss. The tear-jerking world in
which these playgoers journeyed ecstatically was a
world as gleefully in falseface as the minstrels of the

same period were in blackface. It was a world, more-over, that bore about as much relationship to what was true of the genuine problems of a white man's living as the minstrel shows did to those of the Negro.

Our early dramatists did not dream of molding their public's group thinking. They followed the prejudices of that public from a distance respectful enough to be intellectually insulting. If our early playgoers looked upon our early dramatists with condescension it was because these playwrights matched their audiences in the intellectual condescension with which they approached the stage.

The "palmy" years of the American theatre were the lean years of the American drama. Those "good old days" for which the sentimentalists are always weeping, those days when the whole country gave its love to the stage, and the motion pictures and the radio had not yet appeared as homebreakers on the dramatic scene, were the days when the actor was not a means to an end. He was an end in himself and the dramatist the means to his self-realization. They were the days of great stars, incessant "classic" revivals; productions, generally shoddy, which did not as a rule matter much; and new scripts that, historically at least, were significant mainly as they expressed the national adolescence.

Before the last war important forerunners of the new dramatic order had already appeared in this country. William Vaughn Moody, Clyde Fitch, Percy Mac-Kaye, Edward Sheldon were dramatists pointing the way, even as Winthrop Ames and Arthur Hopkins were producers doing the same thing. But it was not really until the twenties that our theatre reached an exciting maturity.

Then it was that the recently filled dramatic libraries of Europe were pillaged in earnest. Then it was that the full fruits of a dramatic renaissance already old abroad were newly brought to America, that experimental theatres turned their backs on Broadway, and that the dramatist in our theatre ceased to be a person necessary because of what he had given someone else to say and became important for what he had to say for himself.

If our playwrights who emerged in the twenties— O'Neill, Maxwell Anderson, George S. Kaufman, Marc Connelly, Paul Green, the late Sidney Howard, George Kelly, Laurence Stallings, Elmer Rice, Robert E. Sherwood, Philip Barry, and the rest—had no common credo of rebellion, there was one faith, one conviction most of them did share. The better of them did want to write their best for the stage. By having their say without condescension, they sought to produce a body of dramatic literature as self-respecting as was the body of literature produced by their contemporary novelists. They invited judgment as writers, not as hacks or artificers. They were not afraid to violate the old canons of public taste, to wound prejudices, to state fearlessly the problems of the individual as they saw them.

The twenties were exciting years in the theatre. Talk

of the art of the theatre was then as common as golden-rod. The New Movement, the new scenery, the new mystery of light, the newly recognized role of the architect, the designer as an interpretative artist rather than as a scene painter, the director as a critic in action and a co-ordinator who by keeping the actor in his place thus insured the values of a dramatist's script, the new dramatists writing with self-respect for new audiences which, having foresworn their group Pollyanna-ism, were anxious to be allowed to remain adults in a playhouse, the whole aesthetic regeneration of the backstage necessary to the theatre's satisfactory expression of these new playwrights' aims—all these "musts," overlooked by Goethe in his literary considerations, were factors contributing to the excitement of the decade preceding the stock market crash.

That crash, the depression which followed, the New Deal, America's sudden awareness that the American dream could also be a nightmare, sobered, enriched, or angered our stage in the ensuing decade. The theatre of the twenties, which had been largely dedicated to perplexed individuals, emerged in the thirties as the theatre of a perplexed people. Our stage became more than aesthetically stirring or intellectually provocative. By deliberate intention it became socially significant. What the artists had labored to perfect for art's sake, a new tribe of propagandists took advantage of in the name of "the good society" for propaganda's sake.

The majority of the dramas written by the special

pleaders of the Left, or even by sturdy democrats who
sought to give Labor a much-needed hearing in the
theatre and dramatized with proper indignation notorious cases of American injustice, were hardly more
adult in their thinking, their orthodoxies, their my-
thologies than such infantile products of our nine-
teenth-century stage as *East Lynne, The Drunkard,
The Streets of New York,* or *Ten Nights in a Barroom.*

The articles of faith of these agitational scripts were
on the whole childlike in their simplicity. In most of
these plays the only right was left. In most of them the
shameful fact that a lady wore an evening dress was
enough to damn her as a Clytemnestra out of Bergdorf-
Goodman gladly living off slain factory hands. A man
who appeared on-stage in a tuxedo could not help himself; he was a villain. His costume proclaimed his social
sins as clearly as Hester's "A" advertised her moral
frailty. Any character who owned a Titian or a Degas
was—ergo—a Fascist. Any person who possessed even a
rowboat or a canoe was in danger of becoming a victim
of imperialist propaganda. Every banker, lawyer, college president, and industrialist was suspect.

Any mention of Herbert Hoover was not only a
command for laughter but accepted as proof that the
dramatist mentioning Hoover's name was possessed of
a wit greater than that possessed by Aristophanes, Lewis
Carroll, W. S. Gilbert, and Shaw rolled into one. All
references to the House of Morgan were held to be

provocations for enough hissing to blow the Dust Bowl to Alaska and back again. Any character not prepared to strike more often than a grandfather's clock, and with the same regularity, was thought to be a reactionary. Every character who, by hard work or good luck, had succeeded in staying off relief was a Fifth Columnist working against democracy.

Conversely, all agitators who wandered into plays were heroes; every mill hand's wife was a potential Saint Joan. Every worker who socked the boss after wrecking his factory was a new Sir Galahad. Readers of *The New Masses, The New Theatre,* or *The Daily Worker* were persons held behind the footlights to be closer to truth than Pavlov, Bacon, Plato, or Aristotle. Any reader of *The Atlantic Monthly, Harper's Bazaar, Vogue,* or *Arts and Decoration* was a Dickensian miscreant. Not to be starving was a dramatic sin. All Party cards were passkeys to paradise. And any character who ate an apple instead of selling one was, for this reason, apt to prove a serpent in the economic garden.

Although there were distinguished exceptions, of course, these were the overstatements and simplicities forming the credo of most of the propagandist scripts written in the early and middle thirties. If the majority of these plays were infantile in their conventions and their thinking, they possessed virtues which cannot be denied and which make one grateful for the feeblest of the lot. Crude they may have been, and most often were. Yet their crudities, like their violence and their simplicity, were a healthy part of our theatre's growing pains.

They could claim a vitality and importance many of the slicker products of our showshops were unable to boast. Childish as they were intellectually and in their means, they were adult in their attempt to bring the theatre into a closer relationship with the nation's problems. Regardless of how they spoke or what they had to say, they sought to speak in a new way for a huge new audience which hitherto had enjoyed no theatrical franchise. Although most of these scripts held "The System," at which they shook their fists, to be their foe, their real enemy, from the standpoint of achieving continued success with America's proletariat, was a lack of humor which exceeded their lack of skill. It was the hilarity of such a healthy and intelligent product of the Labor Stage as *Pins and Needles* which, at the decade's end, won for this sorely needed and astringent revue a passport into the hearts of playgoers of every class and, in various editions, a three-year run on Broadway.

Although the dramatists who emerged in the twenties —Mr. Anderson, Mr. Barry, Mr. Sherwood, Mr. Kaufman, and the rest—have continued to supply our stage with many of its most interesting plays, the theatre of the thirties has produced its important young playwrights. Not nearly enough of them for comfort, but men of true merit, nonetheless. These younger dramatists have not, by any means, been all of one kind. They

have been as different from one another as their predecessors were; as different as Thornton Wilder is from
John Steinbeck (to mention two novelists who have
written plays of genuine distinction); as different for
that matter as Clifford Odets is from William Saroyan.

If social agitation in the sense of the erstwhile Theatre Union, or even of the much more contributive
and lamented Federal Theatre, has largely vanished
from our stage; if some of our so-called radical playwrights have tamed down and reached openly for their
red-white-and-blue bunting, this does not mean our
"new" drama has lost either its social or dramatic significance.

The times have changed with terrifying swiftness.
The clarified needs for internal reform and the hopes
for the abolishment of old and cancerous abuses which
followed Mr. Roosevelt's inauguration have been
eclipsed by the fears and horrors of what Hitler's coming into power on the very next day has meant to men
and nations everywhere. The Russia which promised
much has, under Stalin, been buried with Lenin in his
tomb. Local discontent has been hushed by international terror. Peace has given way to war, war to truces
guaranteeing only future wars. Oceans have shrunk
overnight into ponds; bulwarks of liberty in the old
world have tumbled. The world has been seized by one
of history's greatest convulsions. Democracy, once so
tolerant in its self-assurance, faces through fear the
need to grow intolerant in order to survive. Every-

where the forces of destruction are for the moment victorious.

In such an apocalyptic universe the future of the individual is far from bright. These are the times that try men's souls, indeed! The individual, so long the center of his own universe, has in the modern world become more and more willing to surrender his most cherished prerogatives, to make himself subservient to an all-powerful state or organization. We, who have been brought up to consider government a necessary evil, can now encounter many people eager to believe that individuals are only necessary evils in a government. The illnesses of the world and the weaknesses of man, the individual, have driven the individual man into groups of all kinds in the hope of gaining strength for mass action.

Such mass strength has unquestionably been gained, and the benefits of that strength are many and incontestable. Yet even in this country the individual appears, as an individual, to have lost faith in his own importance and the dignity of his responsibilities. Individual rights seem throughout the world to have gone the way States' rights went here.

Where once man stood up as a biped and defied his God, he is now content to crawl to social protest as a centipede. Not states alone, but individuals, too, are slowly being federalized. The pity of all this, from the point of view of the arts and quite aside from the tragedy of individual men, is that mortals, supposedly

the victims of their own machines, are becoming in
many respects the victims of the protective machinery
they have invented for their group safety. They have
surrendered more than their identity; they have surrendered their wills. Cheerfully, with the best of faith,
they have turned Rockettes in the economic, social, and
military orders. This may well be the final tragedy of
their benevolence, their high dreams, and their despair.

In the storms of such a world the theatre still shines
like a beacon. The drama has no other choice than to
respect those values and those rights upon which we in
the democracies have been raised. Behind the footlights
at any rate the individual remains his own unassailable
citadel. If the free and rational processes of his thinking
are endangered in the world just now, he can still find
a safe harbor in the theatre, so long at least as it survives in freedom. For there, as the following pages
should indicate, the dramatist continues to write of individuals as an individual and by individuals his work
must be judged.

BOB SHERWOOD IN ILLINOIS

THE program names Robert Emmett Sherwood as the
author of *Abe Lincoln in Illinois*. So he is, but he does
not work without collaborators whose aid at times
proves far more potent than any contribution he has

to make. One of these collaborators is the foreknowl-
edge we bring with us, as members of an American
audience, of Lincoln, the man and the martyr. This
endows us with a wisdom no characters on the stage
can claim. By permitting us to measure *what was* by
the tragedy of *what was to be*, it adds a certain weight
to the leanest of lean lines and grants an undeniable
pathos to the sketchiest of undeveloped scenes.

Another of Mr. Sherwood's collaborators is Mr.
Lincoln himself. Had there been any calls of "Author!
Author!" at the Plymouth the other night, Mr. Sherwood would in all honesty have had to lead Abe on
behind the footlights by one of his Borglum hands.
Failing Abe, he would at least have been compelled
to walk on with a copy of the Lincoln-Douglas *Debates* tucked under his own long arms and to point to
that copy, even as Toscanini points with proper gratitude to the members of his orchestra without whose
aid there would have been no audible music. Just as
surely as Mr. Hart and Mr. Kaufman worked together,
so have the Messrs. Sherwood and Lincoln emerged as
a playwriting team in which Mr. Sherwood on the
whole functions as the silent partner. That Mr. Sherwood has been lucky in his collaborator no one can
deny. The Meilhac to his Halévy, or, a trifle more accurately, the Beaumont to his Fletcher, had a gift for
the English language no other biped born on this side
of the Atlantic has equaled, much less excelled.

The best scene in Mr. Sherwood's play is ghost-written by a ghost who haunts all Americans and is the chiefest glory of our dream. This scene is the episode in which Mr. Massey faces Douglas on a public platform to speak some of the fine, free words Lincoln himself delivered during the course of these historic debates. That Lincoln had magnificent things to say on the subject of racial equality, the right to strike, and human liberty, is scarcely news. His words were such that even when they are declaimed by schoolboys they refuse to lose their eloquence. As spoken by Mr. Massey they continue to state in stirring terms principles of which the Union Mr. Lincoln preserved cannot be too frequently reminded.

Timely, reverent, and ultimately impressive as it becomes, Mr. Sherwood's play is not so much written as it is assembled in the best manner of Detroit, though not on the belt. Among the virtues it can claim is that of serving its public as an echo cave. It is capable of giving back to those who sit before it the cries of anguish or hope they may bring to it. From the dark confusion of its hero, audiences can in these dark days derive a certain consolation. To a people at present confused it is doubtless comforting to realize so great a man as Lincoln was once as confused as they are.

Mr. Lincoln is not the only historical figure Mr. Sherwood has relied upon as a collaborator. There is another person, seen or unseen, who always makes his ugly contribution to plays about the Emancipator. His name is John Wilkes Booth. Our constant awareness

that history holds his horse in the alley behind Ford's
theatre distends with tragic meaning, for all of us who
love Lincoln, any references to his future which the
martyred President may utter in plays or books about
him. Let an on-stage Lincoln, after his election, say in
effect, "I'm going to Washington, and I don't think I'll
be quite happy there," and, because of the knowledge
we bring to them, these words take on a pathos that
would not otherwise be theirs. Ask John Jones to say
the same speech and it emerges as a sentence which,
merely as a sentence, would by no means pulverize us
emotionally or tempt us to rank it with "Good night,
sweet prince, and flights of angels sing thee to thy rest."
We have all of us heard of too many people who have
gone to Washington and not been quite happy there to
be surprised by such a statement. Put the same simple
confession of an unheavenly destination into the mouth
of an on-stage Lincoln and the result is, I repeat, different, wonderfully different—not because of what a
dramatist has written but because of the way in which
history has done his playwriting for him.

Such an episode of Mr. Lincoln's writing in Mr.
Sherwood's play as the Lincoln-Douglas debate is not
enough to carry the script's twelve episodes. No matter
how timely or exciting this single scene may be, Mr.
Sherwood's inescapable job as a dramatist is to write
for Lincoln rather than to have Lincoln write for him.
At doing this Mr. Sherwood fails, and fails signally,
until he reaches the two moving episodes in his final

act which find Lincoln expressing his long-smothered hatred of Mary Todd on the very night of his election, and delivering, as a great, gaunt, tragic figure whose shoulders are draped in a shawl, a melancholy farewell to his Springfield friends from the back platform of the Presidential train which was to carry him to the burdens and the tragedy the Capital had in store for him.

Before these concluding scenes are reached Mr. Sherwood writes reverently but without awakening much interest. His subject is the young Lincoln, the tormented mystic of the early days, the raw, unambitious rail-splitter who courted Ann Rutledge. It is the emerging Lincoln, whose friends feared for his sanity when on his wedding day he is said to have dodged marrying the ambitious Mary Todd, and who after his subsequent marriage to her suffered from her nagging and her lack of mental balance. Mr. Sherwood follows Abe from the 1830's in New Salem to that day thirty-one years later when as the newly elected President he set out from Springfield to fulfill his historic mission in Washington.

In his first act, when he is covering the same period covered by E. P. Conkle in *Prologue to Glory*, Mr. Sherwood does less with his materials than Mr. Conkle did. Simple as was Mr. Conkle's drama, it was at least a self-contained play. It did not merely talk. It backed up its words with illustrative action, and caught some of the latent greatness it hoped to suggest in the frontier giant who was its hero.

Unfortunately Mr. Sherwood leaves out most of his illustrative action. He functions like a man who is giving an illustrated lecture and has left his lantern slides at home. He follows neither the straight episodic course used by such a chill dramatic biographer as Mr. Drinkwater nor the freer dramaturgic methods employed by Mr. Conkle. In dealing with Ann Rutledge and Mary Todd, and also with Lincoln, Mr. Sherwood neither justifies nor develops his preliminary incidents. Although he keeps leading up to one big scene after another, he forgets to include these scenes when he reaches them. His script abounds in disconcerting detours of this kind. Taking Lincoln's advice more to heart than the needs of his own playwriting, Mr. Sherwood treats these pivotal moments as obstacles which, since he has not been able to overcome, he has chosen to go around. His intermissions are his most active interludes. It is during them that we are led to believe his characters have their most interesting say. Certainly it is during them that all their growing is done.

For example, Mr. Sherwood does not prepare us for Lincoln's greatness. His greatness overtakes him during an intermission. Abe is an unhappy, mystical, and shiftless fellow in the earlier episodes. Although he is fearless and good, and intermittently witty, he is no more than that. Yet suddenly this same small-town boy is presented by Mr. Sherwood as a national figure, equal to the greatness shown in his debates with Douglas. The result of such uncertain writing is a drama singularly becalmed for most of its first two acts. A record so lacking in tangible proofs of Lincoln's incipient qualities is bound to resemble a portrait of the Great Protector that makes the mistake of being all wart and no Cromwell.

Raymond Massey's Abe is by all odds the most satisfactory visual realization of Lincoln our stage has known. To the life it is the younger Lincoln who has haunted all our eyes. It comes as the best performance Mr. Massey has so far given in this country, marking a healthy advance in his work over the admirable performance he achieved in *Ethan Frome*. Luckily it lacks those sinister gargoyle qualities which, in plays so different as *Hamlet* and *The Shining Hour*, have forced some of us to wonder if Mr. Massey might not have dropped off the roof of Notre Dame. Mr. Massey's Abe manages to be noble without self-righteousness. He is no marble figure resting in a Memorial. His heart is warm, his ways simple.

Although his Lincoln is human, Mr. Massey manages to suggest his spiritual stature. Wisely he keeps his eyes fixed upon Abe's daily problems rather than upon posterity's verdict. His playing boasts many moments of brooding power when, if only the script sustained it, it would completely vivify Mr. Sherwood's hero. Mr. Massey's speech has a rich American tang. If his characterization suffers at moments from its lack of surety and the willful effort by means of which its simplicity seems achieved, let it be quickly stated Mr. Massey

joins hands with Lincoln and with history as one of
Mr. Sherwood's most dependable collaborators. It is
he who rises above the ineptness of an otherwise inept
production and grants cohesion to a script more reverent in its spirit than distinguished in its writing.

October 17 and 25, 1939

MR. SHERWOOD'S WAR PLAY

"WHERE life ends, art begins," said Goethe. So it
does, as is known to dwellers in all the sheltered Wei-
mars on this planet. But the line of demarcation Goethe
drew was drawn at a time less dark than ours. When
he spoke of life ending he was merely establishing a
boundary between reality and creation, fact and illusion. War's havoc was not on his mind. His philosophical serenity was not imperiled by the brutal forces
of a new barbarism. His "where life ends" was only an
aesthetic truism, placidly uttered. It had nothing to do
with the death of individuals, or a death toll of small
nations that has not stopped with Finland, or with the
decencies of civilization now threatened in an appalling
world.

Mr. Sherwood has set deliberately about robbing
Goethe's truism of its appearance of truth, though
not of its truth. It is precisely with all these fresh and
symptomatic disasters of the contemporary world that

Mr. Sherwood's playwriting begins in *There Shall Be No Night*. His drama cannot be separated from the problems and the anguishes of present-day living. It is the proper product of an age in which White Papers matter, and the *Yellow Book* is forgotten. The whole point, and often the theatrical effectiveness, of his play is derived from the way in which it manages to make grease paint and the recent barkings of our radios one and the same thing.

News events now passed into tragic history and unsolved problems, international no less than individual—these are the subjects Mr. Sherwood has individualized in his drama about the invasion of Finland. Whether he has written a play which would be a good play in a sane epoch seems a purely academic question in the presence of so much that is devastating in his dramaturgy at the Alvin. No doubt it is as academic as another question raised by *There Shall Be No Night*. This is, how effective merely as playwriting would his script remain if its scene were Ruretania rather than Finland, and if we did not carry with us into the Alvin these nights the heavy knowledge that civilization is at stake, and that this fragment of recent history Mr. Sherwood has fictionalized is a fact faced by decent people up and down Europe which may yet, God forbid, be faced by us?

In writing of the destruction by the Russians of a cultivated Finnish home, and in describing how a distinguished man of science, a Nobel Prize winner, loses his son, his charming New England wife, and his own life, after having been forced to abandon reason for a gun, Mr. Sherwood unquestionably continues a familiar dramatic practice of his. Intelligent and capable as he is, Mr. Sherwood has often been more of a journalist than a playwright in the creation of his dramatic emotions. He has depended as heavily on outside events to complete his writing for him as he has on music to furnish him with ready-made climaxes of debatable integrity, though of undeniable effectiveness, for some of his bigger scenes.

Shrewd craftsman though he is, he has often functioned more as a lean-to in the field of the theatre than as a self-reliant dramatist. He has seldom hesitated to rely upon either the advance information of his audiences or such public emotions as they may have felt in advance to fill in his playwriting for him. Queen Marie's visit gave point to *The Queen's Husband*. Problems raised by the depression helped complete *The Petrified Forest*. The tension in Europe added to the tension of *Idiot's Delight*. Our love of Lincoln, plus the timeliness of what he had had to say in defense of democracy, did its full collaborative duty in *Abe Lincoln*. Now in the same way, only to an even greater extent, the madness and the tragedies of a world which is all too real serve as a vital part of Mr. Sherwood's playwriting in *There Shall Be No Night*.

If he is functioning as a propagandist, if he has turned sickening headlines into dialogue, and stated the tragedy of a nation in terms of a single family, it cannot be overstressed that, as a pamphleteer, he has succeeded, as no other dramatist heard from in this country has succeeded, in dealing with the topical alarms and abiding implications of Europe's fever chart. Compare Mr. Sherwood's passionately written script with the no less sincerely written anti-Nazi plays—*Birthright*, *Kultur*, and all the rest of them—and you cannot help realizing how much it gains in interest, in dignity, and often in the sheer impact of its results because of Mr. Sherwood's skill.

If at times it is static, it is at least becalmed in the interest of good talk. If its ultimate optimism is hard to swallow; if it gets lost in the scenes between its young lovers; if it suffers toward the end by the introduction of too many new characters; if it indulges in such stale tricks as those employed in the episode during which the scientist tries to frighten his wife into leaving Finland; and if it does not hesitate to do its preaching straight into a loud-speaker or in an abandoned classroom, *There Shall Be No Night* nonetheless proves absorbing for by far the better portion of one of the season's most arresting and moving evenings.

What adds to the complexities of a critical appraisal of *There Shall Be No Night* is that while in it Mr. Sherwood is writing an editorial of genuine forcefulness, the Lunts are managing to work as artists. Never in their distinguished and ebullient careers have they given performances of such admirable and glowing restraint.

If in dealing with his theme Mr. Sherwood has benefited
by his study of Lincoln, the Lunts (as John Anderson
pointed out) have no less plainly benefited by their
playing of *The Sea Gull*. By approaching Mr. Sherwood's topical drama as if it were Chekhov's and its
human revelations at once hushed and dateless; by refusing to meet the script's melodramatics in melodramatic terms, they add incalculably to its effectiveness.

Although Miss Fontanne may have been unable to
subdue her energies to do justice to Irina in *The Sea
Gull*, she now acts Mr. Sherwood's heroine as she
doubtless meant to act Chekhov's. Although her man-
nerisms, delightful and flamboyant as they are in comedies, may have hampered her in Chekhov, in *There Shall
Be No Night* they are not permitted to appear. Both she
and Mr. Lunt work as only brilliant actors could work
who are genuine artists. They fill in the dialogue with
endless humanizing touches. They give it subtleties,
implications, overtones seemingly nonexistent in much
of its writing. In their quiet way, but with manifest
dedication to a cause which has won their hearts, they
capture the heartbreak of all threatened civilization
and suggest the gentle courage which yet may save it.
Richard Whorf, an actor of extraordinary talents, is no
less brilliant as an American radio announcer. Sydney
Greenstreet as a Polish pianist has about him something
of the strength of Sibelius. Mr. Lunt has given the play

a fine production and Mr. Whorf has set it admirably.

Whatever the ultimate literary merits of *There Shall Be No Night* may prove to be (and at the Alvin this is an irrelevant consideration), Mr. Sherwood's play provides an evening not to be missed. It is an evening praiseworthy in its restraint and often genuinely poignant in its dramatization of topical ills; an evening that is frequently as moving as the tragic news it has dramatized. No one can complain about the theatre's being an escapist institution when it conducts a class in current events at once as touching, intelligent, and compassionate as *There Shall Be No Night.*

April 30 and May 11, 1940

THE TOPICAL AND THE ETERNAL

"ACADEMIC twaddle" is the phrase employed by Mr. Sherwood to describe the point made in the preceding paragraphs about his use of newspaper headlines as a collaborator for his plays. "In 427 B. C.," said Mr. Sherwood to an interviewer from the *Times,* "Aristophanes was assailing Cleon, the dictator of the Athenian State, and so insulting was his caricature that he himself had to portray the part, no actor being willing to take the chance. Ever since the drama has reflected the issue of the hour.

"Mr. Brown said that *The Petrified Forest* depended on problems arising from the depression," Mr. Sherwood continued. "Lord Almighty, what recent work of any kind hasn't been concerned with problems arising from the depression? And that goes for *You Can't Take It With You* and *The Time of Your Life!*"

Thus Mr. Sherwood in answer to the foregoing review. I, for one, am delighted he objected to the points I was trying to make. However badly I may have made them they seem to me so far removed from being either twaddle or academic that I trust he will forgive me if I try to clarify them. They merit clarification. Just or unjust as they may be when applied to Mr. Sherwood (and I would not have applied them to him if in my entirely fallible opinion I had not thought them just) they touch upon distinctions quintessential to any appreciation of the theatre not based upon the most naïve form of surrender.

If in a world gone mad one can, in the interests of reason, still be permitted to talk about values more than topical; if it remains pardonable to try to keep our heads while giving our hearts to what the theatre may have set before us; if, even now, it is not impertinent to inquire into the causes of such emotions as the stage may have stirred in us, why then rational response, with all the unpopular differentiations it is bound to make between art and journalism, between the topical and the eternal, between the high excitements of a single evening and excitements which are timeless, continues to be one of the cardinal duties of criticism.

No one has to dwell in an ivory tower, or indulge in *Yellow Book* chatter, or make the absurd claim that art and life are unrelated, or be foolish enough to think all art is not gloriously rooted in the age responsible for its flowering, to insist there are degrees of merit in all artistic achievements, including the dramatic.

As surely as the Grand Central Station has an upper and a lower level (both of which are equally useful, but in different ways), so does dramatic writing boast its levels of accomplishment. If the stationmasters can distinguish between locals and expresses without being damned as Bunthornes or accused of "academic twaddle," perhaps those interested in the theatre can be forgiven if they, too, indulge in such practical classifications.

When Matthew Arnold pointed out that both the ballad and the purely didactic or moral poem are a lower order of poetry than the lyric, and gave his reasons, he was not denying the right of either the ballad or the didactic poem to exist or refusing them a proper welcome. He was merely making a distinction which cannot be avoided if excellence is to be judged by standards worthy of the name. It is precisely the question of standards, safely beyond both the acade-

mies and twaddle, to which so much of Mr. Sherwood's lean-to (yes, I repeat it) playwriting gives
rise.

As a man Mr. Sherwood is one of the finest, most
fearless, and intelligent forces in the modern theatre.
As a playwright he is a vigorous, usually entertaining,
sometimes eloquent contributor, possessed of commendable ideals and often a no less commendable technical dexterity. When he has taken advantage of headlines or relied upon such public emotions as his
audiences may have brought with them into the theatre to do their collaborative service in his playwriting,
he has been entirely within his rights. If in his work he
has often used the passing moment as so much dramatic capital, he has no less often served the moment
well. Certainly the fact that *There Shall Be No Night*
is a dramatization, written at white heat, of the invasion
of Finland and the present-day plight of decent people
everywhere has (as from the first I have rejoiced in
trying to state) resulted in one of the most moving and
effective examples of dramatic editorializing our stage
has known.

Surely the timeliness of an editorial, however force-
ful or welcome, has nothing to do with the qualities it
may or may not possess as abiding literature. Because
we hang upon a dispatch today from Leland Stowe
does not mean that Leland Stowe will take his place
among such historians as Herodotus or Trevelyan. Or
that we will read his dispatches with the same breath-

less interest when the tragic events he is covering are no longer topical. The distinction of Mr. Stowe's brilliant reporting (which like all journalism is anchored to the date line of its writing) is that it fills the needs and satisfies the hungers of its readers when it is sent and read. This virtue of immediacy is, as I see it, not only the point of Mr. Sherwood's most recent script, but gives it distinguishing qualities which more than compensate for its technical shortcomings.

When Mr. Sherwood told his interviewer from the *Times* that ever since Aristophanes played Cleon the drama has reflected the issue of the hour, he was, if he will forgive my saying so, indulging in twaddle, however unacademic. If he had wanted to be academic he would, of course, have mentioned *The Persians* by Aeschylus as a somewhat more accurate antique parallel to his present drama. Surely Mr. Sherwood did not mean to confound his solemn approach to a solemn theme with an Aristophanic satire luxuriating in topical gibes.

Even so, unless Mr. Sherwood means the temper of the times as opposed to specific dates or contemporary occurrences in any age; unless he has in mind the question of enlightened living; or such dateless topics (however restated they must always be according to the pulse beat of any period) as the nature of man, his relationship with his God, his neighbors and himself; the pursuit of happiness and justice; the anatomy of love and laughter and death; of heroism and of

black despair; of passions belonging to no one day in
any age but to all men in all time, I must admit I find
it impossible to see how Mr. Sherwood can contend
that ever since the Greeks the drama has reflected the
issue of the hour, especially in the sense he gives the
word issue when he relates it to a news-worthy event
not only in his reference to Aristophanes but in his
own practice in *There Shall Be No Night.*

Most plays worthy of the name and of respect are
expressions, direct or indirect, of the issues (by protest or acceptance) of the age which contributed to
their birth. Scores of dramas, much needed and much
admired, have served their welcome journalistic purpose by saying intelligently and provocatively in
dramatic form what the forums, the coffeehouses, or
the newspapers have been full of. They have had their
day and more than justified themselves by perhaps re-
shaping the days to come.

But from the Greeks through Shakespeare right
down to Mr. O'Neill, the plays which have remained
contemporary with audiences through time have not
been those which speak, however eloquently, only of
public events contemporary with their writing. For
the life of me I cannot remember a play by Marlowe
or by Shakespeare warning England of the dangers of
the Spanish Armada. Even when Shakespeare wrote
about history he did not follow it; he supplanted it by
all the quickening wonders of his imagination. What
had been became, after he had touched upon it, not

what was but what he had sensed it as being. And as such we remember it.

Even such postdepression scripts of Mr. Sherwood's naming as *You Can't Take It With You*, or *The Time of Your Life*, or his own *The Petrified Forest*, did not depend upon any one date to fill them in dramatically. They were self-reliant in a way *There Shall Be No Night* can neither claim nor needs to be. They were concerned with the depression but could boast an interest not dependent upon their reliance on facts, however horrible or worthy of interests. In Mr. Sherwood's own phrase they "arose" from the depression rather than leaned upon it.

Should Mr. Sherwood answer me by saying he is not Shakespeare, I will be the first to agree with him. I still insist, however, upon congratulating him and our theatre upon his being Mr. Sherwood. My sole and simple point is that it is possible to swear by the eternal without underestimating the values of the topical. The main thing, for the theatre's well-being, is not to forget how seldom they are one.

May 18, 1940

GOD IN THE TWO-A-DAY

MR. BARRY'S *Here Come the Clowns*

ALTHOUGH *Here Come the Clowns* is not apt to win him many new admirers or even satisfy his old ones, Philip Barry's fable about a stagehand who goes searching for God among a group of vaudevillians has its interesting points. It is a difficult play, written as enigmatically as the second half of *Hotel Universe*. Its exposition is complicated, its action often static. Sometimes it is willfully obscure, especially when one considers the very simple point reached at its conclusion. Yet the play has its virtues.

They are not the glib, smiling virtues which made Mr. Barry's early comedies so popular. They have nothing to do with the sentimental charm which characterized his writing of such a romance as *Tomorrow and Tomorrow*. They are not the result of the high spirits which distinguished such a rollicking allegory as *White Wings*. They are not born of any of those delectable verbal felicities or those half-smiling, half-sobbing tangential scenes upon which Mr. Barry has long since put a trade-mark, recognizable even in *Hotel Universe*.

Nonetheless, they are there. They are real ones, too. And they demand your respect for Mr. Barry as a man who is bravely continuing his struggle to find his place in God's universe. You cannot fail to sense he is doing more than writing to please you. Like his stagehand, Dan Clancy, you know he is embarked on an agonizing quest of his own.

You are conscious of the anguish which has sent Mr. Barry straying into Pirandello's domains. Even when you are hopelessly lost, you listen. And listening, you find yourself pleased by the play's many proofs that *Here Come the Clowns* is written by a man who really knows how to write. He may confuse you. He may be confused himself. He may have chosen the most elaborate of all trick ways in which to arrive at a very simple conclusion. But he has style. He has a perceptive mind. He is sensitive and adroit. He can put dialogue to uses truly revelatory. And he is a painstaking craftsman capable of ingenious planning.

In his latest play Mr. Barry needs all of his skill, and I am afraid more than even he has. For *Here Come the Clowns* is his attempt to state dramatically the same theme he has stated in his recent novel, *War in Heaven*. If the novel leaves you feeling it would make a better play, you leave the play convinced it would make a better novel.

Mr. Barry's drama is an allegory of the forces of good and evil. It is the story of how a good man, who has been cruelly abused by life, finally understands the reason behind the world's evil. For the benefit of his stagehand who is looking for God, Mr. Barry has a mysterious Illusionist persuade a group of vaudevillians to reveal their hidden tragedy or meanness. These few people—the midget (in one of the most poignant scenes in the play), the ventriloquist and his Lesbian wife, the press agent, the dancer and the orphan who will not marry her, the stagehand, his unfaithful wife, her lover, and her sister—these people are to Mr. Barry symbols of the world's sufferings and joys. In this two-

a-day world an unseen old gentleman who owns the
vaudeville theatre is presumably God. The Illusionist
represents the forces of evil.

When the Illusionist makes himself up and imper-
sonates the old theatre owner, the stagehand finally
sees through the masquerade. Dying by a pistol shot
meant for the Illusionist, the stagehand reaches the
conclusion that men have abused the greatest gift they
have ever had—the free will which God has given them.
The woods are full, says he, of men of ill will such as
the Illusionist, who are bad by their own choice. Men,
not God, are responsible for evil. They have willed it.
"The rule of the world's in no hands but our own—
if we've ruled it one way, we can rule it another!"

The major difficulty with Mr. Barry's play, aside
from its frequent talkiness and its obscurities, is that
his vaudevillians fail to speak for more than themselves.
They are individuals who refuse to fit easily into Mr.
Barry's final generalities. Then, in spite of the high
skill of such episodes as the scene of the midget, or the
moment when the ventriloquist turns on his wife, or
when Clancy discovers he was not the father of the
dead child he loved so dearly, one somehow finds it
hard to accept the owner of a vaudeville house as God.
One wishes, too, Mr. Barry's conclusion was not only
more closely related to what has gone before but stated
so that its exaltation could not be resisted.

Here Come the Clowns is not helped at the Booth
by the relentless monotony of Robert Milton's far too

deliberate direction. But John Koenig has equipped Mr. Barry's script with an excellent setting, rich in atmospheric detail. Jerry Austin, Russell Collins, Ralph Bunker, Frank Gaby, Hortense Alden, and Madge Evans are all of them actors who contribute helpful characterizations. And Leo Chalzel is admirable as the diabolical Illusionist.

It is Eddie Dowling, however, who as Dan Clancy, the God-questing stagehand, gives the evening's best performance. Mr. Dowling's voice is rich with all the music of Irish speech. His playing is sensitive, tender, and completely understanding. If he succumbs to the uncertainties of the final scene, his characterization is at all other times possessed of genuine authority and depth. Its simplicity is haunting in its rightness.

You may suspect, when the last scene of *Here Come the Clowns* is reached, that Mr. Barry has made you take a ride in a dirigible to get no farther than across the street. Still you respect his intentions and much of his writing, even if you do not admire the whole of his play and cannot really claim to have enjoyed it.

December 8, 1938

The Fabulous Invalid

TO THOSE who are in love with it, the theatre has always been more than an art or an amusement. It has

been a disease—a kind of blessed lovesickness from
which there is no cure. It is a malady which eats its way
into their blood streams; an obsession which haunts
their sleeping and waking hours; an illness which so
affects their vision that the very word THEATRE invariably spells itself for them in capitals.

Cheerful or distressed as they may be, the truly
stage-struck are among the happiest of mortals. What
they suffer from is a distemper lying safely beyond
the skill of doctors. The more hopeless is their ailment,
the happier they are. Theirs is a complaint which may
touch the minds of its victims (from the outsider's
point of view), but which feeds their spirits. It does
more than that. Although it may do ruinous damage
to their tear ducts and force a new language on their
tongues, it fortifies its incurables with a religion; it
provides their hearts with a new beat; and it creates
among all who suffer, or have ever suffered, from it a
joyous freemasonry in time and space.

That Moss Hart and George S. Kaufman have long
been afflicted with this blessed lovesickness is everyone's good fortune. Even those of us who have had to
content ourselves with loving the stage from afar have
had to admit, without any of the usual jealousies of
courtship, that the theatre has smiled on Mr. Hart and
Mr. Kaufman. Of recent years they have, indeed, taken
their place among her favorite suitors.

Much as they have cared for the stage, even these
talented swains have never made such open love to it

as they make in *The Fabulous Invalid*. The cruel trick
of fortune is that they prove Romeos who lose their
voices in the balcony scene. They become tongue-
tied in milady's presence. They know she is threatened
now, and always has been. And they rise gallantly to
defend her. But as playwrights they unfortunately
turn out to be knights who have forgotten their armor
and left their weapons at home.

The theatre itself is the fabulous invalid of their inspired title; that theatre which, though rumor has announced its imminent death since the time of the
Greeks, has always managed to elude its gravediggers.
For one silly scene in the middle of their disappointing defense, they drag poor William Shakespeare into
their script. For the most part, however, their discussion
of the theatre's trials is more immediate. It is limited
to, and centered on, the misfortunes which overtake a
single New York playhouse from the night of its glamorous opening in the last century to the time that one
of Broadway's younger groups has recently come into
possession of it.

That playhouse—the Alexandria by name, and presumably a proud aristocrat ravaged by the cruel
changes which have overtaken Forty-second Street
—provides Mr. Hart and Mr. Kaufman with their plot.
Little by little this theatre loses its prestige and its
glamour when such familiar enemies as the War, the
silent movies, the talkies, the radio, and the depression
batter inexorably against its doors. From having been

a landmark comparable to the Empire, the Alexandria dwindles into a cheap movie palace, a place for "Screeno contests," and a burlesque house. Then, just when it seems ready for the housewreckers, a band of youngsters, dedicated to the drama, take it over, and we are led to believe it will come to life again.

Truly this is all there is to the plot of *The Fabulous Invalid*. That is, if one is capable of forgetting the creaky ghost story upon which Mr. Hart and Mr. Kaufman depend for their continuity. Do you wonder what that ghost story could be? Naturally you do. But even after learning it, you will still have cause for wonder.

Mr. Hart and Mr. Kaufman introduce us, in a charming second scene, to a great star (Doris Dalton) of a vanished epoch. She dies of a heart attack on the night the Alexandria has opened, and is joined in death by her handsome young actor husband (Stephen Courtleigh), who promptly commits suicide. From a ghostly stage doorman (Jack Norworth) these two players learn that dead actors do not have to go to heaven until the theatre has also died. They are free to visit it at will and to keep up with its happenings. As the theatre is no deader nowadays than it ever was, these three unplanted cadavers continue from then on to wander into the boxes and onto the stage at the Broadhurst until you could scream at the mere sight of them.

The Fabulous Invalid is really no play at all. It is a pageant, written with unquestionable affection, but

with a skill no more advanced than you would expect
to find in the writing of a high school senior's dramatization of "Why We Must Be Loyal to Our Princi-
pal," or "Thomas Jefferson—That's the Spirit." In
form it is reminiscent of the Federal Theatre's *Living
Newspapers*. In fact its reliance upon a single playhouse as its major character is often suggestive of the
illustrated lecture form used by the producers of
...*one-third of a nation*...when they permitted a single tenement house to tell their story for them. The
only difference is that where...*one-third of a nation
*...was vitally alive, *The Fabulous Invalid* is almost incredibly naïve—and ailing.

Although, as in the auction scene, its writing has its
valid moments, most of it is superficial and obvious. It
has little to say to the theatrically lovesick, and even
less to those to whom the theatre of Dodie Smith is the
end-all and the be-all of the drama. The final comment
on its well-intentioned weaknesses is that the evening
ends up by being a defense attorney turned prosecu-
tor. It defeats the very case it hopes to make for the
glory, glamour, and importance of the erstwhile theatre. One may shed a few sentimental tears at *The Fabulous Invalid's* badly staged and poorly impersonated
flashbacks of the famous productions of yesteryear.
Such tears are not the result of what is being done behind the footlights. They are the tears any stage-struck
mortal might be induced to shed (with the proper
musical cues and stimulation) by turning over old pro-

grams, looking through a summer issue of *The Stage*,
or listening to old tunes which stand for bygones which
cannot be relived.

The trouble with the flashbacks at the Broadhurst is
that they end up by being humorous. They come across
not as samples of greatness but as laughable black-outs.
Instead of being impressed by them, one snickers at
them. If their false climaxes and hollow lines were all
there is to the theatre, a movie-trained youngster would
rightly argue the theatre might as well die. The irony
of Mr. Hart's and Mr. Kaufman's scenario is that the
Alexandria's most living moments come not when it
is supposed to be in its heyday but when it has been
given over to its "Screeno contests" and its strip-tease
artists. In its neon moments it becomes vital; in its supposedly glamorous past it is almost as dead as its ghosts.

What about the fine words in which distinguished
dramatists have expressed their ideas? What about the
new forces which have revitalized our stage from the
coming of the New Movement right down to the time
of Mr. Odets and *Pins and Needles*? What about the
maturity our theatre has achieved since the War? What
about Mr. O'Neill's thoughtful contribution? Or the
rebirth of the poetic drama Mr. Anderson has brought
about? And social impulses? And Miss Cornell, Miss
Hayes, Miss Claire, the Lunts, Mr. Gielgud, Mr. Evans,
Burgess Meredith, and innumerable other glamorous
performers in our own times? Surely the importance
of the theatre is based on more than a sentimental mem-

ory of players who once were, or a schoolgirl's fondness for the smell of grease paint, or a carriage trade
that no longer exists. Yet all these questions, and many
more, are left unanswered by Mr. Hart and Mr. Kaufman as they stutter to express their unchallengeable
love for the theatre.

The only living character in *The Fabulous Invalid*
is provided by Donald Oenslager. Though the designer, he is the hero of the occasion. He performs for
the eyes all the graphic and poignant writing Mr. Hart
and Mr. Kaufman fail to supply for the ears. His reali-
zations of the interior and the exterior of the Alexandria Theatre take their place among the finest realistic
backgrounds of our time. They are perfect in their
details, admirable in their lines, and excellent in their
execution. They say everything the play fails to get
said, and say it with such eloquence that Mr. Hart and
Mr. Kaufman might well have used them as their
model. They are nine tenths of a lavish but misguided
show.

Miss Dalton is charming in her first scene. Neither
she nor Mr. Courtleigh and Mr. Norworth can be
blamed if they prove negative thereafter. As ghosts,
they are left for the rest of the evening with nothing to do truly worth the doing. The trouble with
The Fabulous Invalid is that it suffers from the same
complaint. It is a poor sermon affectionately addressed
to converts. Or, if you prefer, a pep talk delivered with
a woeful absence of pep, perception, and depth to those

who do not need it. It finds two lovers of the stage
with little more to say than, "You poor sick thing, I
love you. You will never die."

October 10, 1938

RE-ENTER MR. ODETS, UPPER LEFT:
Rocket to the Moon

IN *Rocket to the Moon* Clifford Odets continues to
enlarge upon the instructions of the Scottish songbirds
by taking both the high road and the low at one and
the same time. His new play, his first purely romantic
drama, is a tantalizing mixture of faults and virtues.

Its initial act, when he is establishing the unhappy
married life of the little dentist who is his hero and
preparing for the love affair this dentist has with his
office assistant, is the finest Mr. Odets has yet written.
It is warmly human and revealing. In no time it takes
an old theme and makes it new. It does this without
depending either upon its setting or upon any labored
professional details to gain its effects. By the sheer
magic of his dialogue, by the almost dental precision
with which he can lay bare the nerves of his characters,
by the skill of his planning no less than of his portrai-
ture, Mr. Odets fills his stage with people quiveringly
alive.

When the curtain lowers you feel the exhilaration which can come only from the theatre when it is functioning admirably. You are fascinated—to a certain extent stunned—by the impact of the man's skill. You are conscious of the vigorous perception of his writing, and no less aware that what you have been listening to are words only Mr. Odets could have used in this particular manner. They are not flamboyant words, at least in this act. Their very simplicity is fierce and unveiling. They show Mr. Odets' genius for putting the commonplace to vivid and creative use. They sting you into awareness by their sweaty humor, their acidity, their crude humanizing force. The people who speak them appear to be turned inside out until the very seams of their beings are exposed.

In the next two acts of *Rocket to the Moon* you lose your way exactly as Mr. Odets appears to have lost his. You wince at the bad lines which begin to crop up with increasing frequency. You can feel Mr. Odets' script slipping away from him, as, instead of traveling toward a visible moon, it takes a pitiful tailspin in the opposite direction. You wish he had not done this. Or that he had had the fortitude to cut whole hunks of that. When the Pollyanna ending steals upon you, and the dentist is presumably going back to his wife, and his secretary has turned down both him and his Mephistophelean father-in-law, and everyone has apparently been awakened to life—though God knows how—you shake your head, wondering what under the sun Mr. Odets is trying to say, if, as appears questionable, he really has anything to say.

Yet even when you are wincing, shaking your head, and despairing, you cannot blind yourself to the fact that, though *Rocket to the Moon* is a bad play, it is a bad play written by a man who, when he writes well, can write with exceptional skill. Just when you feel the script has turned you out in the cold for good, it suddenly invites you to sit with palms outstretched before a roaring fire. You listen to Mr. Odets, even when you deplore what he has dashed off, or his manner of saying it. You sit up and take notice because the lightning of Mr. Odets' extraordinary talent continues to flash long after an appalling darkness has begun to set in. In such scenes as the sudden appearance of a traveling salesman, or the heartbroken outburst of a penniless dentist who has turned blood donor, or in a hundred lines scattered through the murkier passages, you are coerced into realizing this man Odets is no everyday dramatist—when he is writing as he should and as only he can.

Certainly the Group Theatre has done everything it, or any other organization, could do to emphasize the virtues in Mr. Odets' new play at the Belasco. It has been no less industrious in trying to obscure the shortcomings which become increasingly apparent. Morris Carnovsky captures perfectly the anguish, weakness, and helplessness of the lovesick dentist who is the victim of his routine and his marriage. Eleanor Lynn is excellent, especially in her earlier scenes, as the pathetic secretary who in a world of fantasy lives on the cocaine of lies. Luther Adler, beneath a gray wig, gives one of the suavest and most satisfying performances of his career as the enigmatic rich man who is the dentist's father-in-law. And Art Smith, Leif Erikson, Sanford Meisner, William Challee, and Ruth Nelson all contribute vivid characterizations executed in the Group's best tradition of ensemble playing. Even they, however, cannot make one forget that *Rocket to the Moon* is a disappointing play; indeed, the most exasperating kind of failure, a play which has so many good things in it that there seems to be no excuse for its being as unsatisfactory as it ultimately proves to be.

November 25, 1938

Awake and Sing

IT WAS a happy idea of the Group's to let us see Mr. Odets' first long play again. For there seems to be little room for argument on this point—*Awake and Sing* is unquestionably the best play yet to have come from Mr. Odets' pen. It is warm, tender, and compassionate, written with that wizard's mastery of dialogue which sets its author apart from any of our younger dramatists. Its picture of the squabbles, the tragedies, and the frustration of a Jewish family in the Bronx throbs with that vigor which is Mr. Odets' alone.

The method of *Awake and Sing* may be Chekhovian in its indirection but the mood is as authentically American as is the humor which heightens the play's tragedy and gives a final, tingling quality to Mr. Odets' admirably drawn characters. The script literally quivers with vitality. If anything, it is more absorbing now than it was four years ago when first the Group produced it with a company that was bettered then by the presence of Jules Garfield and Stella Adler.

In none of his subsequent long dramas—in *Paradise Lost*, in *Golden Boy*, and not even in *Rocket to the Moon*—has Mr. Odets shown such a sure mastery of his materials as he shows in *Awake and Sing*. Here he controls his plot with the firmest hand he has so far brought to storytelling. Here, too, his writing seems more maintained in its virtues than it has been since. He avoids the confusion which overcame his tale of duplex woe in *Paradise Lost*, his hopeless last act of *Golden Boy*, and the many murky moments that mark his second and third acts of *Rocket to the Moon*.

The magnificent vigor of his talent (it is really genius when Mr. Odets is functioning at his best) does not lead him into overstatement in *Awake and Sing*. The two Odetses—the superb realist of the human spirit and the self-conscious romanticist who can overstuff his dialogue shamelessly—do not fight in his first play the

Dr. Jekyll and Mr. Hyde struggle which has marred his subsequent scripts.

Awake and Sing is a drama of more than one season's validity. Its Jewish idioms are at once racy and hilarious, and put to heartbreaking use. Its people are observed and projected with such completeness that they seem to have lived full, if meager, lives long before the first curtain has risen, and to continue to live them after the final curtain has fallen. Here is a play which bears not only seeing and reseeing, but seeing again. Such is its uncommon persuasion and distinction. Most assuredly *Awake and Sing* is a drama, written in the form of realism, which cannot be accused of dwelling in the dust. It can claim those qualities of "self-renewal" which, in A. B. Walkley's phrase, grant, and are the proofs of, permanence in a work of art. It does not exhaust its say with one hearing. It has new pleasures, new subtleties, new revelations to yield with each seeing. There are not many contemporary scripts for which such a claim can be made.

March 8, 1939

Night Music

WHEN, at the ripe age of thirty-three, Clifford Odets wrote a preface to the Modern Library's one-volume edition of *Waiting for Lefty*, *Awake and Sing*, *Till the Day I Die*, *Paradise Lost*, *Golden Boy*, and *Rocket to the Moon*, he seemed to have persuaded himself a definite phase of his career was over. If he was willing to place his earlier work historically it was because he was convinced that since writing those dramas he had become "a better craftsman" with "his horizons lifting wider." These early plays he dismissed as being "part and parcel of a 'first-period' group." He was so definite in writing "finis" to a phase in his development that those of us who admire his work were forced to look forward with especial eagerness to the promised maturity of his second period.

This maturity was not present in *Night Music*. Obviously the play belonged to a new development in Mr. Odets' career. It still had about it that vitality in phrasing and attack which is the unique stamp of Mr. Odets' talent. Its writing was frequently pungent. Its images were often driven home as with a pneumatic drill. Its characters were from time to time established with incisive vigor which is Mr. Odets' pre-eminent aesthetic possession. But the old dogmatism, which in large part was responsible for the force of the earlier Odets dramas, was missing.

Without it Mr. Odets seemed lost. So was his play. The absence of the erstwhile cocksure conviction may be taken as a proof of intellectual growth. It is a good thing always for an artist to realize that black and white are not the only colors. Still, without his former blinders, Mr. Odets appeared to be looking out on a world which (for him) was strangely gray. His tale of the adventures of two young people on Manhattan found him doing the very thing which in the Modern Library he quotes Oscar Wilde as having said about another author; that is, having nothing to say and saying it.

Mr. Odets' final preachment in *Night Music* (because, of course, he did seem to feel duty-bound to get around to some preaching in his concluding episode) was no more revolutionary than that all young people are entitled to marriage, a home, and a comfortable way of life. Somehow, as one listened to these pallid words crudely stated, one missed the old, brave dream of a new world; the angry cries of "STRIKE, STRIKE, STRIKE!!"; and the sudden spiritual rebirths which, in the pattern of Mr. Odets' earlier plays, have put in their appearance almost with the regularity of the marines.

If Mr. Odets (like Mr. Rice in *Two on an Island*) struck one as being strangely tamed, *Night Music* came across the footlights as being even more confused dramatically than politically. It had all the earmarks of a play dashed off in a hurry and of having paid the penalties of extreme haste. Still one misses it. One hates to have it close so abruptly because indifferent or poor Odets is far more exciting to listen to than what the majority of playwrights can turn out. The man's writing may have grown in unevenness. But when it is good—in its sudden eruptive moments of high virtue—

it keeps one wondering when the lightning will strike
next. And strike it did from time to time through the
uncertain, sentimental, and undisciplined course of
Night Music.

March 12, 1940

ON MR. SAROYAN'S TRAPEZE
My Heart's in the Highlands

"SEEING is believing" is an adage we have all been
brought up to respect. This is one of our personal limitations; one of the limitations of our theatre, too. It
holds our stage down to the literal and the superficial.
All too frequently it forces it to function as a realm of
verifiable but flat reality where everything aims at being rational and no more than that, and where there is
no such thing as a line, a character, a scene, or a plot,
which does not possess a meaning easily explained.

That other world, that world of unprecise meanings
and yet genuine emotions which musicians have long
ago invaded and into which the *surrealists* have strayed,
is not one to which humdrum Broadway often leads us.
But last night, when it turned to William Saroyan's
My Heart's in the Highlands for a series of extremely
interesting experimental performances at the Guild,
the Group Theatre did succeed in making playgoers
realize there can be more to seeing than believing, that

seeing can mean feeling, too, even when you do not understand exactly what you have seen.

Far be it from me to pretend that I understand precisely what Mr. Saroyan is up to. Yet what he is saying with deliberate vagueness, and what the Group Theatre has staged with a formalism which turns its back skillfully on everyday reality, interested and moved me more than most of the productions I have sat before this winter. This much I do know. And, from those around me who had tears in their eyes, I surmise they were no less touched than I was by what is poignant, charming, and yet indefinable in *My Heart's in the Highlands*.

To try to reduce Mr. Saroyan's drama to a synopsis is as futile as it would be to claim to have captured the quality of an opera's score by relating its plot. What is important about his fable is not that it tells a story but that it strikes several chords. Although its formlessness is intentional, in its wanderings it does things to you which a host of dramas, following a straight and narrow path, cannot pretend to do.

My guess (for I am certain about nothing that has to do with *My Heart's in the Highlands* except my pleasure in its really distinguished moments and its power to move me) is that in telling how a starving poet and his son are visited, to the delight of their poor neighbors, by a great, gray-bearded old Shakespearean actor who plays beguilingly on a silver bugle, Mr. Saroyan is writing an allegory of sociological significance.

I presume he is leading us among the gay dispossessed to tell us, without naming names, something is radically wrong with the world. I gather, too, his heroes are a father and son who are one and the same person; that he is showing how starved, yet constant, is mankind's love for beauty; and urging us to realize the great people of the earth are not the "big" men whose greatness is measured by the numbers they have slain, but the little men who rise to greatness by the gallantry with which they meet their privations and sustain their dreams.

Personally, I wish Mr. Saroyan had been surer in the writing of some of his single scenes. I regret he chose to kill off his venerable bugler with the ineffectual jumble of Shakespearean speeches he assigned to him. Yet, hazy as the meaning of this or that scene may be, and elusive as the whole play's concrete significance is, I congratulate Mr. Saroyan upon having employed his symbols so that all of them combine to establish a mood and evoke emotions, even when they defy exact comprehension.

Without being freakish or objectionably arty, Mr. Saroyan has managed to widen the theatre's horizons by escaping from facts and reason and making the unintelligible seem intelligible. In doing this he has been abundantly aided by the Group, by Herbert Andrews' admirable *surrealist* settings, by Robert Lewis' inventive direction, and the heartwarming performances of Philip Loeb, Sidney Lumet, William Hansen, and Art Smith.

Although Mr. Saroyan's play is frankly an experiment, it is an experiment of which not only the Group but all genuinely adventurous theatre lovers should be proud. It throws open some welcome windows, even if it opens them upon a fog. The air it admits may be cloudy, but it is moving and fresh, and a joy to inhale.

April 14, 1939

SECOND THOUGHTS ON SAROYAN

ALTHOUGH *My Heart's in the Highlands* is not a play which says a precise thing in a clear-cut manner, its whole point and glory is that it does something to you—something poignant and exquisite and indefinable. I suspect that those of us who liked it and were touched by it were doing both the play and ourselves an injustice when we said we neither knew nor cared about knowing exactly what Mr. Saroyan was up to. This was merely our clumsy way of suggesting what is at once distinctive and arresting in the intention and the execution both of Mr. Saroyan's writing and the Group's production.

We really knew more than we confessed, only we

had been brought to this knowledge in an untraditional way. We had been delighted and moved, as Mr. Saroyan and the Group wanted us to be, in that realm of consciousness which lies beyond mere rationality.

We were aware Mr. Saroyan was telling us all is not right with the world. We were no less aware that he was making us feel in the bugle notes of his old actor how beckoning is beauty and how starved for it are the dispossessed of the earth as represented by his unknown poet, his gallant little son, and their kindly neighbors. We sensed, too, that Mr. Saroyan had led us into a new country, a hazy land beyond the confines of the literal where moods are facts—a gay, anguishing territory of blessed innocence, sweet irrelevancies, and courageous lunacies.

Although we groped toward *surrealism* as a symbol for our reactions, I suspect what we were really trying to say was that in *My Heart's in the Highlands* Mr. Saroyan and the Group have extended the theatre as a medium. They have done more than produce a joyous, yet heartbreaking, fable as naïve as a primitive and no less touching. They have fused words and actors and colors and sound and design into an evening's entertainment which enables the stage to evoke in an audience those tangible, yet intangible, sensations which are among the wonders and delights—indeed among the liberating compensations—of music.

April 19, 1939

The Time of Your Life

WILLIAM SAROYAN continues to serve the theatre well. He has much to bring to it—his vitality, his compassion, his originality, his courage, his genuine writing skill, his love of people and of words, and his magical ability to create a mood which in itself not only makes a comment but takes the place of plot.

My Heart's in the Highlands showed what Mr. Saroyan could do to extend the theatre's dimensions. In it he wrote a fantasy about mankind's eternal hunger for beauty which was more of a melody than a play. In it he got happily beyond the Q.E.D.'s of playwriting *à la* Pinero. He orchestrated his theme instead of plotting it. He kept it floating in the happy realm of music where it should have remained unchallenged by those literalists in our playhouses who are so busy trying to find out at every moment what this-and-that is about that they never give either this or that a chance to do anything to them in its own emotional rights.

What Mr. Saroyan did charmingly about beauty and the dispossessed in *My Heart's in the Highlands* he has done even more charmingly on the subject of the purpose of existence and the pursuit of happiness in *The Time of Your Life*. His new play is, one suspects, the kind of drama Philip Barry meant to write and came near to writing in last season's *Here Come the Clowns*. It, too, finds a playwright looking into the heart of life. Where Mr. Barry lost his way in the philosophical confusions of his brave allegory, Mr. Saroyan steers a surer, simpler course, if only by virtue of the ever-warming compassion of his writing.

To respond to *The Time of Your Life* one does not have to know precisely what it is about. What matters in Mr. Saroyan's playwriting more than what is being done is our willingness to have something done to us. If Mr. Saroyan has dispensed with plotting as plotting is commonly understood, it is because he wants mood in the theatre to serve as the equivalent of melody in music. He is well aware that none of us in the presence of a symphony would think of holding up a white-gloved hand like a traffic cop to insist the music be stopped before the next bar is reached because of our impatience to find out if the second violin has honorable intentions so far as the oboe is concerned.

To relish such a play as *The Time of Your Life* one has only to be willing to feel. It is a quickening play—gay, tragic, and filled with revelations even when it may seem meaningless. Its people—all characters wandering in and out of a saloon on San Francisco's waterfront—are not grease-paint creations. They have blood in their veins, fresh air in their lungs, and joy in their hearts. They leap to life as Mr. Saroyan, with a vigor matched only by the suddenly revealing sensitivity of his perceptions, states their small hopes, their secret pleasures, their mean worries, and minor tragedies.

For those who suffer, as most of us do in our theatre-going, from a Guy Fawkes phobia on the subject of plots, who insist upon knowing exactly what is happening at every moment during a play, who feel cheated if they are not told precisely what Jack is doing to Jill, or, in a more modern script, what Jill is doing to Jack, Mr. Saroyan offers the compensation of a story of some sort. It is not much of a story. So far as action is concerned it could be told in one act. But action, surface action, is the least of Mr. Saroyan's interests. His fable is no more than how a man, a strange, kindly, and inquiring fellow, a delectable, heartsick, Irish Mr. Fix-It, whose search, between gulps of unexplained champagne, is for happiness and an answer to the far-reaching enigmas of life, manages to marry a two-dollar prostitute off to his amiable henchman and thus save her from the pryings of an odious busybody on the Vice Squad.

To pretend that *The Time of Your Life* is only concerned with such a story is to miss its point. It is a formless play. It suffers somewhat by the unnecessary change of scene in the second act which for the moment removes it from its saloon setting. It has its undeniable moments of monotony. And it includes two characters as feebly written as are its two unfortunate rich people.

Yet, formless or not, Mr. Saroyan's script has enormous vigor. It has beauty, too. Its compassion is as irresistible as its humor is gay or as its insight is exceptional. Such scenes as the ones in which the policeman describes his hatred of his duties; or the prostitute is brought a mechanical toy, symbolical of what is wrong with the machinery of life; or a longshoreman talks of literature and brawn; or an Arab plays on an harmonica music revealing his race's sadness long ago—these are outstanding moments in a rewarding evening.

Nor is Mr. Saroyan, with all the fine, eruptive beauties of his impromptu writing, the only contributor to the evening's many pleasures at the Booth. The Theatre Guild, with Eddie Dowling's and Mr. Saroyan's aid, has staged *The Time of Your Life* extremely well in an admirable setting by Watson Barratt. Mr. Dowling is touching and winning as the Mr. Fix-It whose quest is for happiness. Gene Kelly proves himself a dancer of remarkable grace and versatility as a job seeker on the waterfront. And Charles De Sheim, Edward Andrews, Len Doyle, and Michelette Burani are among the many others who add to the delights of a production both touching and joyous.

The character most symptomatic of Mr. Saroyan's methods and intentions is the prostitute played by Julie Haydon. Obviously Miss Haydon, an actress possessed of a quality of almost phosphorescent innocence, is not meant to represent the conventional fallen woman in Mr. Saroyan's play. To find Miss Haydon playing a prostitute is certainly not to find the American theatre indulging in what is known as type casting. To cast her as the regulation on-stage chippie would be as absurd, if the traditional results were aimed at, as it would be to cast Shirley Temple as Thaïs or Diamond Lil. The mere fact Miss Haydon is playing such a part should be warning enough, to those accustomed to thinking in terms of theatrical stencils, that Mr. Saroyan is not writing conventionally.

Yet some people, seeing Miss Haydon, will doubtless not take the hints given to them by her very presence in the cast. Disregarding such hints, their impulse will be to say, "Julie Haydon is not right—she is not like a prostitute." One of the most interesting things about this country is that in it every man, woman, and child, regardless of how ignorant he, she, or it may be on any other subject, seems to know exactly what a prostitute should be like, at least on the stage. The reason is, of course, that the expectations of most playgoers are the victims of their memories. Almost all of them have seen Lenore Ulric as Kiki and Jeanne Eagels, or someone else, as Sadie Thompson. If, therefore, the actress asked to play a fallen woman behind the footlights does not follow the Sadie-Kiki tradition; if she does not emerge from the wings suffering unmistakably from curvature of the spine; if her voice is not whisky-soaked enough to sound like an asthmatic foghorn; and if she does not wear in her hat an ostrich plume which has been over-exposed to California's climate, why, in the presence of such a sport among sports, most conformists in an

audience feel swindled so far as their on-stage prostitutes are concerned.

With Miss Haydon, who is palpably so unlike the
majority of the grease-paint Everleigh Sisters, this is
not only the explanation of her radiant rightness for
the part, but in itself an explanation of what is unusual
in Mr. Saroyan's aims and methods. Unlike most of our
dramatists, Mr. Saroyan does not content himself with
surfaces. He gives us a bifocal exposure in time, inviting
us to look behind the present into the past. He asks us
to consider not the prostitute who is, so much as the
girl who was. In other words, his challenge is to make
us realize how, in the case of such a character as the
one Miss Haydon plays, the machinery in the toy of
life has failed to operate. What is true of Mr. Saroyan's
writing of his prostitute is no less true of the constant
spiritual disclosures, the spurts of revelation, which
add to the joys and fascination of such a sample of the
originality he has brought into the theatre as *The Time
of Your Life.*

October 26, 1939

Love's Old Sweet Song

ONE by one, Mr. Saroyan's by now familiar virtues
put in their appearance in *Love's Old Sweet Song* at
the Plymouth last night. They were all there. But as

they crept in singly, like conspirators misinformed as to the time of an important meeting, and as each one disappeared before the next could make a cloaked entrance, there were never enough of them on hand to establish a quorum in Mr. Saroyan's favor.

The result was less like sitting before a play than having dropped in one's lap from the stage a series of fragments from a torn *surrealistic* valentine Mr. Saroyan had forgotten to deliver. Obviously his new comedy benefits at moments from Mr. Saroyan's very genuine and most welcome gifts as it runs its moonstruck course. However mad, incomplete, or downright tiresome it may become, it is plainly the work of a man blessed with imagination.

If, as *Love's Old Sweet Song* trots and stumbles, stumbles and trots throughout the evening, it seems by all odds the least ingratiating of Mr. Saroyan's plays yet to have been produced, the reasons are not hard to find. Much as I hate to confess it, his newest offering has about it all those slipshod, slightly balmy qualities which those who do not admire Mr. Saroyan are fond of ascribing to his plays.

Where, in *My Heart's in the Highlands*, Mr. Saroyan pointed out man's inescapable hunger for beauty, this time he has again turned to the dispossessed to show nothing more or less than that love conquers all. A pitchman is finally lifted out of his charlatanism by falling in love with a good woman. Love does not win, however, until a huge family of worthless Okies have taken over the good woman's home, appropriated her clothes, eaten her food, burned down her house, and a Greek wrestler, his messenger-boy son, his old father, and a cousin of uncertain standing have all played their part in the sentimental proceedings.

Mr. Saroyan's Yearlings are not to be confused with Mr. Steinbeck's Joads. Although both families are described by their creators as being Okies, the Joads would have a hard time recognizing the Yearlings as fellow creatures. Oklahoma cannot be blamed for them. Neither can California for that matter. They are the products of no state except Mr. Saroyan's original state of mind. Truly, the Yearlings are like what the Vanderhoff tribe might have become if it had deserted *You Can't Take It With You* for *Tobacco Road* and indulged in lower mathematics.

Mr. Saroyan's writing can be very funny at moments, even in such a hastily dropped egg as *Love's Old Sweet Song* turns out to be. His gift for caricature has not deserted him. When he is mocking the effect of the movies, rolling off the names of *Time's* editors, spoofing the curiosity of a photographer from *Life*, or laughing at a wrestler's physical prowess, his exceptional talents continue to make themselves felt.

His new play lacks, however, the magic of its predecessors. It holds jokes until they have not only lost their humor but died of old age. It grows tiresome and thin. Its silliness is redeemed by no point. Its confusions have no real beauty behind them. It suffers from the manifest speed of its composition, a speed which has spared it none of its faults and emphasized only the defects and uncertainties in its point of view no less than in its execution.

Mr. Dowling and the Theatre Guild have done their best to hide the flat-footed writing of Mr. Saroyan's newest ballet. Mr. Saroyan and Mr. Dowling have staged it inventively. Walter Huston gives a winning performance as the pitchman. Jessie Royce Landis does the best work of her career as the good spinster. Arthur Hunnicutt and Doro Merande are excellent as the charter members of the talented Yearling clan. And Alan Reed, John Economides, and Peter Fernandez appear as Greeks bearing gifts no one has to beware of. Still, haste has made cruel waste in the case of Mr. Saroyan's newest script. The only writing of a bad evening which achieves and sustains the quality Mr. Saroyan must have had in mind is the excellent work Paul Bowles has done in the composition of his fascinating incidental music.

May 3, 1940

Six

OVER THE WATER

WHERE FREEDOM DWELT

"THE theatre of war" is a grim phrase, all too common in European dispatches. It is a theatre which, to the world's tragedy, has of late wandered up and down Europe with a mechanized precision unknown to the happier bands of strolling players that once carried the theatre with them. It, and the no less grim rehearsals which have preceded it, provide reasons, eloquent in their finality, for the meagerness of the old world's contributions to the new world's drama of recent seasons.

Twenty years ago in Burns Mantle's annual compendium, five of his ten *Best Plays*—Sacha Guitry's *Deburau*, William Archer's *The Green Goddess*, Molnar's *Liliom*, Barrie's *Mary Rose*, and Galsworthy's

The Skin Game—were foreign plays competing for honors with such native scripts as *The Emperor Jones*, *The First Year*, *Nice People*, and *The Bad Man*. The next Broadway season, as Mr. Mantle sent it down to posterity, divided its trophies Solomon-like between the American and the transatlantic best. Clemence Dane's *A Bill of Divorcement*, Andreyev's *He Who Gets Slapped*, Mr. Milne's *The Dover Road*, Mr. Maugham's *The Circle*, and Paul Geraldy's *The Nest* were among the successfully produced dramas from the old world to vie with such native plays as *Anna Christie*, *Dulcy*, *Six Cylinder Love*, *The Hero*, and *Ambush*.

For 1922–23, Mr. Mantle found only two scripts from abroad—Karel Čapek's *R.U.R.* and Galsworthy's *Loyalties*—to put on his favored list along with *Rain*, *You and I*, *Icebound*, *Merton of the Movies*, *Mary the Third*, *The Old Soak*, yes, and I regret to confess it, Channing Pollock's *The Fool*. Sixteen years later the Critics Circle's second successive award for the winter's best foreign play went to Paul Vincent Carroll for *The White Steed*. And last season (1939–40) no foreign drama was deemed prizeworthy by these same sages in solemn conclave met.

Although the war and the exhausting years of tension which preceded it offer silencing explanations for Europe's diminished role in the American theatre, there are other explanations which insist upon being out. The fact that the great dramatic renaissance Europe knew

from the nineties through the twenties appears to have
run its course may be one of these. In the decade before appeasement faded into war, the democracies—
England, France, and Ireland—continued to have their
say. Noel Coward, John van Druten, Mr. Shaw,
André Obey, Jean Giraudoux, Jacques Deval, Sean
O'Casey, and Mr. Carroll (to pick at random) were
playwrights who commanded transatlantic audiences
with new plays.

But dictators and the drama do not seem to get along.
Pirandello survived Il Duce's March on Rome but he
was the sole Italian to write plays of international interest after Mussolini's rise. However exciting the
Soviet theatre may have been in its backstage innovations and the vigorous stunts of its showmanship,
its stage, which functions only as a house organ for a
one-party government, has produced no new playwrights of distinction.

"What is needed before everything else in the life of
the German theatre and especially in that of the capital
city is freedom!" Fifty-one years have passed since
Maximilian Harden wrote those words. Fifty-one years
have passed too since Otto Brahm, working side by side
with Harden for the establishment of the famous *Freie
Bühne*, announced, "We are erecting a free theatre for
modern life. . . . Truth it is which we strive in every
way to reach."

Goering and Goebbels, Himmler and von Ribben-
trop do not seem to share Harden's and Brahm's en-

thusiasm either for freedom in or out of the theatre, or for truth. The Czechs who, after the last war and in the first flush of a nationalism long waited for, enjoyed a robust theatre, know this. The Viennese, so proud of the Burg Theater in the old days and from whose ranks Schnitzler, von Hofmannsthal, and Hermann Bahr once emerged, know this, too. So do the Danes whose Oehlenschläger long ago hymned beauty and hated barbarism and oppression. So do the Norwegians in whose fjords such a grim champion of truth and independence as Ibsen was cradled. So do the Dutch whose Heijermans was a writer without fear. So do the Poles; so do the Belgians. So do the Parisians whose eyes for centuries have rested upon billboards reading "Liberté, Égalité, Fraternité." So do we all as we watch the progress of a certain house-painter, turned Genghis Khan, whose dream seems to be to paint the swastika large upon the edifices of every nation which has loved either truth or freedom. So, too, must even the Germans.

Yes, fifty-one years have passed in Berlin since Brahm and Harden championed a free theatre and truth. With them in Germany, and because of Germany like a black plague over Europe, the whole splendid concept of these ideals has vanished, that concept which before and after the war made the stages of Berlin and of Frankfurt, of Dresden and of Leipzig, of Mannheim and of Stuttgart, of Darmstadt and of Munich one of the great glories of the modern world.

The German harvest of forty years' splendid frui-

tion was a rich one. It was rich in the lean financial years
of the Republic and no less rich even under the Kaiser.
No one could pretend to know about the theatre fifteen
years ago who was not acquainted with it as it had
flowered in the Fatherland in the years following the
founding of the *Freie Bühne*. Germany was the country to which every stage-struck student was drawn.

There was Reinhardt; Reinhardt, the virtuoso; Reinhardt, the realist; Reinhardt at Salzburg, in Vienna, and
Berlin. There was Jessner and his *Jessnertreppen*. And
Ernst Stern, Linnebach, and Pirchan as designers. Then
there were Moissi, the Thimigs, Hartmann, Bergner,
Pallenberg, Wegener. These were actors to conjure
with. Among the dramatists Hauptmann, Sudermann,
and Wedekind still represented the older group. And
Toller, von Unruh, Hasenclever, and Kaiser were lead-
ers of the younger.

One person, unfortunately a person who matters,
was not impressed with the German theatre in the days
of its strength and freedom. Ironically enough, as a
boy of twelve in Upper Austria and shortly before
Lohengrin was to "captivate" him, he was taken to see
Wilhelm Tell. In *Mein Kampf* he does not say what he
thought of Schiller's dramatic ode to liberty. Obviously
it must have been Gessler, not Tell, who struck him as
being the play's hero. Obviously, too, he must have
been taken home before the play reached its end.

He is definite, however, on the subject of the German theatre when it was free. He was horrified by it,

appalled by its frankness. The plays produced in it were not fit for the education of the young. They did not remind Germans of their past glories. "The performances . . . were such that for the sake of the nation it would have been useful to avoid visiting them altogether."

Inevitably he preferred "the theatre of war." But such a peacetime theatre as would meet with his approval does not augur well for the drama's immediate future in a Europe under his domination. Even before his emergence cut the once vital arteries of civilization's cultural interchanges, America had turned less and less to Europe for its plays.

Our stage, so long no more than a colonial institution, borrowing first from England, then from the Germany of Kotzebue, then from the France of all the tawdrier contrivers, and often borrowing (especially from the Continent) without bothering to acknowledge the debt, awoke slowly to its dramatic independence.

It took tardy advantage even of the huge body of dramatic literature produced in Europe just before the turn of the century and in the seasons preceding the first world war. Seventeen years had elapsed before the *Liliom* which Budapest had seen took New York by storm as a daring, experimental play in the memorable first production it was given here by the Theatre Guild in 1926. *John Ferguson* was four years old before the same Guild, then a truly adventurous band of young people, had the good luck to stumble upon it. *Jane Clegg* and *He Who Gets Slapped* were each of them seven years old before the same pioneering organization produced them locally. Chekhov, now so frequently revived and at last so justly admired, was no less slow to win an American hearing. Twenty years divide the Moscow Art Theatre's demonstration with *The Sea Gull* of the high virtues of Chekhov's dramatic method, from the Washington Square Players' hasty and ill-fated production of the same play in 1916. Truly it was with such performances in the middle twenties as Miss Le Gallienne's productions of *The Three Sisters* and *The Cherry Orchard* down at the Civic Repertory Theatre that Chekhov's dramas, written before and just after the turn of the century, began to take their place along with the works of Shaw and Ibsen among Broadway's perennials.

This, perhaps, is a fair sample of the different times upon which the American theatre before 1918, and the European theatre after 1890, were operating. The Guild's first years were made easy, at least so far as play selection was concerned. At its disposal was a whole library of important dramas which commercial Broadway had not dared to produce. When the Guild's standards proved successful, hence contagious; when other experimental producers and, finally, hard-boiled Broadway itself began to take dramas of the same kind from precisely the same shelves, the first great reserve of European plays was soon exhausted.

Meanwhile America had come of age. So had American dramatists. The United States, once so dependent upon its dramatic imports, was becoming more and more self-sustaining. America slowly replaced Europe as the scene of young Americans' *Wanderjahr*. The Europe which had once drawn them as a cultural "must" had changed tragically in the thirties.

However isolationist sentiment in the United States may have been in politics in the fateful years following 1933, it is not now and has never been isolationist in its theatre. New York, as a dramatic capital, is large enough both in mind and curiosities to be interested in the best, regardless of where that best may come from. It knows that excellence needs no passport and admits no frontiers. As a city sustained by its cosmopolitanism, and sustaining because of it, New York has been saddened by the decline in Europe's dramatic output. In this decline it has seen only another tragic proof of the Old World's plight, and another reason for treasuring the more dearly the proud privileges of freedom and truth which our theatre nightly reminds us are still ours.

IRELAND AND *The White Steed*

YOU have to turn to the Irish for such a play as *The White Steed* or a proper production of it. Joxer in *Juno and the Paycock* had a name for it. It's a "darlin' " play, not in a saccharine or silly way, but "darlin' " in the sense of winning the heart by its eloquence, its radiant faith, its humanity, its rollicking humor, its wit and turmoil, and in the proud fiery manner of its breathing, in the oppressive air of this sorely troubled world, tales of legendary heroes who have never died.

As in the case of *Shadow and Substance*, Paul Vincent Carroll has written in the best Celtic tradition a play which is not only a drama in its own right but an allegory of Ireland. Once again his subject is a major problem of his country advanced in terms of a conflict waged within the Church itself. This time Mr. Carroll's pivotal character is not a proud aristocrat of the cloth, out of touch with his rough curates and his ignorant parishioners. He is Canon Matt Lavelle, a wise, lovable, peppery old codger who, paralyzed though he is, manages to triumph over the inhumanity, the rigid Calvinism, the committee of moral vigilantes, and the other snooping and coercive methods of such an essentially un-Christian force as Father Shaughnessy represents.

Out of this battle, fought in such a favorite setting of Mr. Carroll's as the living room of a Canon's Parochial House in County Louth, emerges a fable which, more than speaking dramatically for Ireland, has its unmistakable bearing upon the struggle men of good will are fighting everywhere at present against men of evil will.

What also emerges at the Cort in the person of Mr.

Carroll's heroine is a rebellious maiden restoring the pride of the servile schoolteacher who falls in love with her. He has been brave only in his cups. Her bravery is nurtured on dreams of her country's ancient glories. As Niam did for Ossian in the days before the Christian Era, when Ireland was peopled with mighty warriors and the land had not come to teem with a race of little black-haired men, Mr. Carroll's heroine makes room for her schoolteacher on the white steed she rides.

To synopsize Mr. Carroll's new play is to make a script, at once simple and effective, sound like the fuzziest of fuzzy allegories. It is to lose sight of the gaiety underlying its overtones; to ignore the pungency of its dialogue; to fail to indicate the compassion with which its meaning is pointed; and to overlook unfairly some of the characters Mr. Carroll has drawn with genuine skill.

Above all, it is to forget Mr. Carroll's wisdom as a dramatist. He is a propagandist, attacking egotism, persecution, and cruelty, who knows and avoids the dangers of "raving" and "raging." By his own confession, he is well aware of what he has described as man's "love of this battered imperfect thing called life." In the presence of a serious subject he does not forget the curative and persuasive powers of laughter. No wonder that in last Sunday's *Times* he could write with affection of the Aristophanes who is "still laughing," of Boccaccio and Rabelais still dancing, of Voltaire's "grand guffaw that still blows up the Seine and over the tops of Paris," and of Chaucer who "still goes roaring down to Canterbury." Mr. Carroll is himself a merry sage. His laughter, like his humanity, is a proof of his sagacity, even as *The White Steed* is a proof of how much he has grown in authority as a dramatist since he wrote so good a play as *Shadow and Substance*.

If he still has difficulty in establishing his young lovers, if he cannot quite make us believe in their affection for one another, or if once in a while his machinery creaks, if some of his village snoopers remain no more than broad types, Mr. Carroll, nonetheless, shows he is a man who can write from his heart and set ideas spinning in dramatic form. His dialogue is rich with all the music and wit of his race. Moreover, when it comes to his drawing of Canon Matt Lavelle and Father Shaughnessy he works with a master's skill.

The two performances of the evening which are unforgettable are George Coulouris' brilliant and unsparing playing of the detestable Father Shaughnessy, and Barry Fitzgerald's Canon Matt Lavelle. That very mortal saint, the Canon, may be a surefire part. Although from the certainty of his appeal he may seem the *Abie's Irish Rose* of stage clerics, Mr. Fitzgerald does not content himself with letting the part do his work for him. Dodging the obvious, he brings all his unction and his skill to giving a performance both lovable and memorable.

January 11, 1939

MR. MORLEY'S *Oscar Wilde*

WHEN the real Oscar touched these shores he delighted a nation never overly fond of its customs of-
ficials by informing them he had nothing to declare—
except his genius. In their *Oscar Wilde* it is Oscar's
genius which Leslie and Sewell Stokes allow him to
declare for himself. They go further. They permit him
to declare his tragedy too. So does Robert Morley, who
as Wilde gives a performance at once so brilliant and
revelatory that it must be described not as a performance but as a definitive biography which just happens
to be acted instead of written.

Cannily enough the Stokeses turn to Oscar as a collaborator no less than as a subject. Without ever boast-
ing of their brightness, in Jack Horner's much pub-
licized fashion, they have stuck their thumbs into the
pie-crammed shelf of Wilde's epigrams and pulled out
a whole orchard of his ripest plums. At its outset their
play is almost a compendium of Wilde's wit, a continu-
ation in dialogic form of the collection of his aphorisms,
known as *Oscariana*, which the luckless Mrs. Wilde
once made. About its introductory badinage there is
all the nimbleness of mind which contributed to Oscar's
superlative powers as a conversationalist. Yet even when
they are permitting Wilde to speak at the dangerous
height of his career in terms of those paradoxes at which

he excelled, the Stokeses are advancing his tragic story which has many times been told.

In Algiers they introduce Oscar and Lord Alfred Douglas, explaining the Marquis of Queensberry's valid objections to their friendship. Next they follow Oscar into Old Bailey, first when he is bringing his ill-advised suit against Queensberry, then when he is on trial himself. In both instances they rely heavily on the actual testimony to do their writing for them. Thereafter, when Wilde has served his term in Reading Gaol, they follow him to France, permitting us to sample the final wretched days of his lost glory, when penniless he was at the mercy of his few remaining friends, and drink and suffering had rotted his mind.

As a biographical drama the Stokeses' play is certainly less inventive than was Parson Weems' maraschinoed version of the life of Washington. Often its writing is no more creative than was Bartlett's when he was making some of his better quotations. Both as drama and as biography it is guilty of curious omissions. No mention is made of *De Profundis*. Constance Wilde and the two children are never referred to. The barbarous treatment to which Wilde was exposed at Clapham Junction is ignored. The full tortures and the temporary spiritual awakening of the prison years are passed over. Still, in spite of its patent limitations, this *Oscar Wilde* which the Stokeses have brought together, and which has received the blessing of such a survivor of the wreckage as Lord Alfred Douglas, is one of the most engrossing attempts at dramatized biography our theatre has seen in many seasons.

Its honesty is at all times compelling. It does not mince matters. It has the wisdom to realize, as Mrs. Roosevelt stated so incontrovertibly at one of those moments when *My Day* was functioning as the modern *Poetics*, that "After all, the story of Oscar Wilde is always bound to be—the story of Oscar Wilde." The Stokeses do not try to change this story so that it could cover the career of Shirley Temple. They let bad enough alone. Their play gives the complete picture of Wilde's shameless degradation, his escapades with grooms, etc, etc. Except for one unfortunate curtain line about the navy, it dodges cheapness and sensationalism in retelling a chronicle which, if grossly told, would cause most playgoers to reach for their Mothersill before the first act were over. Its spirit is essentially clean in its record of ugly facts. Without leers it puts before grownups an unflinching adult interpretation of one of the most scandalous tragedies known to literature.

If the Stokeses have not hesitated to gain assistance by dipping their pen into Wilde's own inkwell, they are no less fortunate in the aid they receive from their actors at the Fulton. John Buckmaster as Lord Alfred Douglas and Harold Young as Frank Harris are among the many capable performers who add to the evening's vividness and good taste by the suave accuracy of their characterizations.

What makes *Oscar Wilde* memorable, however, is Mr. Morley's playing of Oscar. Mr. Morley is best known to American audiences for the historically inaccurate but impressive half-wit he created when, in *Marie Antoinette*, he was playing Louis XVI to Norma Shearer's Norma Shearer. Skillful as was his Hollywood Louis, on the basis of what he did rather than what he was given to do, Mr. Morley's royal locksmith was the epitome of the obvious compared to his Oscar Wilde.

As no actor I have ever seen in a Wilde revival has been able to do, Mr. Morley gives point, charm, even naturalness to Oscar's epigrams. He purrs with pleasure as with seeming spontaneity he rolls them out. His heavy-lidded eyes dilate with surprise as he startles himself into pride by the unexpected turns of his own wit. His paradoxes appear never to have been memorized. They are thought up on the spot. The look of unmistakable authorship steals across his face as his aphorisms ooze from his rosebud mouth. He does not merely utter them; he walks the floor with them, subjecting them paternally to a vocal lullaby. He speaks them in the rich velvet tones of mock innocence with which Mrs. Patrick Campbell disguised her most devastating comments. Like her, he seems to relish playing Malice in Wonderland.

Mr. Morley's Oscar is no static creation. He is at all times the product of Mr. Morley's thinking and planning. He takes possession of Mr. Morley's eyes, his lips, his hands; and he changes with the times. At first he is the arrogant *flâneur;* then the immoral decadent; next the witness witty in his self-confidence; then the cornered wretch in a state of pitiable collapse; and finally the bloated ruin of the last years in Paris. It is not likely that anyone who has been privileged to sit before Mr. Morley's Oscar will see Wilde in any other terms.

October 11, 1938

THE DODIE BIRD

TO EVEN her best friends it is improbable that Dodie Smith seems destined to disturb Shakespeare in his Stratford tomb, Ibsen in his Norwegian grave, or Chekhov as he rests in Moscow. Were she a novelist, the author of *Autumn Crocus, Call It a Day*, and now *Dear Octopus* would unquestionably be on more intimate terms with Kathleen Norris and Frances Hodgson Burnett than Tolstoi. One doubts if Miss Smith herself is fooled on the subject of Dodie. Certainly she does not write as if she thought herself a genius, or were anxious to have anyone else so consider her.

She makes no pretense of having big things to say, or of saying little things in other than a little way. As a dramatist Miss Smith is the theatre's cricket on the hearth. What she chirps is a song of domesticity doubtless doubly welcome because of its familiarity. She is frankly sentimental in an age which likes to pretend it is hard-boiled. In a day of angry issues, economic change, social awareness, and international cataclysms, Miss Smith goes serenely on her mittened way, thinking in terms of crumpets and tea, nursery memories, sweet romance, and the fireside worries of average people. She even dares to write affectionately about what, in some quarters, is such an unmentionable subject as a happy family. This is the boldest thing about her. It makes her placid mediocrity appear revolutionary. Still, there are plenty of playgoers whose minds are not marshmallows who feel warmly toward her for being what she unashamedly is.

It is crystal-candy clear that La Dodie does not suffer from what Clare Boothe has described as an allergy to decent people. She has so sweet a tooth that often she bites off more than other people can chew. Her characters are sometimes saccharine to the point of being slightly diabetic. Both her men and women might almost be the Five Little Peppers grown up. Miss Smith does not attempt to write as a sophisticate. Her playwriting is as simple as a pair of old bedroom slippers, and no less comfortable. Indeed, it is downright "home-y." Her thinking never proves exhausting. She is neither cynical nor witty. You feel that she still believes in Santa Claus, and, what is more, are willing to swear that he believes in her.

Plainly she is in tune with the infinitesimal. She does

not lift her pen either to protest or to reveal. She merely records, in popular magazine terms, the domestic concerns of the *bourgeoisie*, serving suburbia as its Sappho. Her obviousness is as plain as the signs in florists' windows announcing Mother's Day.

Naturally the success of this English spinster has been as small with the critics as it has been large with the general public. Miss Smith writes not for individualists but for those who have a tribal instinct and who, whether they can explain why or not, feel sentimental about their families. Mr. Nathan, a bachelor, was doubtless right in describing such a play as *Dear Octopus* as whiffle-poofle by any cold critical standards. Mr. Watts, another bachelor, may have felt embarrassed by its unblushing pleasantness, but most reviewers who are family men found it amusing enough to spend the evening glancing at Miss Smith's latest album. Although they did not think of taking it seriously as a play, they were touched by it. Like many theatregoers of a certain age, mellowness, and experience, they were grateful to have been asked to warm themselves at the fireside of characters who were decent, unexceptional, and agreeable. Surely there is room for a play dealing with such people.

Maybe La Dodie's chief accomplishment is that, even when we roast her, she does manage to make marshmallows of us all.

January 12 and 20, 1939

MR. MORGAN's *The Flashing Stream*

ALTHOUGH dramatic criticism cannot pretend to the absolute truth of which mathematics is capable, still truth—however personal—is one of its constant aims. It is truth which forces me to take my little ax in hand when confronted with such an almost budless cherry tree of a play as Charles Morgan's *The Flashing Stream.*

Mr. Morgan is well known in this country as the dramatic critic of the *London Times* and the author of such novels as *Sparkenbroke* and *The Fountain.* Last night at the Biltmore he was heard from for the first time as a playwright. Perhaps—you see I cannot tell a lie—it would have been wiser if he had not been.

His drama is an earnest one; a hymn sung without music to "the soundless passion of a single mind." Plainly it is written by a man who cares about words even if he has not mastered the "austere art" of dramatic dialogue. No less plainly it is the work of a man who has thought, and is trying to have, his sincere say. Yet, as it traces the relationship of a great woman mathematician and the group of British naval scientists with whom she is working to perfect an aerial torpedo, *The Flashing Stream* proves to be not only an unconvincing story but a strangely pretentious and empty one.

It is a philosopher's drama in which Plato appears

to have been living on a diet of vegetable marrow. It is a play of ideas in which the ideas prove to be either nonexistent or difficult to support. Although its subject is passion, its writing—even when high-fallutin'—is so cold that at any moment you are prepared to brush penguins off the dialogue.

Presumably Mr. Morgan is concerned with a group of mathematicians who can do everything except multiply. This is his whole point. For he sings not of arms and the woman but of a productive celibacy. He is trying to dramatize what Mr. Thurber has illustrated with far more success as the battle between the sexes, the warfare between such "personal animals" as women and, of course, such "impersonal" Titans as men. He does this in a play, at once phony and pointless, which leaves you feeling as if you had been reading a learned essay on Casanova by Calvin Coolidge.

Although not nearly so attractive as she was as Mrs. O'Shea in *Parnell*, Margaret Rawlings works honestly and well, with a deep voice no doubt supposed to make science vocal, as the lady mathematician. The others do better than might have been expected. At least they ward off laughter. And Felix Aylmer, as a witty Lord of the Admiralty, is very winning in the kind of part which, with its every entrance, comes in retriever-wise with another bid for popularity in its mouth.

Godfrey Tearle is less fortunately cast as the tormented male mathematician. His playing is effective enough in a superficial, utterly stagey manner. But spiritually he fails to suggest the character Mr. Morgan's script indicates. Visually he came near to breaking up the polite solemnity of the evening on many occasions last night by his incredible resemblance to President Roosevelt. Mr. Tearle, I suspect, would have been happier at a revival of *I'd Rather Be Right*. So, for that matter, would the rest of us.

April 11, 1939

MR. MILNE PASSES BY

TEN years ago when, as a blissful pair of British newly-weds, Edith Barrett and Henry Hull were calling each other "Binx" and "Bubbles" and thus causing spinsters and bachelors out front to congratulate themselves on being isolationists, Mr. George Jean Nathan sounded off in no uncertain terms. "A. A. Milne, the Chelsea Pollyanna, the chain candy-stores of English literature and the Happiness Boys of the drama" wrote he, "is with us again in an exhibit called *Michael and Mary*. Attending it is much like going to a marshmallow roast with Dr. Frank Crane's ghost, Jane Cowl, J. M. Barrie's boyhood Sunday School superintendent, the Messrs. Page and Shaw, the man who first thought of putting cream in an Alexander cocktail, Ada Mae Weeks and Ethelbert Nevin. It is the *Nachtasyl* of over-sweetened sentimentality, the *King Lear* of virtuous pap, the *Old Oaken Bucket* of the grease-paint E-string. It is so good, so pure, so moral, so tender, and so damned noble that it hurts."

That, as I say, was ten years ago. Now Mr. Milne is with us once again, this time not as a dramatist but in the library, allowing us to look over his shoulder (as he would put it) at the pages of his *Autobiography*.

The reader (once described by Mrs. Parker as the "Tonstant Weader") cannot be blamed if he approaches this record of Mr. Milne's life expecting to find Christopher Robin chinning himself on the clauses or Winnie-the-Pooh darting from comma to comma.

It is not Mr. Milne's fault if Winnie and Chris do appear. Mr. Milne cannot help himself. He is right when he says the title of every autobiography should be *It's Too Late Now*, and complains that modern critics make the silly mistake of condemning one author for not writing like another. He is no less correct when he insists "One writes in a certain way because one is a certain sort of person," conditioned by his childhood and the life he has led.

Now Mr. Milne is very definitely a certain sort of person. It's far too late for him, or us, to do anything about that. He is sensitive. He can write charmingly. He can be witty in the fluffiest tradition of English wit. His prose is at once facile and precise. And, unmistakably, he is Winnie-the-Pooh's father.

It is not surprising to find that in his *Autobiography* Mr. Milne's childhood occupies one half, and by far the better half, of the book. The hard thing to determine is where the child leaves off and the adult emerges.

Mr. Milne has some good things to say now and then on writing. He gives a vivid account of his working hours in *Punch*. He paints an amusing picture of William Archer and a vivid one of E. V. Lucas. But, except for his description of the technical problems he faced and solved in creating the Victorian poet who was the central figure of his *Truth About Blayds*, Mr. Milne allows the reader to do precious little peeking over his shoulder into the secrets of his desk or his life.

He makes it clear he is an author. He mentions the titles of his better-known plays, novels, and nursery books. He discusses contracts. He tells some literary anecdotes. To no one's surprise, he names Barrie as his friend. He suggests how a few of his plot ideas came to him. And he confesses he is hard to live with when he is writing. But, like his own Mr. Pim, he passes by at the very moment one would like to have him sit down and talk.

During all the years of his success as an author of whimsies what does Mr. Milne do in the pages of his autobiography? Why—

> *Christopher Robin goes*
> *Hoppity, hoppity,*
> *Hoppity, hoppity, hop.*
> *Whenever I tell him*
> *Politely to stop it, he*
> *Says he can't possibly stop.*

No wonder the reader is tempted to start skipping, too.

October 5, 1939

MURDER AS A FINE ART
Ladies in Retirement

ALTHOUGH crime is not exactly unknown in this country, the common run of our homicidal plays do not treat it with the respect to which our newspapers would persuade us it is entitled. Our criminal melodramas go gaily about the gruesome business of murder. They refuse to take it seriously. No one can deny they spill blood freely. As a rule, however, they take pains to water this blood before they shed it. They do this by making the action more important than the characters; by forcing life to take a holiday while overworking all the possible means of dying; by removing death, as it were, from life and by taking it for a ride (sometimes a gloriously exciting one) on what amounts emotionally to the equivalent of a roller coaster in an amusement area.

These melodramas of ours in which death plays so active a part in the plot and yet so small a one in the sympathies are what is technically known as "thrillers." They belong to a special category in the theatre. Whether they are as good as was *The Bat* of happy

memory, or as silly as was *Goodbye in the Night* of
recent failure, they have won their group classification
justly because their sole aim is to thrill, by foul means
if not by fair.

So special is their form that were Polonius alive today
he would have to revise his tiresome drum roll of
dramatic categories to include them. As a fellow with
a sharp eye for the differences between the species,
Ophelia's father, that "Jephthah, Judge of Israel" of
matters theatrical, would no doubt be precise enough
in his thinking to distinguish, as critics and audiences
really should, between such types as the aforesaid
thriller, the detective or Master Mind play of the "who-
dunnit" or Cock Robin variety, and the psychological
murder melodrama.

It is the English who excel at psychological murder
melodramas even as in seasons back our playwrights
have excelled at "thrillers." Often, as in *Night Must
Fall* or *The Perfect Alibi*, the British can stalk murder
psychologically at far too leisurely a pace to satisfy
their more frenetic American cousins. When, however,
they are writing well; when they are writing as well as
did Mr. Priestley in *Dangerous Corner* and Jeffrey Dell
in *Payment Deferred*, as brilliantly as Patrick Hamilton
did in *Rope's End*, or with the invention Mr. Percy and
Mr. Denham have shown in *Ladies in Retirement*, the
English can demonstrate at once how literate, well-
observed, and cannily constructed their blood-letting
scripts can be.

De Quincey in a famous essay once playfully suggested that we look upon a murder—when it is once committed and there is nothing we can do to undo it or aid in tripping up the culprit—as a fine art. "What's the use of any more virtue?" he wrote. "Enough time has been given to morality; now comes the turn of taste and the fine arts."

De Quincey asked us to waive moral worries and to consider crime with a coldly professional and critical eye; in fact, to take the attitude toward it that Aristotle took when he spoke of "the perfect thief"; that Dr. Howslip took when he mentioned a "beautiful ulcer"; or that Coleridge maintained when, returning with his disciples from a fire, he delivered himself of this verdict, "Oh, sir, it turned out so ill that we damned it unanimously."

De Quincey noted the conditions of the perfect crime, saying scornfully in passing, "As to old women and the mob of newspaper readers, they are pleased with anything, provided it be bloody enough. But the mind of sensibility requires more." First, the person murdered ought to be a good man. Secondly, he ought not to be a public character, no doubt because goodness is rarer among such characters. Thirdly, the subject chosen ought to be in good health, "for it is absolutely barbarous to murder a sick person, who is usually unable to bear it."

The authors of *Ladies in Retirement* may not be psychological melodramatists who take De Quincey too literally. As anyone knows who has sat spellbound before Mr. Percy's and Mr. Denham's well-characterized and shrewdly plotted murder play, its concocters have ignored De Quincey's stipulations in several respects.

It is a nice woman, not a good man, who is done in at the Henry Miller Theatre. Furthermore, she is strangled after we have made her acquaintance and when we have come to like her so much that we are tempted to trip up the culprit. But the crime committed in *Ladies in Retirement* is almost as "beautiful" as was Dr. Howslip's "ulcer." Certainly Mr. Percy's and Mr. Denham's melodrama can claim the high virtue of scorning those people condemned by De Quincey as being satisfied with anything, provided it be bloody enough. *Ladies in Retirement* meets the more exacting requirements of "the mind of sensibility." It is no childish thriller. It does not depend for its shuddery suspense upon any such easy tricks as sliding panels, clutching hands, shrieks in the dark, or ghosts who air their bedding under green spotlights. The basis of its excitement is a set of believable characters, shrewdly observed and well established, who move and are moved through a plot that doubles its tension by refusing to follow an expected course.

Mr. Percy and Mr. Denham are partners in a business devoted only to incorporating horrors. Still, they go about that business as if it were legitimate. And the yield is excellent. They have mastered the higher mathematics of grease-paint murder. Although one knows, soon after the curtain has risen and their nice old lady has been seen near a Dutch oven, that before long she will be stuffed into it, the interest is derived not from surprises which cheat, but exclusively from the psychological relationship of the stuffer to the stuffee. When Mr. Percy and Mr. Denham pull crimson rabbits out of their melodramatic hat, one could swear it is with blood and not red ink that these rabbits are stained.

The authors of *Ladies in Retirement* are no less fortunate in their actors than they are capable in their plotting. Flora Robson, who is making her New York debut as the companion-housekeeper, is a brilliant performer. She has a personality of extraordinary force and a technical resourcefulness of infinite fascination. She is as arresting to watch as she is to listen to; a Lady Macbeth in Victorian dress; a person who by the quietest of hushed means can not only create tension but grant it dignity.

As the giddier of her two daffy sisters Estelle Winwood gives one of the oustanding performances of her career. She is willowy, undulant, rattle-brained, and yet at all times precise in her effects. Jessamine Newcombe is likewise admirable as the gruffer of the two touched sisters, the one who is always cluttering up Miss Fiske's parlor with dead birds found on the beach, bits of driftwood, feathers, flowers, and shells.

Isobel Elsom plays the red-wigged and ill-fated Miss Fiske so vividly and with such a perfection of detail that one hates to have her done away with. In short,

Gilbert Miller has assembled throughout a flawless cast for a melodrama which offers its full rewards both in murderous excitements and in fine acting. It may not let much blood, but it does its welcome damage to the blood pressure.

March 27 and 30, 1940

DANTON AND ORSON WELLES

ONCE again Vladimir Sokoloff is facing the French Tribunal as Robespierre, the "Old Incorruptible," in a New York production of *Danton's Death*. The last time he played the part was when Georg Buchner's revolutionary drama was being staged here in German by Max Reinhardt as a huge mass spectacle up at the Century Theatre some eleven years ago.

Time has erased most of the details of the Reinhardt production. Even the memory of Mr. Sokoloff's Robespierre has blurred. But there was one moment in that performance at the Century which no one who sat before it is apt to forget.

It came when Paul Hartmann as the Danton who had sentenced countless people to the guillotine faced the mob himself and realized that, in the name of liberty, he too would be condemned to the very same death to which he had sent his victims. It was at this breathless moment that Mr. Hartmann laughed. At first his laughter was the merest chuckle. It sounded low and dreadfully alone. Little by little it began to grow. Suddenly someone else was carried away by its daring and its contagion. Soon several people had joined in it. Finally everyone, from the on-stage rabble to the members of the mob scattered throughout the auditorium, had begun to laugh hoarsely, derisively for what seemed to be an age of disillusionment. So Gargantuan was this mob laughter, so ironic was its cause, that for once the gods and mankind appeared to be laughing at the same thing and at the same time.

I mention this example of Reinhardt's virtuosity in connection with the Mercury's revival of *Danton's Death* only because Buchner's drama is obviously a director's play. It is a technician's holiday, a feast for the *régisseur*, a barbecue for the fellow who lives to demonstrate his wizardry by attempting to say for a script, in terms of his handling of crowds and lights and visual effects, what that script fails to get said for itself.

That *Danton's Death* is not much of a play was made clear when Reinhardt staged it here in German. What Orson Welles has done is to make this melancholy fact even clearer by presenting it in English in a whittled form lasting no more than an hour and a quarter.

Like Reinhardt before him, Mr. Welles seems to have been interested in Buchner's script primarily because of the challenges with which it presents him as a director. As a director he meets these merely technical problems again and again with uncommon brilliance. Furthermore, he has found his own original and provocative ways of solving them.

Unlike Reinhardt the realist, who is a master of huge mobs, Mr. Welles gains his most striking visual effects by producing a French revolutionary drama on a stage free of the usual supernumeraries. His imagination is forced to operate on a smaller budget. His crowds, living or dead, are evoked by suggestion. They are creatures, hideous, ominous and haunting, created by the innumerable blurred masks that dot the huge cyclorama with which Stephen Jan Tichacek has surrounded the scant properties employed in each of the quickly shifted individual scenes.

Upon this sea of indistinct faces Mr. Welles throws, often with fine effectiveness, the excellently modulated lights at the Mercury's command. The many-headed mob is the ever-present background of masks. It is bathed in blood red, or diminished to pale rose and gray in dramatic conflict. It is even shown in its full green and deathlike horror when Robespierre, the heartless executioner, boasts he is alone only to be surrounded for a splendid second by the death masks of the thousands he has killed.

Interesting as these effects are in their own rights, and no less visually exciting as is much of Mr. Welles' direction, one soon begins to realize that what Mr. Welles is doing is no more than playing upon Buchner's drama as if he were Thomas Wilfred giving a recital on his clavilux.

You tire of looking and begin to want to listen. You can follow the switchboard but you cannot locate the human heart. You become painfully aware that, admirable as *Danton's Death* may be as a technical demonstration, it is all stunt and no play. Inventive as the stunt may be, you begin to resent the absence of a play. You are forced to feel as if, having sailed on a boat filled with interesting passengers, you found that, in addition to having to sit at the captain's table three times a day, you were permitted to talk to no one else except the captain in between meals.

Although Martin Gabel is an effective Danton so far as the script permits him to be, and Mr. Welles speaks quite finely whatever his farewell lecture can nowadays be taken to mean, the evening as a whole is as disappointing as Mr. Sokoloff's Robespierre when he is hampered by English.

It becomes increasingly apparent that Mr. Welles' virtuosity, though capable of results as stirring as his modern-dress *Caesar*, is not only the source of his strength but also his greatest weakness. The ever-exceptional Mr. Welles is not content to play Samson in the theatre. He must also be Delilah. Yes, and the Philistines, too. He is the personification of strength dramatically, until, in the course of his Protean act, he reaches for his shears. It is when he starts to cut that he not only weakens the plays which have tempted him, but allows them to fall into the hands of the Philistines.

November 3, 1938

BURYING *The Three Sisters*

"READ him in the kitchen of life, and you will find nothing in him but the simple plot, mosquitoes, crickets, boredom, and gray little people. But take him where art soars, and you will feel in the everyday plots of his plays the eternal longings of man for happiness, his strivings upwards, the true aroma of Russian poetry, in no smaller measure than it is felt in Turgenev."

Thus wrote Stanislavsky in a well-known passage about Chekhov and his plays. Never did his words seem truer than on Saturday night at the Longacre where the young ladies and gentlemen of the Surry Players were all dressed up—fit to kill, as a matter of fact— trying to persuade themselves and others they were giving a performance of *The Three Sisters*.

That their production was paved with good intentions, regardless of the goal to which it led both the audience and Chekhov's script, is beyond dispute. But good intentions are not enough. In the world of the arts at any rate it is still reasonable to assume they are among the generating forces lying behind all effort. They deserve to be taken for granted, not praised. Yet

seldom have such commonplace commodities as good
intentions resulted in a sadder fiasco than at the Longacre.

The Surry Players did not take Chekhov "where art
soars." They did not even give him a reading "in the
kitchen of life." They simply led him blindfolded into
the darkest subbasement of incompetence; into a veri-
table Hades of amateurishness; into an Inferno of non-
comprehension. There they proceeded to smother him
by kindnesses murderous in their heavy-handed ineptitude.

The glory of Chekhov's plays consists not in what
lies on the surface of his writing but in that rich sub-
soil of his emotional statement with reaches down to
the bedrock of human character and frustration. His
apparent lack of design is the surest proof of his planning. His seeming irrelevancies are all relevant. They
are more than parts of the pattern. They are the pattern itself. They are the most magical illusion of his
method, his means of escaping from the externalities
of the well-made play, of orchestrating a mood, of allowing us to listen to his unlistening people as they
speak the autobiographies of their hopes and sufferings, of endowing the insignificant with its true significance, and of achieving a new dimension in what appears to be the medium of realism.

Unless this interrelation of parts is made clear, unless
a director is at work who understands and stresses the
hidden design, unless he is helped by actors who can

build their characterizations from within, any of Chekhov's long plays is bound to seem worse than baffling when encountered on the stage. It is fated to appear as downright silly—as much a cruel parody of itself—as did that touching tale of the three sisters who want to go to Moscow and never get there, which the Surry Players thought they were acting at the Longacre.

Neither Chekhov nor Mr. Wiman's young protégés were aided by the meaningless stylization of Johannes Larsen's ceilingless interiors, with their senseless use of steps and levels. As well play *King Lear* on a roller coaster as try to produce Chekhov in such a stunt setting which, by its very ground plan, imprisoned the action of *The Three Sisters*, denied it fluency and focus, and turned the evening into a hopeless traffic jam. Lucinda Ballard's overrich costumes were equally inappropriate. So was Samuel Rosen's utterly unilluminating direction. So, if one excepts such potential Chekhovians as Robert Allen and Hume Cronyn, were all the members of the Surry Theatre.

If these actors became somewhat confused in Arden when they tried to do *As You Like It* two seasons back, they lost their way completely in Chekhov Saturday night. Katherine Emery, Anne Revere, Shepherd Strudwick, Dorothy Mathews, Jabez Gray—all of them exceptionally high-minded, well-meaning, and as a rule gifted performers—were playing a hopeless game of blind man's buff. Their ignorance as to what they were about created no bliss. The curtain was up but they kept it steadfastly down, at least so far as the real values and subtleties of the play were concerned. Nor were they helped by a text which, in such a cut as the one occurring in the drunken doctor's speech, betrayed that it, too, was lacking in comprehension of Chekhov's intentions and his genius.

No two dramatists in the world have been more dissimilar than the gentle author of *The Three Sisters* and gruff Ben Jonson. But had Chekhov been personally exposed to the Surry Players' revival last night he would undoubtedly have understood what Jonson meant when, after the failure of one of his comedies, he described it as having been "never acted, but most negligently played." Most of us out front could not help thinking back to the virtues of Miss Le Gallienne's production of the same play, to the American Laboratory Theatre's revival with Germanova and Ouspenskaya in the cast, to the great and unforgettable wonders of the Moscow Art Theatre's performance, and, above all, to the script itself. And thinking back, the fault was not ours if we were possessed by a feeling of outrage.

October 16, 1939

Seven

MADNESS WITH MUSIC

"MOONBEAMS FROM THE LARGER LUNACY"

WOULD you, at a musical comedy or revue, know how irresistible are the comedians whose duty is your pleasure? Would you have proof incontrovertible that they are as unoriginal as on occasion your worst fears may whisper they are? Or final confirmation that they are as convulsing as your laughter or your hope insists they must be?

The test, the acid test—if a generous hostess, an anniversary which has downed the budget, the open sesame of press tickets, or your own reckless affection for these worthies should seat you as near them as you have always dreamed of being—is to look away from the stage—yes, even from them—and grudgingly steal some glances at the orchestra pit.

If, between songs, when the musicians are at liberty though still confined in their abyss, these same musicians are staring only at themselves (which may explain their dejection), or snickering openly at a customer out front (because their manners can be as sour as their music is sweet); if, as the comic enters, there is no more light in their eyes than can be found in an abandoned cellar; if they busy themselves emptying their trombones, reading newspapers, or mothering their instruments when the zany's best quips are being effortfully released, why then, with the certainty of death and taxes, you may be sure the person you are laughing at does not belong to the blood royal in the realms of inspired nonsense.

In the presence of such Andrews as are truly merry, indifference is as impossible as was chastity to Casanova. Those moles of music in the theatre, the fiddlers and the saxophonists, the drummers and the pianists, must be pardoned if boredom, tolerant or belligerent, is the expression with which they welcome what may be convulsing us. We are novitiates; they are old-timers. By the end of a long run they have been as overexposed to what still startles us into smiles as wives are to their husbands' stories after years of married life. The mortality of jokes is always high among hearers. It is only the tellers who believe their chestnuts must have been watered in the Fountain of Youth.

There is more to the theatre's better jesters than their jokes. Much more. Their memorized gags can be a source of wonder and delight. They can put the match of laughter to our unsuspecting risibilities as if these risibilities were so many giant firecrackers, and every night on which we heard their stories for the first time the Fourth of July. But the genuine entertainers of our stage are not the by-products of librettists, however good. The best of gag men, of plot makers, and of lyricists are their friends, not their masters, and seldom their equals.

This is why, when a true chieftain of laughter's tribe appears, even the musicians wake up and permit their attention to go off union hours. They are not like other mortals, these men and women who send our worries galloping down a dead-end street which stops with themselves. There is a boldness about the overdrawing of their features; a simplification in their spirits; an exaggeration, personal as it is peculiar, about their gestures, their walks, and their expressions which happily removes them from what can be precious or dull in the life class conducted by the theatre, and makes them cartoons drawn by a benevolent God.

These Pagliaccis in reverse, these clowns who weep with hearts that are always bound to break—into smiles —soon after the reversals or the separations preceding the intermission have been forgotten, can claim many things in common, although only with one another.

What each develops in costume, personality, or facial geography is a trade-mark of his or her own which we would cheerfully sue another of them for were he or she so foolhardy as to copy it. Taste being what it is, we may be no more susceptible to the individual commodities these entertainers have to sell than we are to spinach. Yet they turn us isolationists to this extent. None of us would tolerate encroachments on what each one of them has clearly established as his or her own dominions in the hemisphere of our sympathies.

Male or female, they are a privileged lot; the most privileged people in a world notorious for its underprivileged. Equity's domains do not admit their equals in good fortune. Theirs is the joyous prerogative of looking, and having to continue to be, only like themselves—at least as we have come to cherish them on-stage. Their one grave duty, in a world as serious in its madness as ours is mad in its seriousness, is to keep alive the people their past performances have told us that they were in public. Their one unpardonable infidelity would be to be unfaithful to the legendary creations they have devoted their lifetimes to making real.

They are not actors, these mountebanks. They are self-performers, duty-bound to project what we and they have come to envisage as unique in each of their on-stage selves. The stern realities of their trade touch them as little on the surface as do the realities of our living. An audience is the only jury they seem to know. A jest, rapturously received; a grimace that wows the house; a caper that commands a howl; a lyric that has to be repeated; an exit that provokes the thunder of applause—these are at once the *Mein Kampf* and *Das Kapital* of their confessed ambitions.

To them a black-out is patently something which happens only in a revue. Everything for them is as gay and forgetful as they can succeed in persuading us it must be. We love them for their humility or their energy, their arrogance or their pathos. Most of all we love them because theirs is the right, of which they take glorious advantage, to turn the dull values of our living inside out.

They can make foibles endearing, silliness sane, parochialism a comic virtue, vulgarity desirable, stridency beguiling, bad manners irresistible, stupidity endearing, sex a scream, frustration convulsing, politics sidesplitting, ambassadors human, dictators hilarious, and even democratic corruption and ineptitude the finest of fine jokes. It is because they hold nothing sacred except their duty to be amusing that, when they succeed in being so, we greet them with hymns of approval. The sadder the world, the more comforting and welcome are they. Stephen Leacock, a wise man in his humor, must have had them in mind when he wrote of "Moonbeams from the Larger Lunacy." Even in the present darkness, their lunacies can lighten our hearts.

VICTOR MOORE

THAT there is a Dickensian quality about Victor Moore would be easier to maintain if his spirit were not so obviously wrapped up in bunting. Although he is Mr. Pickwick up to a point, the point comes mainly at his waistline. The resemblance is more dimensional than intellectual. Mr. Moore is naturalized in every one of his fears and instincts. He may look like Mr. Pickwick but his spirit remains that of a Caspar Milquetoast who has grown jolly by swallowing the Capitol dome.

Although the flag he carries is red, white, and mainly blue, it is always rain-soaked. Or is it tear-soaked? He is the nation's idea of the vice-presidency. It is his fault if we have forgotten such men as John Adams, Thomas Jefferson, and Theodore Roosevelt ever held the office. He made Mr. Throttlebottom a figure who for most of us will always be timidly objecting to the Senate's actions.

We have long known him for a career man in politics. From the vice-presidency he rose to Public Enemy Number 13 in *Anything Goes!* And when he left off carrying "Putt-Putt-Putt," his sawed-off machine gun, he bobbed up as "Stinky" Goodhue, our Ambassador to Russia in *Leave It to Me!* Now in *Louisiana Purchase* Mr. Moore finds himself back in the Senate again. He is no longer the gavel-swinger. He is not even a floorwalker. He does not stay in the chamber. He is a sort of house detective among the Solons, and he goes about the business of investigating corruption in Huey Long's state much as Mary's little lamb might go about the same job had he been assigned to it by J. Edgar Hoover.

Once again his voice has the heartbreak in it that might be heard in the bleat of an asthmatic ewe that had just learned for the first time about a Judas-ram. Once again his pale face shines like the smiling countenance of a humanized moon in a cigar ad. His figure continues to boast those portly lines in which the male equivalents of Helen Hokinson's dowagers rejoice. His gestures have not lost their shyness. His hands steal to his face with the fear a kleptomaniac's might show were he surrendering to his collector's interests for the first time. Yet even when he is a Senatorial snooper, Mr. Moore's brown eyes flash with their erstwhile good nature. They light up, as they have always done, with an endearing love of a joke—a love which, in his case, can be as slow to kindle as it is irresistible when once awakened.

What is so beguiling about Mr. Moore is that he has never lost his innocence. He is a judge whose spirit is in diapers. He combines the decorum of the bench with the distresses of the cradle. The ugly realities of

life seem as happily out of his reach as if they were
black butterflies he could never quite catch in his net.
Although his simplicity is always laughable, it is never
merely foolish. It has about it the wisdom of virtues
unlost, of faiths unsurrendered, of a guilelessness that
is incorruptible. When laughing at him, one wants to
protect him, to lead him by the hand through the
crowded traffic of the plots in which he is poignantly
involved.

In reality the character he creates (even when as in
Louisiana Purchase he turns up as a person capable of
temporarily outwitting some crooks) is a pathetic figure. He is frustrated, naïve, and credulous to an eye-
moistening extent. That this fortunately recurring
character happens to win laughter instead of tears is
due to the brave fact that he is without self-pity. He
does more than enjoy jokes on himself—when he understands them; he invites them. Always he meets them
smilingly, with a gallantry as timid as are his approaches
to life.

If, as Senator Loganberry in *Louisiana Purchase*, Mr.
Moore has changed his Throttlebottom-Public Enemy-
"Stinky" Goodhue pattern somewhat, and done it ably
with a new calculation in his gentle eyes, he has not
altered it too much. He has amended the Constitution
rather than thrown it out. He remains the perfect smiling symbol of everything baffling in us all. We have
other funny fellows as hilarious as he is, but we have
none we love so much. What he does without senti-

mentality is to turn the funnybone into a rib placed directly over the heart.

June 3, 1940

ETHEL MERMAN AND JIMMY
DURANTE

WHEN Mr. Wiman and his authors agreed upon *Stars in Your Eyes* as the name of their new musical comedy, they hit upon the happiest of titles. At the Majestic two stars really are in your eyes, twinkling so brightly that you are more than willing to overlook the routine qualities of a book which is only serviceable and of a score by Arthur Schwartz that is singularly undistinguished. Inasmuch as the stars in question happen to be Ethel Merman and Jimmy Durante, it would perhaps be more accurate to describe them as planets. Certainly in the firmament of Broadway, they blaze with an effulgence uniquely their own.

They are hilariously likeable performers, these totally different zanies. Their personalities are nothing short of epidemic. Theirs is the energy which, in the language of contemporary Bulfinches, is supposed to be American. Although they are always in high, and make you run until you practically trip on your tongue trying to keep up with them, they never wear you out, any more than they exhaust themselves. They have more than enough vitality to take care of everyone. They do not borrow from an audience. They give to it until that audience is bubbling over with their same exuberance.

Both Miss Merman and Mr. Durante have wisely gone their way ignoring that "Abatement of Noise Campaign," which once upon a time the Little Flower, known as La Guardia, was so foolhardy as to launch. A buzz saw is as quiet as a sylvan nook compared to Miss Merman. Mr. Durante can make the foghorn of the *Normandie* sound like a child's whistle. The two of them are city folk, blessedly free of the rickets, anemia, hookworm, snake bites, and other countryside threats to health. Mr. Durante's pallor may indicate he has seldom given the sun a chance to see him. But hard as this is on the sun, both Miss Merman and Mr. Durante are possessed of that healthy exuberance which can only belong to "East Side-West Side" Spartans who have been exposed to the tests of Manhattan and have survived them triumphantly.

Miss Merman for some strange reason has never been able to do full justice to herself in the movies. Perhaps the mere fact that she has been so far away from New York has depressed her even as it has depressed countless New Yorkers. More probably it is because no camera has yet been invented large enough to capture the charm of her personality and the sunny gaiety of her spirits. Her joyous and magnificently accurate stridency is of a special sort. She needs a large auditorium, precisely as for everyone's comfort certain horsey men require the open air. Miss Merman has a kind of flashy style which behind the footlights can be infinitely more ingratiating than chaste elegance. She is so likeable in a big-hearted, good-natured manner that she can make a heroine even out of the hellcat she is asked to play in *Stars in Your Eyes*.

Her black-eyed surety would be impudent if it were not so beguiling. As well demand Sophie Tucker to dwindle into a schoolmarm as ask Miss Merman to subdue herself until she proves as colorless as a debutante. There is, incidentally, a pronounced spiritual affinity between Miss Tucker and Miss Merman. They are runners in the same joyous relay race. Like Miss Tucker, Miss Merman has a fine musical ear, and a marvelous power of full-throated, yet informal, projection. Young though she is, Miss Merman has always had a happy way of suggesting she was just about to become a red-hot mamma. The proof—the final proof—of her skill as a singer is that, while she is singing them, even Mr. Schwartz's songs at the Majestic seem to be almost as good as were such of her past masterpieces as *Eadie Was a Lady*, *Sam and Delilah*, *You're the Top*, and *I Get a Kick Out of You*. It is only when she has stopped that you realize how flat most of them are.

As for Mr. Durante, he roams through *Stars in Your Eyes* more furiously than the wind has ever blown, even in the old days, around the Flatiron Building. He swings

into action with his eyes gleaming behind that mountainous nose of his like twin moons rising above Pike's
Peak. There is nothing of the Little Lord Fauntleroy
about him. He looks like the whole of the Dead End
gang grown up into one sweet-tempered toughy. His
rowdiness is superb. Mr. Durante is a volcano in bum's
clothing. No swinging doors have ever swung as he does
his head when he vibrates with entirely justified self-
confidence through the boastful lyrics of *A Self-Made
Man.*

Although some people may not surrender to the
Durante spell, the whole point of a democracy is that
it expresses the will of the majority. The minority in
this instance must be limited to those whose thyroids
are not operating as they should. Mr. Durante is a
first-rate comic; untamed, untiring, unhousebroken,
and (to those of us who are ardent Jimmy-ites) irresistible.

Both he and Miss Merman are to be seen at their incredible best in *Stars in Your Eyes.* If the evening had
no other justification, it would find an abundant one
when the final stanzas of this musical are reached and
Miss Merman and Mr. Durante go to town hand in
hand, and in a big way. When these two let down their
hair (of course, this is only a figure of speech so far as
Schnozzola is concerned), the outside world ceases to
exist for fifteen jubilant minutes. Theirs is the kind of
captivating madness one wishes had taken possession of

certain of the earth's rulers. Had it been, this would be a Panglossian universe indeed.

March 10, 1939

DU BARRY WAS NO LADY

THAT *Du Barry Was a Lady* has sex on its mind cannot be denied. That it revels in jokes meant for playgoers whose sensibilities are well tiled is no less obvious. But that most of the elegantly dressed Minsky-isms, in this saga of an attendant in a men's washroom who dreams he is Louis XV, are amusing is no less incontestable. It is Miss Merman and Mr. Lahr who must be thanked for this.

Miss Merman sweeps through the evening with that bright-eyed, shining vitality which is always such a captivating feature of her playing and her singing. She needs no vitamins; she has plenty to spare. Her throat houses as beguiling a calliope as Broadway knows. The Midas touch is upon her tonsils because she can turn brass to gold. She can do more than that; she can keep it brass. No one can match her in putting a song across, in trumpeting its lyrics, in personifying its rhythms.

All the bright lights of Broadway seem to shine from behind her face. Hard-boiled she frankly is, but she makes toughness itself an irresistible virtue. She possesses not only great energy but a kind of shimmering dignity, too; a dignity born of her poise, her skill, her honesty, and her magnificent professionalism.

Give Him the Oo-La-La and *Katie Went to Haiti* may not be Cole Porter's masterpieces, but Miss Merman sings them with just as much verve and authority as if they were. While she is saxophoning them on her vocal cords they are satisfying enough.

Mr. Lahr proves no less helpful. He is a hugely funny fellow, a comic who grows more and more comic with the years. Like Miss Merman, he has boundless zest. His crossed eyes, the bullfrog croakings which emerge from his pondlike mouth, his hilarious travesties of the operatic manner or the ritual of court etiquette—all these prove reliable ammunition in his comic shotgun.

Give Mr. Lahr a scene in a Men's Room or let an arrow hit him so that he is forced to stand up, and he can do plenty. He may not be a Puritan, but he belongs to the aristocracy of perfect fools.

December 7, 1939

BILL ROBINSON

THERE are those who insist Bill Robinson cannot read or write, except to sign his name. Although the rumor is of course false, I, for one, am entirely willing to believe Bojangles is no base addict of the printed word. His dancing offers conclusive proof that he is not. It is more than the performance of an expert. It is the work, and play, of a profoundly modest man. One trembles to think how even this vast modesty of his, which is one of his most beguiling attributes, might have been imperiled had Bill been able to spend much time perusing the ecstatic paragraphs which all these many years the reviewers have had no other choice than to write about him.

But when it comes to Bojangles' not being able to write—such a rumor is a palpable lie. Everyone knows Bill Robinson can write his name. His signature is written large, and with magnificent flourishes, on every dance he executes. Nor do his literary gifts end with his signature. He may carry his John Hancock in his shoes, which is somewhat irregular. But what he signs his name to, when he begins to step, is a literature which gets along quite nicely—thank you—without the aid of words. He taps his feet as an artist, where hacks must content themselves with tapping a typewriter. Because he is at once his own "message" and machine does not mean he has not more to say than the majority of scriveners ever manage to get said.

Bojangles serves jazz as its joyous metronome. Obviously he has just bitten off a fragment of the Comic Spirit as if it were a hunk of watermelon. Although he subjugates sweet music as if he were its Emperor Jones, his feet supply him with his own tom-toms. When, at sixty-one, he capers into *The Hot Mikado,* no one can doubt the accuracy of the operetta's new title.

Nothing can apparently be done in any swing version of the Gilbert and Sullivan classic about getting the Mikado on the stage soon after the rise of the first curtain. The libretto sentences him to be a second act figure. At the Broadhurst, however, Bill Robinson is decidedly worth waiting for. It cannot be counted an irrelevance that the first words his Emperor is heard to sigh from the wings are "Get along, Little Doggies." Without his doggies, Bill's most humane Mikado never would exist, in or out of Japan.

With them, however, he invades Titipu as if it were Manchoukuo. Only so agreeably does he do it that it does not seem to be an occupation at all. As the potentate of Oriental potentates, Bojangles has only to emerge as an end man in a minstrel show to turn his conquered province into an annex to the Cotton Club. Since he is dipped in gold from the neck down, his conquest is bound to be visual before it is aural. But after reciting a few feebly revamped Gilbertian lyrics, Bill goes to work. Thereafter one precise foot begins to follow another down onto the stage. Words—even what is left of Gilbert's words—cease to matter. From then on they become mere impedimenta. Bojangles not only speaks, he writes with his feet. And with his feet he writes such captivating lyrics and music that my own guess is Gilbert and Sullivan would have forgotten all about that carpet at the Savoy if only they had been lucky enough to hear and see Bojangles.

This veteran dancer with the body of a cadet has

swung into action. His feet have begun to write for him—and for the Savoyards, too. A smile is on his face; the kind of serene smile which has always been his, long before he proved his greatness by managing to maintain it in Shirley Temple's presence. Although his arms may be spread or at his side, the balance he maintains betrays him as a master of grace. His every movement is as effortless as only fun can be to those who know how to live and are lucky in their living. But what ebullient scores and lyrics his shoes—his golden shoes in *The Mikado*—manage to beat out as they wander from routine to routine! Theirs may be of necessity a somewhat limited vocabulary. Yet with what precision Bojangles' feet employ it until it gains an inexhaustible variety! In their suspensive tapping, they manage to make the conclusion of a measure seem as important as the fate of nations. What they create is not a single masterpiece but a Golden Treasury of footbeats.

For this man Bojangles is one of the most articulate men of our time. He is more than mortal. He is a titan —not of literature, but with his toes. Our theatre knows few artists of his caliber. In his chosen field he is a superb master, which is something that can be said with a coward's safety about precious few of his contemporaries in their different, if more ambitious, lines of endeavor.

March 27, 1939

MR. WEBB, MISS HOLMAN, AND
LA LUPE

EVEN when it was first produced here as a play back in 1929, with Reginald Owen, Gertrude Lawrence, and Leslie Howard, *Candle Light* did not shine like a good deed in a naughty world. Its dullness was on the monumental side, scaled to Borglum rather than Cellini. Turning it into a musical comedy has not helped, as *You Never Know* made irksomely clear at the Winter Garden last night. In the process, the play's story of the valet and master who temporarily change places has grown considerably duller.

The book Roland Leigh has adapted from a European libretto does not make for gaiety. It snuffs out whatever wit gleamed in *Candle Light*. I do not mean to say there are no jokes in *You Never Know*. There is a steady barrage of them. I only mean to hint that the thud of them as most of them fall flat in the orchestra pit is not a cheering sound.

Although Clifton Webb attempts to characterize the amorous valet, he remains for the most part Clifton Webb. He has grown considerably as a comedian since the days when, lean, lank, dapper, and immaculate, he used to go dancing down the polished floor of the

Château Madrid in hot pursuit of the Dolly Sisters with
his coattails flying behind him like advertising streamers
tied to a plane. In *You Never Know* he is given scant
chance to indicate his growth. He remains immaculate
imperturbable, sleek; and is forced to go his way with as
little aid from the book as Haile Selassie received from
Geneva. He sings drily and dances in his usual un-
ruffled manner. But Mr. Webb is no longer content to
limit his capering to a ballroom kind. Unfortunately,
in some of his more sinuous contortions he appears to
take himself as seriously as if his mother had been
frightened by Isadora Duncan.

Miss Holman is as deep-throated as ever. She remains
the Mrs. Siddons of Tin Pan Alley, a songstress ever-
ready to serve jazz as its Lady Macbeth. With almost
terrifying poise she wanders through a script giving her
little to do. Flagstad at the Metropolitan could not have
more manner. Miss Holman can be effective in the
sultry way so uniquely her own. Although she is a
great one for arranging her draperies as if she were
about to be photographed by Ira Hill, and striking an
arrogantly forlorn pose, her skill with a limited type of
song cannot be disputed. It is not her fault if she does
not reverberate with maximum effectiveness in *You
Never Know*. To succeed even a torch singer must have
something more in her torch than Cole Porter has
remembered to put there.

Still, I must admit the Sisterhood of Solemn Saxo-

phones to which Miss Holman belongs and which
she serves as High Priestess is not a favorite order of
mine. I prefer my torch singers to have some sense of
humor. Although I am in a decided minority, I find I
tire easily of those smileless female baritones who, with
their dropped voices, are all heartbreak and no play.
I quickly weary of the militant self-pity with which
they can prop their shoulders against the proscenium
while imploring someone to give them something to
remember them by. My interest chooses the nearest exit,
and runs there instead of walks, as I watch them following their abdomens around the stage while chanting
gutturally whatever would be the opposite of Negro
spirituals, as if they were wandering up and down the
banks of the Volga.

Speaking of geography, needless to say, Lupe Velez
is all over the place. Let it be quickly admitted she is
very amusing when she takes to her imitations. Subtlety, however, does not appear to be a word included
in the overbright lexicon of Miss Velez' acting. Attractive as she is in her *South of the Border* way, and hot
as are the tamales upon which she has unquestionably
been fed, she makes the fatal mistake of behaving as if
she were going to be given only one evening in her
whole life in which to show how attractive she is. The
result cannot help being a somewhat painfully over-
crowded hour. Miss Velez writhes, grimaces, pouts, and
smiles in terms so unmistakable that beside her a whole

row of posters would seem obscure. Then she is so constantly wigwagging with her body that one tires of reading the message.

September 28, 1938

MR. GAXTON, MISS TUCKER, AGAIN MR. MOORE

WHAT this country needed in simpler times may have been a good five-cent cigar, but what New York is always happy to have around is a musical comedy it can take to its heart. If Manhattan is a more cheerful place just now, it is because in *Leave It to Me!* it can boast precisely the kind of gleeful exhibition for which it has been looking these many months.

This musical comedy, which the Spewacks have concocted and which Mr. Freedley has presented in his best tradition of expert professionalism, is a mad and delectable affair. Its tale of an American Ambassador to Russia, whose one official hope is to get recalled so that he can go home to Topeka, is a pleasant saga, filled with comic possibilities. It is amiable in its humanity, daring in its international impertinence, and lusty in its humor. Mr. Alton has kept its choruses busy. Mr. Johnson has backed it with some of his handsomest settings. And Cole Porter has provided it with some lyrics in his most ingenious and unblushing manner.

As the correspondent whose job it is to get Mr. Moore dismissed from his ambassadorial post, Mr. Gaxton is his jaunty and ingratiating self. As ever he is as full of pent-up energy as a boiling kettle. He moves around the stage in a state of happy torment. His body swings as if it were responding to the cries of a swallowed saxophone. His heart seems always to be giving his spirit a pep talk which his tongue cannot work fast enough to translate. His joyous agony is a source of delight. A mannerism it may be, but it is a dependable one, eloquent in its very inarticulateness.

As for Miss Tucker, she remains a red-hot mamma both as a comedian and a singer. Once again she serves jazz as its Schumann-Heink. Her authority is equaled only by her warmth. She has the kind of full-blown personality not often encountered in our theatre nowadays. Neither the Spewacks' lines nor Mr. Porter's intricate lyrics and music cause her any difficulties. The minute she rolls onto the stage you know she has everything under complete control, including the audience.

Miss Tucker is the ambitious wife in *Leave It to Me!* She is the millionairess who finds herself our embassy's first lady in Moscow; the breezy American who is taking the steps to Russia, and whose high resolve it is to serve the Soviets by putting red ants in their pants. Her husband is different—very different indeed—as Mr. Moore makes hilariously clear. He is without pretensions. His only ambition is to get back to Kansas. He is just plain "Stinky" Goodhue; a timid, wistful, and uproarious character; Mr. Throttlebottom gone into diplomacy.

He is, in other words, precisely the kind of little fellow Mr. Moore has been delighting us with all these many years. If *Leave It to Me!* seems at times like a sequel to *Of Thee I Sing* or *Anything Goes!*, it is of course because Mr. Moore is in it. The characters he plays from season to season may have different names. One year he may be known as Public Enemy No. 13; the next, Mr. Throttlebottom; and still another, as just plain "Stinky." But no less surely than the Rover Boys kept on being the Rover Boys from book to book, so does Mr. Moore keep on being Mr. Moore as he wanders from libretto to libretto. He is always the same, and no one would have it otherwise. One would almost—I say almost—as soon see our form of government change as have Mr. Moore alter in any respect.

November 12, 1938

Eight

VOICES OFFSTAGE

ATKINSON VERSUS ARISTOTLE

ANY modern, caring for beauty, believing in freedom—aesthetic no less than political—and anxious to feel the hot pleasures of participation made possible by the theatre, cannot avoid being irked at times, as our friend and neighbor on the *Times*, Brooks Atkinson, has recently been, by the arctic chill of that miraculous ice floe of rationalization known as the *Poetics*.

Aristotle's pre-eminence in dramatic criticism is truly one of history's strangest ironies. Although he is often referred to as the father of criticism, he was no critic at all as criticism is commonly understood. There is not one line of appreciation, one evocation of beauty, one example of joyous surrender or reaction, one true spiritual reflex to a specific drama or dramatist in the dry but amazing pages of the *Poetics*. Nor was there meant to be. Even so, no critic has ever exerted so wide an influence as Aristotle.

No wonder Mr. Atkinson has been tempted to dismiss the *Poetics* as "a curious relic of a dead civilization," and accuse the Stagirite as a dramatic critic of stead-fastly averting his eyes from the main business of the artist. Aristotle was in many ways the last man in the world to whom fate should have relegated the dubious honor of being the first dramatic critic. Not only did he distrust the theatre in performance, but his approach to the work of the great Greek writers who provided him with his materials was almost purely scientific.

The drama, as he surveyed it in those incomplete, often spurious lecture notes of his which have come down to us, was no more than an annex to his already incredibly extensive laboratory. He took care in his report (which might have been better understood, and would certainly have done less damage, had it traveled under some such name as *The Origin of Species* rather than the *Poetics*) to remain cold even in the presence of beauty's heat, to keep his findings impersonal, and to bisect the writings of the poets as if they were so many frogs he had found in his dramatic pool.

Had Charles Darwin or Pavlov or Einstein become aesthetic arbiters through accident or priority, the re-sults could not have been in many respects more un-fortunate or disconcerting than they were when, for centuries, Aristotle was forced into the role of being a critical pontiff whose edicts (rightly understood or twisted beyond all recognition) were deemed to be un-challengeable.

If Aristotle's influence was pernicious, as it unques-tionably was for centuries; if the neoclassicists ham-pered all true creation in the name of a bogus Stagirite of their own invention; if the "Three Unities" were wished upon him and are inaccurately associated with his name; if his spirit was essentially unromantic; if he never enjoyed the advantage of sitting before Shake-speare's plays, and was spared the embarrassment of try-ing to fit Shakespeare, Ibsen, Shaw, O'Neill, or Saroyan into his neat pigeonholes; if as a demon deductor he would have headed, even in his own day, almost any-one's list of undesirables when it came to choosing a companion to take to the theatre; and if he did not understand the function of criticism as Dryden, Less-ing, Hazlitt, Sainte-Beuve, Shaw, Walkley, or Anatole France have understood it, the fault was not his; and we should, I think, be cautious in condemning him for not being other than he was. No one blames Vitruvius for failing to mention chromium, or Quintilian for omitting Marx, or Jeremy Collier for overlooking the Brothers Minsky; yet condemnations of this kind are not uncommon in the case of Aristotle.

Another misunderstanding, even more widespread on the subject of the Stagirite, is to damn him as a rule-giver because the rule-givers have always done him the injustice of traveling under his name. Much as I agree with many of the points Mr. Atkinson has made against the *Poetics* in the *Times*, still I hate to have him base his whole sly argument on what strikes me as being this very same and all-too-familiar misconception.

I may be entirely wrong, but as I read the *Poetics*, Aristotle's last intention in them was to establish a set of inflexible laws by which the drama was always to be governed. His lecture notes were not, as I see them, meant to serve as the basis of a theatrical Code Napoleon. They were merely the astonishingly clairvoyant observations, findings, classifications, and deductions of an amazing mind. They were the brilliant results of the researches of a physicist who loved the drama more than, as a superrational man of science, he may have cared to admit. One feels that, almost as a hobby, he was trying to organize from the evidence he had on hand the same kind of general truths on the subject of dramatic poetry—both comic and tragic—which his ever-co-ordinating spirit of inquiry had led him to discover as a biologist, an astronomer, a meteorologist, a sociologist, and a philosopher.

He was not endeavoring to write a handbook on dramatic technique. He never once pretends to be telling anyone how to write a play. Certainly his classroom notes cannot be condemned because in them you will find nothing "to explain why Shakespeare was a great dramatic poet and Thomas Bailey Aldrich a poor one." He did not even get around to appraising or appreciating what it was that contributed to the greatness of the Greek plays he was talking about.

When he said a play should have a middle, a beginning, and an end, he was making an observation the sense of which some of our own dramatists might well take to heart. He was no more passing a law than he would have been had he observed that most people have two legs. His method was explanatory, not pontifical. Even his "musts" (which multiply as the *Poetics* proceeds) seem more in the nature of saying "on the basis of past and present practice this must be so" than trying to dictate future performances. No scientist of his greatness would have ever surrendered to the unscientific folly of believing for a moment that knowledge ended with him. Like many another man of science, however, he had the courage to classify the specific instances at his disposal and arrive at general deductions he hoped would be illuminating.

It is true, of course, that Aristotle did not belong by training or interest to the happily anarchic and emotional world of the drama as we now know it. He was temperamentally a misfit even in the theatre of his own day. He made it his duty to remain passionless in the *Poetics* in his very discussion of the tragic passions. Yet he had the courage to probe deeply into the ever-tantalizing question of the origins of dramatic beauty. We who drift around on frail aesthetic skiffs at the populous mouth of the drama's mighty river cannot but

admire him for his brave pioneering feats at its source.
He had, moreover, an athletic toughness of mind which
enabled him to make deductions that, if some of them
are bromidic now, have become so only because of the
accuracy with which he could cut his way to lasting
essentials. The world's blessing was the cold precision
of his giant mind; the theatre's tragedy, especially from
the days of Castelvetro and Scaliger down to Diderot's
and Lessing's rebellion, was that Plato could not have
written the *Poetics* instead of Aristotle.

Plato was an artist, by gifts and instinct, in spite of
the moralizing which found him, almost against his
will, exiling artists from his state. And Aristotle was
essentially a man of science. Still, in certain respects he
had a clearer understanding of the wonders of artistic
creation than Plato himself. It was he, after all, when
answering Plato in the *Poetics*, who dared to insist
"poetry is more philosophical and a higher thing than
history: for poetry tends to express the universal,
history the particular." In other words, he was never
unaesthetic enough to judge beauty in terms of such
criteria as morality or reality.

If the *Poetics* proves less vitalizing to Mr. Atkinson
than a walk across Central Park, it can still claim its
virtues as a diligent, though chilly, pursuit of the very
kind of truth Thoreau admired. In it Aristotle may seem
to be taking pains to conceal his reactions to any single
drama. At least in one place, however, he lets us glimpse
the human being and the playgoer rather than the scien-

tist turned esthete. This is when he speaks, rightly or wrongly, of the purgation of emotion through pity and fear. The man who stumbled upon such a phrase was not a person who had merely thought about the drama in test-tube terms for classroom consumption. He was a theatregoer who had surrendered to it, even if, unfortunately, both surrender and combat were, of course, very far from his intention in the case of the *Poetics*.

January 20, 1940

A PROFESSOR'S LOVE STORY

IN THE realms of research Professor George C. D. Odell's *Annals of the New York Stage* is a monument which on the local skyline deserves a place alongside Grant's Tomb, the City Morgue, the Hall of Records, and the Empire State. Merely contemplating the labor that has gone into it is enough to break the spirit of lesser men, however accustomed they may be to marveling at those ancient Egyptians who toiled to raise the pyramids. What the diligent professor has done in his eleven stout volumes is to perform, singlehanded, an antiquarian chore that would exhaust a whole labor union of recording angels.

He has not finished yet. Over seven thousand pages (not counting the indexes); more than three million, six hundred thousand words; and Mr. Odell has even now sandhogged his way no nearer to the present than the seasons between 1879-82! No city's stage has ever had so faithful a chronicler; no chronicler of the theatre's past has ever lived so happily in a city of the dead. Professor Odell's love of the theatre's yesteryears is unrivaled. His devotion to things which theatrically are GWTW is more epic than anything that has come out of Hollywood.

If the result of his excavations and his sweepings is not a place where anyone can dwell too long with comfort, it is certainly one of the greatest and most indispensable consulting rooms known to dramatic history. For the theatrical Pompeii Professor Odell has recovered from the ashes of time is a site no student of our stage history can ever hope to get along without visiting.

With a relish, almost necrophagous, the good professor asks us to feed on a diet of faded programs and tattered reviews. No fact is too small to win his interest. No actor or performance is too insignificant to gain admittance to his heroic repository. Wherever men and women have been gathered together on the site of the drama—Variety, lectures, or music on Manhattan, in Brooklyn, or on Staten Island—Professor Odell can be counted upon to be on hand. He loves the statistics of past entertainment as Mayor La Guardia loves contemporary fires. There is no keeping him away from them.

His new volume is, in a way, more interesting to present-day theatregoers than his previous tomes have been. It reveals Mr. Odell matching reviews by William Winter and J. Ranken Towse with memories and opinions of his own. It covers the seasons which found Gilbert and Sullivan in New York presenting their own versions of *Pinafore* and *The Pirates*, and during which Oscar Wilde started out on his transcontinental lecture tour. It mentions such great foreign stars as Bernhardt and Salvini. Its honor roll of illustrious performers includes Maurice Barrymore, "Lotta," the elder and the younger Sothern, Mary Anderson, Rose Coghlan, Fanny Davenport, Ada Rehan, and Clara Morris. And among the men and women, still with us or of vivid memory, to whom it refers are John Drew, Daniel Frohman, William Gillette, Lillian Russell, Mary Shaw, De Wolf Hopper, Henry Miller, and Otis Skinner.

In other words, Mr. Odell's new volume brings him almost within hailing distance of the modern stage. But the differences between the theatre which is and the theatre which was are so fundamental that it is almost impossible to see how the one ever grew out of the other. Magnificent as were the actors with whom Mr. Odell deals; important as were such managers as Daly and Wallack; far-flung as was the older theatre's empire of often childish make-believe, those of us trained in the shrunken but adult playwright's theatre of the present find it difficult to shed the tears Mr. Odell sheds so readily over the vanished stage of the early eighties.

In spite of his reverence for cold facts and his giant's appetite for statistics, the professor is quite a sentimentalist. "Alas! the good old days, the rare old actors," he writes at one point, and obviously feels this at a thousand others. No doubt in his untiring fondness for what has been lies the real explanation of the heroic task to which he has set himself and which he has performed heroically.

Although every research worker in American theatrical history stands enormously in Mr. Odell's debt, I, for one, wish that instead of crying so voluminously over old programs, Mr. Odell had devoted the space he now dedicates to sighs and tears to relating the past theatre to the times and society in which it flourished. I wish at many moments that he had looked up from his faded files to survey life itself; that his critical comments were sharper; that his point of view were richer, his human curiosity greater, and his own personal appearance in his narrative were not only less frequent but less like the caperings of a ewe he has mistaken for Lamb.

Such profound interruptions to his lava flow of data as "What a thing life is with all its chances," or "Let us hurry through October and November, noting, as our chariot rolls along, etc," or (this for some minstrels) "So welcome, my merry men all," or "Even as I write the names of those actors, I feel a glow," or "Ah, Daly's, love of our hearts, when comes there such another theatre?"—such interruptions as these do, I suggest, wear down the gentlest reader after a while. They are as out of place as Winnie-the-Pooh would be in the Congressional Record.

So please, please, professor, when next you lift your fortunately "unwearied pen," do try to get a steadier hold on yourself. A little bit of such "ah-ing" and exclaiming and glowing and charioteering and philosophizing goes too long a way. Your *Annals of the New York Stage* is much too valuable a reference work to be turned into a dead-letter office for valentines of such a kind.

January 6, 1940

THE FOUR GEORGES
G. P. Baker At Work

HAD there been only one George Pierce Baker, and had he been the arbitrary teacher of playwriting that some of his critics have imagined he must be because he dared to give courses in the writing of plays, his influence would not have extended beyond his classrooms, if indeed it would have stretched that far. But there were at least four Bakers functioning simultaneously in the two great universities which claimed him. And at Yale, as at Harvard, all four of them were significant.

First, there was the Baker most widely known to undergraduates at Harvard, at Radcliffe, and at Yale; the formal classroom Baker whose business it was to teach the history of the drama to anyone who might care to learn it. He chose his materials so wisely (they were new when he first presented them) and showed such a happy instinct for limiting his attention only to what was theatrically most significant in each man or period he dealt with, that hundreds of those who have sat under him, and then turned teacher, have been compelled to follow in his footsteps down the straight trail he blazed through history. This classroom Baker, seated behind a broad desk, with a sheaf of faded notes before him, and a black brief case stuffed with dusty books beside him, was the most professorial of the four Bakers, and, for that very reason, of later years the least important of the lot.

For some years he was a slightly bored and tired man. Even in his last terms at Harvard, his lectures on the essentials of a play, the four tellings of the Electra story (this was before O'Neill had raised the number to five), Aristophanes, *The Cid*, Victor Hugo, or what have you, showed the long-run system can be as dangerous for teachers as it is for actors. When he spoke of Lope de Vega or Tom Robertson he did so in tones as mechanical as Joseph Jefferson's must have been when, after countless seasons of playing Rip, he called for his dog, Schneider.

There was much good stuff in these outline courses. Whether the subject was the English drama from its beginnings to the closing of the playhouses in 1642, or from the Restoration to modern times, or a general survey of the world's drama, the facts were all there, earnestly investigated, and set forth with the precision of the man who had edited the *Belles Lettres* series, who had published an interesting batch of Garrick letters, performed the same service for the Charles Dickens–Maria Beadnell correspondence, written in *The Development of Shakespeare as Dramatist* the most penetrating study of Shakespeare's technique that has yet appeared, and helpfully set forth the common-sense essentials of playwriting in his *Dramatic Technique.*

Yellow as his notes may have been, and slightly bored as he may himself have seemed in the classroom, these lectures of Mr. Baker's had the decided advantage of being delivered by a man whose primary interest was the theatre. He never abused dramatic literature by treating it as if it had no connection with the stage. He kept it smudged with grease paint. Even in his weariness, he managed to give the impression that the desk behind which he was lecturing was surrounded by footlights.

Witty as many of his comments were, clarifying as his perceptions proved, and amusing as he used to be when he would roll out long sentences and make a classroom roar at their intentional involutions, the moments one remembers best were those in which he forgot all about facts and tendencies, and, abandoning his professional calm, began to make his points as an actor. He had his favorite characters by means of which he would expose the virtues or the follies of a type of playwriting.

Sir Fopling Flutter in *The Man of Mode* was one of these. When he came to him, Professor Baker's blue-gray eyes would deepen behind his pince-nez, his face would beam with pleasure, his portly body rock with mirth. Still seated at his desk, with his coat, usually dark gray, tightly buttoned, he would begin to assume the airs and graces of a Restoration fop. His voice would change and take on the mincing tones of Ethe-rege's hero. His hands, which he always used swiftly, would begin to race in circles. Artificial gallantries would be slightly indicated in a way which seemed so courtly and was so deliciously right that one could have sworn his sleeves were fringed with lace.

Professor Baker was no less happy when, during his talks on Henry Arthur Jones and Arthur Wing Pinero, those transitional dramatists who were his friends, he could show the strides they had made as playwrights by quoting from their earlier works. In Mr. Jones' *Saints and Sinners* he used to give as admirable a per-formance as he did in *The Man of Mode*. By doing so he pointed out all that was absurd in the older melo-dramas. Standing up, with his left hand pushed far into the pocket of his coat and still holding a copy of the play in his right, he would act the scene in which Fan-shawe, the extremely wicked villain of the piece, con-fesses in a soliloquy that his intentions toward the parson's daughter are not honorable. A terrific scowl would spread across Mr. Baker's face and seem to take possession of his vocal cords. As he leaned against the blackboard, imitating Fanshawe who was supposed to be resting against a tree, flicked ashes off of an imaginary cigarette, and indulged in chuckles far more diabolical than any Jones had dreamed of, the classroom turned into a theatre. On that academic stage, a melodrama of not-so-long ago was spoofed far more entertainingly than have been many of the older melodramas which have recently been revived.

To those who took his historical courses at the same time they were working with him in other capacities, the reason for his coldness in the lecture hall was clear enough. He was a teacher who had tired of teaching in the ordinary way. His notes were left yellow and unadded to because his heart was no longer in them. They held as little interest for him as a train does for the person who has left it after it has carried him safely to his destination. From the fall of 1903, when he was first allowed to experiment at Radcliffe with a course in playwriting, he must have realized with an ever-increasing clarity that the drama's present, and not its past, was his goal. Undoubtedly he felt indebted to these historical courses he continued to give, because it was by means of them he had been directed to his new field of interest. Perhaps he also hoped they would perform the same service for those who took them

that they had performed for him. From an intimate
knowledge of the theatre's past might come a desire
to contribute to its present-day practice. Be that as it
may, the Baker who "walked through" these courses,
year after year, was much too much of a New Englander and far too well trained as a professor to succeed in faking what he did not feel. In this respect his
acting talents, even his theatrical instinct, failed him.

The man who met his incipient playwrights in an
upper room in Harvard's Widener Library did not
have to act. He was doing what he liked, and his liking
for what he had to do was plain from the moment he
hurried in, deposited his black actor-y hat on a near-by
bookcase, took off his dark coat, pulled some blue-
covered manuscripts out of his bulging brief case, and
seated himself at the circular oak table around which
the students were grouped informally. This second of
the four Bakers was beholden to no notes. The job
ahead of him required patience, but for some miraculous reason he did not look upon it as a chore. The
forbidding, unget-at-able Puritan who put the under-
classmen off was beginning to thaw. The chalky mask
of professordom was being laid aside. A new man was
emerging.

This Professor Baker who dared to teach such an
unteachable subject as playwriting was the least dog-
matic of men. He had no Golden Rules of Dramaturgy.
He did not pretend to be able to turn out playwrights

in ten easy lessons. He did not claim to be able to turn them out at all. He was among the first to admit dramatists are born, not made. But he did hope to be able to shorten the playwright's period of apprenticeship by granting him the same instruction in the essentials of his craft that the architect, the painter, the sculptor, and the musician enjoyed in theirs.

There was nothing oracular about his methods in these seminars. He did not lecture. He dodged the absolute. He issued no proclamations and passed no laws as to what dialogue, or plotting, or characterization should be. His distinctions between the materials available to the novelist and the dramatist were given in his book. So, too, were his common-sense pleas for clarity, for the scenarios he felt it advisable for playwrights to draft before beginning their actual scripts, and his endless illustrations of what was good and bad in dramatic practice and why.

But what was inelastically stated in *Dramatic Technique*, with that finality which can attach itself to words set down in black and white, was flexible and free when spoken by Mr. Baker and applied to a case in point. His verbal comments had another advantage over his written ones, inasmuch as they could keep pace with tastes of changing years. Where the date 1919 on the title page of his book was bound eventually to seem printed on many of the pages which followed it, Mr. Baker's point of view remained undated. Born

a contemporary of Jones and Pinero, he managed to
continue as the contemporary of each class that came
to him.

When he had hurried into that upper room at Widener and seated himself at the table, with the window
behind him and the light pouring down on the manuscript he held in his hands, it was obvious that his
belief in "the play's the thing" was stronger than any
Hamlet's has ever been. He spoke briefly, except at
the early meetings of the class when he was making
his initial assignments and waiting for his playwrights
to turn in their first scripts. His custom was to let the
plays speak for themselves.

His program for his beginners was as similar each
year as the results were different. Invariably the course
would start off with a one-act dramatization of a short
story. Three short stories, culled from anywhere, could
be selected by each of the tyros for Professor Baker's
approval (or his demon assistant's). Always the one
presenting the most insurmountable technical problems was the one chosen. Next came an original one-act
play, and, finally, by spring, a long play. As many
others as the students happened to write and wanted
comment upon were gladly received.

A sure test of the merits of a play was Mr. Baker's
reading of it. He was an exceptional reader, and he
made a point, whenever possible, of reading a manuscript at sight, without revealing the author's name.
Naturally enough, he got scripts of all kinds and was

forced to be as ready as an old-fashioned stock actor with quick-study characterizations and every conceivable dialect. He was compelled to vary French with Irish, Irish with Italian, Italian with English, English with American. Even as an American he was called upon to suggest tough guys of the toughest sort undergraduates could imagine, prostitutes who made Mae West seem virginal, Indians who grunted about Manitou on the mesa, Negroes who put Mrs. Stowe to shame, and Southern colonels who were more Southern than the Confederacy. He had to rip out oaths that only occasionally pinkened his cheeks or caused him to hasten madly through a speech, which was his other way of blushing. He had to read love scenes that must have disturbed everything New England in him. The number of pleas he was forced to make to imaginary juries would undoubtedly have captured Max Steuer's envy.

The wonder was he never succumbed to the temptation of making fun of the stuff he was reading. He could spoof the classics, real and pseudo, in his history courses, yet he never made sport of his young playwrights' work. He was on their side. He was fully aware that their fellow students would tear them limb from limb when the time for comment came. Accordingly he acted as their defender. He would plunge into the first manuscript on the pile before him (neatly typed in black and red, of course, in order to distinguish the dialogue from the stage directions) and read it through in the dialects required. Or, if none were needed, he would give it the benefit of that deep Boston voice of his which had a surprising way of going Brooklyn in its pronunciations every now and then. Perhaps it should be added that everyone thought Professor Baker was a good reader except the person whose play he happened to be reading. It was not hard to identify the dramatist in question. Author's vanity and a poker face are not compatible.

When the last page was finished and the final curtain read, the class had its merciless but helpful say. Mr. Baker merely presided over these discussions, throwing a word in here and there and waiting for his private conference with the playwright to give his own opinion or to make suggestions. Come to think of it, there was not any teaching, as teaching is ordinarily understood, in English 47. The course was as free from pedagogy as is the MacDowell Colony. There were only twelve or fifteen people who shared a common interest, who knew as they sat informally around that table that they were aiming at the same goal, and who were aided in their writing, first of all, by the simple knowledge that they had to get their stuff in on a certain date, and, secondly, by the reassuring thought that Mr. Baker somehow believed in them, for reasons which were not always clear. There was, of course, more to it than this. All-important was that indefinable evocative gift of Professor Baker's which

made him a great teacher even when he did not seem
to be teaching at all.

The third of the four Bakers known to his Cambridge
students was the tireless Baker, who, when he had
lectured to his history courses at nine in the morning,
spent several hours dictating letters in his small cubby-
hole of an office, met with two of his four playwriting
courses (he gave an elementary and an advanced course
both at Harvard and Radcliffe), conferred with his
dramatists, worked in the garden of his Brattle Street
home and eaten a hurried dinner, used to come rattling
up to Massachusetts Hall in the dusty Dodge his energy
and his driving had aged so prematurely that it had
begun to resemble his wrinkled brief case. Once ar-
rived at the Johnson gate, and looking slightly surprised and pleased at having made a safe landing, he
would wriggle out from behind the steering wheel,
jump to the street, bang the door behind him, rush
into the yard as if a host of demons were pursuing
him, give a presidential salute to the men and women
who were inhaling their last cigarettes and going over
their lines beside the unperturbed bust of James Russell Lowell, and scurry through the two-story room
which was the Cain's Warehouse of his past productions, prepared to spend the evening rehearsing the
better plays his course had yielded.

Outside, Massachusetts Hall was (and still is) one

of the truest architectural joys of the Harvard land-
scape. As one of the oldest structures in the Yard, it
could boast that trim grace which early New Eng-
landers were able to give to their buildings. Inside it
was, at least in the days when Mr. Baker and his designers worked in it, a fascinating nightmare. Its hollow
shell, cluttered with flats and drops which stretched
to the ceiling, and smelling strongly of paint and glue,
was a defiant contradiction of its chaste exterior. If
Bernhardt's heart had beaten in Priscilla's body the
effect could not have been more startling than it was
to find this topsy-turvy, grease-paint kingdom enclosed
by brick walls which had housed troops during the
Revolution.

In the center of this confusion was a space cleared
for a rehearsal stage. Facing it, with innumerable little
paint-specked chairs flanking it on either side, was an
equally spattered black table behind which Mr. Baker
sat with the author. As he took up his position there
night after night, half in the shadows and half-blinded
by the light that beat down from above on the script
he held in his hands, the Baker who in his youth was
supposed to have resembled Edwin Booth came to life
once more. His scraggly gray hair was darkened by the
shadows. His long, sensitive face had a rapt intentness
about it. There was something about his straight, tight
lips which gave him an expression startlingly similar to
the one that forever repeats itself in Booth's photographs.

At rehearsal, as in his sessions in Widener, Mr. Baker was the most stalwart defender his playwrights could find. His job was a far harder one than anyone realized, even as his work as a director was far more skillful than many people gave him credit for. Not only was he working with scripts which as student offerings had the right to be bad and for the most part took advantage of their right, but he made it his duty to protect these plays from actors who generally were inexperienced amateurs.

His faith in his dramatists was endless. He never forced them to rewrite, even when it was as obvious to him as it was to everyone else (except the playwrights in question) that drastic rewriting was necessary. His hope was that his playwrights would learn by having had a real production in front of a selected audience, every member of which was supposed to turn in a criticism. Those productions of his were, he knew, his surest means of instruction. They could teach more to dramatists possessed of any instinct for the theatre than hours of idle theorizing.

With his actors, as with his playwrights, Mr. Baker's patience knew no bounds. With them, too, though officially it was not supposed to be among his duties, he functioned as a teacher. He was an excellent judge of acting. He was blessed with that alert inner ear all good directors must have. It allowed him to hear a line as it was being read at the same time that it enabled him to hear it as it should be read. He had a sure sense of timing, a shrewd eye for character, and the all-important ability to get results from beginners.

When things got too bad, when his actors failed completely to give him what he wanted, he would push his chair back, dig his hands deep into the pockets of his coat, and rush onto the scene, with short, mincing steps and with one foot put before the other as if he were walking the tightrope, to illustrate how this or that part should be played.

He did not scold. In fact, he hardly ever lost his temper. But when he did, it was an impressive display; horribly dignified, chilly as the banks off Newfoundland; devastating as Cotton Mather's threats of brimstone. Almost always he was equability itself. This man who could straight-arm strangers so effectually, could be warmly intimate with the few to whom he gave his friendship each year. There was nothing of the palaverer in him. He kept his friendships, like his work, on the gold standard. As a scholar he valued the real meaning of words. As a dyed-in-the-wool New Englander he had an honest detestation of those amiable phrases which most people render meaningless by squandering lightly.

He was sparing, almost stingy, with praise. His thanks for something he liked or appreciated was a slight pat on the back, a hastily muttered "That's fine." This was all. Yet it was by means of these few words, as treasured by those who earned them as if they were public testimonials, that he reared the astonishing organization which flourished at Harvard; that he persuaded men and women, who received no pay and little credit for it, to sit up night after night to slave on his stage crews; that he got his actors, in spite of the courses they might be taking and the fact that the 47 Workshop counted for nothing as an undergraduate activity, to feel duty-bound to come promptly to all rehearsals; that he mesmerized designers into competing for the privilege of setting one of his productions; and that he built up and held together that loyal Cambridge audience (he did the same thing in New Haven) which felt itself honored to be allowed to sit in at the performances of what were usually very bad plays.

It was this Baker who inspired more active loyalty than any other teacher at Harvard (not excepting the great "Copey" himself) who was the fourth of the four Bakers. This man Baker, with his extraordinary personality, was the keystone upon which everything else rested. He may have put people off. His seeming coldness may have terrified some and antagonized others. Yet everyone who actually worked for him, and hence knew him—because he was the kind of man who revealed himself only in his work—felt affectionately toward him. He was not Professor Baker to them. He was "G.P.," but always, significantly enough, he was "G.P." only when he was safely out of earshot.

It is because these four Bakers existed side by side that there was—and can be—only one George Pierce Baker,

as Yale has doubtless learned by now, and as Harvard
discovered some years ago when Mr. Baker put the
Cambridge elms behind him for New Haven and what
Harvard was foolish enough to think at the time was
"blue obscur-i-tee."

January 9, 1935

THOMAS WOLFE AS A DRAMATIST

WHEN Thomas Wolfe fell like a giant pine before
the ax of a wasteful death, most of the newspapers com-
mented upon his early interest in the theatre. They
mentioned his having worked with Professor Koch at
the University of North Carolina, and having then continued his studies with Professor Baker at Harvard.
Quite naturally, it was the novelist who had fathered
such sprawling, though exceptional, books as *Look
Homeward, Angel* and *Of Time and the River* rather
than the young playwright whose scripts were never
professionally produced that won their attention.

Still there is something to be said about Thomas
Wolfe the dramatist who was and might-have-been. In
spite of the fun he made of Mr. Baker's playwriting
course in the bitterly sarcastic pages of *Of Time and the
River*, the Tom Wolfe I remember at Harvard was one
of the most earnest of Mr. Baker's dramatists.

To those of us who were stage-struck undergraduates

at the time, Tom loomed large under the Cambridge elms as a man who had grown and grown until he was already as huge as his own legend. He was even taller than his talk. Words poured from that small head of his as red-hot lava flows down the slopes of a volcano whose top is almost hidden in the clouds.

His talk was hesitant at first, but could become brilliant, fevered, and exciting. Where most of his contemporaries were proud of having a thought to state in a single sentence, his ideas rolled out even then in chapters. What added to the color of his conversation was the frenzy which burned in his black eyes, and the vehement intensity with which all he had to say was said. His speech was nervous. It was halting and jerky in its separate cadences, and filled with suddenly asked questions which were thrown out without waiting for answers or expecting them. Yet it achieved smoothness by the very magic of its volume, by beating down upon his astonished listeners like a cloudburst of improvisation. It was made the more impressive because Tom himself called to mind a titanic hillbilly, a Paul Bunyan of the Southern mountains who, in the course of his protracted feuds with an idea, might stoop down above the door at any minute and reach for a shotgun with which to punctuate his sentences.

The mountains were very much in Tom's thoughts when he first reached Harvard. He had already written for Professor Koch a lurid one-act tragedy called *The Return of Buck Gavin* for which, at Chapel Hill in

1919, he had pasted on some false whiskers to play his own mountain outlaw. If you doubt me, you have only to turn to the second series of Mr. Koch's *Carolina Folk Plays* and, before reading Mr. Wolfe's early effort, look at a picture of him in make-up. In this photograph you cannot fail to notice in the man the "suggestion of . . . pantherlike power" which Tom asked for in his stage direction. Though some of this power is "veiled" behind his beard, it flames in Tom's tortured eyes.

Tom carried the mountains with him to the Workshop. The first of his plays Mr. Baker produced was an utterly conventional little one-act, known accurately enough as *The Mountains*. Although it might almost have served as a mountain play to end all mountain plays, unfortunately it did not. Its hero, as is the custom in hillbilly scripts, was an unhappy young fellow, anxious to get away from the mountains. As I remember, the curtain had not been up two minutes before he walked to a window and shook his fists vehemently at an inoffensive peak painted on the backdrop, crying "Goddamn you, Baldpate (for that was the mountain's name), yuh hemmin' me in!"

Two years later, in May, 1923, Mr. Baker staged the first of Tom's plays to bear signs, however faint, of his genius. It was *Welcome to Our City*, a long, occasionally Expressionistic drama in ten scenes. It was not a good play. Although it was as undisciplined as you would have expected a play by Thomas Wolfe to be, it contained some promising writing. It boasted,

moreover, one hilarious satiric scene, written in dumb
show (amazingly enough). In this episode a phony
Carolina governor was shown up in all his phonyness
by the simple act of permitting the audience to watch
him undress. He had retired alone to his hotel bedroom,
full of political pomposity. First he surveyed himself
in a mirror, making fine oratorical gestures. Then little
by little he shed both his clothing and his dignity. First
he removed his padded coat. Then his layer-after-layer
of vests. Then he took off his toupee. Finally, just as
he was getting into bed he slipped his false teeth in a
tumbler. Before this scene was over more than the body
of this governor was unclothed. His character was
naked.

Tom must have been amused as he watched the
Cambridge performances of *Welcome to Our City*.
His play was deeply concerned, among other things,
with the way in which a proud young Southern aristocrat seduces a pretty young mulatto. In choosing his
actors Mr. Baker could never have been accused of type
casting. New England was conscripted, much to its surprise. It was Cambridge's Dorothy Sands who assumed
a sweet potato voice to impersonate the wronged mulatto. And it was Senator Henry Cabot Lodge's grand-
son, John, since turned movie actor, who played the
rebel seducer.

Welcome to Our City came near to being done professionally in New York. Tom submitted the script to
the Neighborhood Playhouse which was very much

interested. As I recall Helen Arthur's telling of the story, she sent Tom a letter expressing her enthusiasm for the play, and saying the Neighborhood would like to do it. As a matter of routine, she suggested some necessary alterations. But she did not then know her author. Practically by return mail she received an irate letter from him, filled with expletives, demanding the immediate return of the script, and asking who the hell she thought she was anyway to know more about his play than he did.

If Miss Arthur had been a mountain named Baldpate, Mr. Wolfe could not have been angrier at her. Had he gone on with the theatre Tom would always have been shaking his huge fists at it. It would have hemmed him in. Even in his novel-writing he was hemmed in, and fought like the genius he unquestionably was for a complete freedom he never quite found. Of such geniuses, however, the theatre stands permanently in need.

September 21, 1938

INDEX

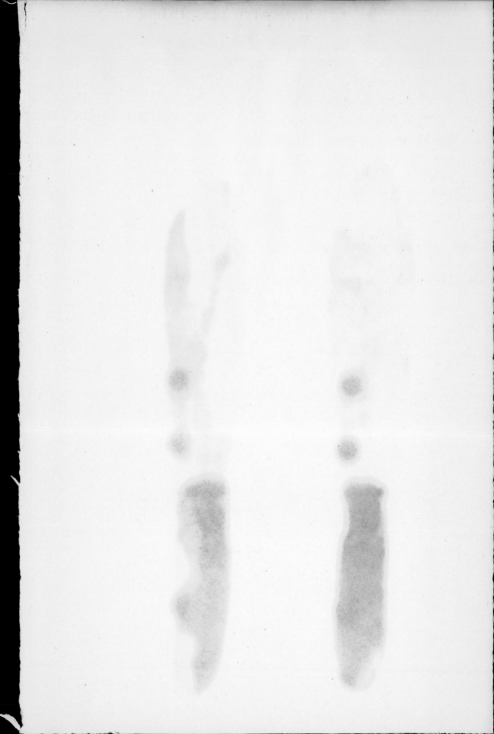

DATE DUE

GAYLORD

PRINTED IN U.S.A.